The Brotherhood of Secret Darkness
and Other Cults, Cabals, and Conspiracies

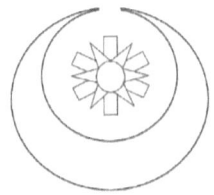

by
Jason J. McCuiston

From
Dark Owl Publishing, LLC

Arizona

For Andrea. Thanks for always having my back.

TABLE OF CONTENTS

INTRODUCTION

Growing up in the seventies and eighties, it's no surprise that I developed an acute interest in conspiracy theories, mystic cults, and shady cabals of evil-doers. I had already cut my teeth on Marvel Comics, the Savage Sword of Conan, and the Super Friends by the time an actor occupied the Oval Office. Hydra, the wizard cults of ancient Hyboria, and the Legion of Doom were always working in the shadows to cause problems for the good guys. Meanwhile on TV, Leonard Nimoy was ever *In Search Of* the facts about UFOs, ancient mysteries, and other seemingly impossible phenomena, and Carl Kolchak was stonewalled every week by some government official in his quest to uncover the truth about the monsters among us.

Later, Cobra Command secretly operated out of a little town called Springfield somewhere in Middle America to spread their particular brand of terror across the comic book world. My own favorite pastime of Dungeons & Dragons became the focus of the now infamous Satanic Panic. And everyone knows the Government framed The A-Team for a crime they didn't commit. Even in the heyday of the Greatest Decade Ever, something sinister was going on behind the scenes. We all sensed it, but we didn't quite *know* it.

Not until *The X-Files* told us The Truth is Out There. Sure, the Cigarette Smoking Man and the Well-Manicured Man weren't as ominous nicknames as Black Manta or The Scarecrow, but the Syndicate was far more terrifying than the Legion of Doom by virtue of being all too believable. Maybe it was because I turned twenty during the Clinton Years, but it seemed like there was a tidal shift in the zeitgeist. We—or at least, I—started to sense that things were not as we'd always been told. Maybe the good guys hadn't won. It was like we lived on the surface of a big old onion, and if we dared start peeling back the layers, the rottener it got.

But somewhere between the era of "Trust No One" and that of "Trust the Science," conspiracy theories stopped being about urban legends and started becoming headlines. They weren't fun anymore. At least not for me.

This collection is my way of taking back that spirit of fun those old mysteries, legends, stories, and adventures once inspired. In the summer of 2022, I was struggling on a novel manuscript, crushed by a terrible bout of writer's block brought on by stress. Much of that stress had to do with the current shape of the world as I headed full tilt into middle age. Instead of forcing myself to finish my WIP, I decided to write five new stories.

Somehow, it worked.

Since all five tales had something to do with a conspiracy, a cult, or a secretive cabal, they became the core of this collection. Well, four of them—"Brotherhood of Secret Darkness," "Ragnarok n' Roll," "Ouroboros," and "Reign of the Annunaki"—did. (The fifth is looking for a home elsewhere at the time of this writing.) Checking my catalog of unpublished and previously published stories, it was easy to fill out the roster for the rest of the book. "Majestic Dawn," a prequel to my novel *Project Notebook*, first appeared in Pole to Pole Publishing's *Not Far From Roswell* anthology (2019); "The Graysville Train Robbery" previously appeared in *Fake News* from Old Sins (2020); "Nephilim Phenomenon" was published on the Tell-Tale Press website in 2020; and "The Feis" first appeared in Dark Owl Publishing's *A Celebration of Storytelling* (2020). The remaining four shorts and novella are unique to this collection.

Apparently, I love a good conspiracy.

And to really tap into that love, I decided to illustrate the collection as an homage to the comics and magazines that inspired me as a kid. I am no Frank Frazetta, Sanjulián, Bernie Wrightson, Arthur Adams, or Bill Sienkiewicz, but I do my best. I had a lot of fun putting this book together, and I certainly hope you have as much fun reading it. In any case, I thank you for picking it up and giving it a try.

Take care and God bless,
Jason J. McCuiston
South Carolina, 2023

THE BROTHERHOOD OF SECRET DARKNESS

Nashville, Tennessee, October 26ᵗʰ, 1888—

N The bullet grazed Professor Wyrd's brow as it carried his top hat to the train station's tiled floor. It took him a moment to connect his pain with the sudden thunderous boom and the startled screams of his fellow travelers. In that moment, he caught a glimpse of the man in the dark derby and green plaid suit behind the haze of gun smoke. The assassin was short, narrow, and grim, with a thin moustache. Those were the only details Wyrd registered before toppling into his friend's arms.

If Professor Phinehas Wyrd was stunned into inaction, he was blessed that his companions were not. Quicker than his own collapse, Catherine Yeltzen's knives were in her hands and in flight. A heartbeat later, the gunman gave a cry of pain and disappeared into the chaos orchestrated by his single shot.

"You all right, Professor?" Hiram Jones asked as he steadied Wyrd back on his feet. "You're bleeding a fair bit." One of the aging gunfighter's own nickel-plated revolvers was in his free hand as his pale, hawk-like eyes scanned the emptying platform for more attackers.

"I'll live." The professor touched the crease above his left eye with his gloved hand. He winced at the sharp pain that turned heavy and throbbing as it raced through his skull. "Where's Catherine?"

"I am here." The Russian knife-thrower handed Wyrd his hat and silver-headed cane. "The man got away, but not unscathed. He carries one of my blades in his wrist and he left his own weapon behind. He should not get very far if we pursue."

"I fear that is not likely to happen, my dear." Professor Wyrd sighed as he caught sight of a pair of Nashville policemen. "We must first make the acquaintance of the local constabulary."

Hiram holstered his weapon and said in his deep drawl, "Well, the first place we start looking is the local Mason's Lodge. That feller was wearing a watch fob with their sigil engraved on it. If I hadn't had to catch you, I'd have put a bullet right through the middle of it before he could have taken another step."

Professor Wyrd donned a practiced smile as he stepped to meet the policemen. Under his breath, he said, "Thank God for small miracles. If you'd have killed him, Hiram, we would no doubt be locked up as the aggressors in this little fracas."

Catherine lit a black cheroot in defiance of social custom and the astonished glares of the two policemen. "Obviously, the Brotherhood of Secret Darkness knows we are here."

"Which puts us at least one step behind in the game," Hiram observed. "As usual..."

After dealing with the police and convincing them that the attack was a foiled robbery attempt, Professor Wyrd and his two colleagues adjourned to the nearest hotel to plan the next step in their investigation.

"Who'd a thought taking down a vampire in Knoxville was the *easy* part of this caper," Hiram Jones said as he rolled a cigarette and looked out the third-story hotel room window. "As much as I enjoy being back home in Tennessee, I thought we'd a-been done by now."

Professor Wyrd rubbed the bandage on his brow and pondered the tumbler of whiskey in his hand. The wound and the alcohol served to dim the ever-present pain in his left thigh, the pain he'd carried since he was twelve years old. He sat in one of the suite's two upholstered wingbacks across from Catherine. The blonde beauty smoked one of her black cheroots and wore a bored expression in the same casual manner she wore men's clothes.

"Yes," Wyrd said. "I had thought Ravenscroft was working alone as well. But the documents we found in his lair seemed to validate my belief that the Enemy is currently engaged in a far-spread conspiracy of coordinated evil. It is my hope that once we uncover and expose this Brotherhood of Secret Darkness that the Order will accept my hypothesis and commit more resources to rooting out and destroying this conspiracy."

Catherine rolled her green eyes. "I fear, Professor, that your Order suffers from a complacency borne of centuries of perceived superiority. The hierarchy believes the myth that the monsters and demons of this world are random and chaotic, undisciplined with no direct plan or coordination. And why should it think otherwise when the Church itself is so fractured and so often at odds with its own disparate parts?"

Wyrd frowned but could not deny the truth of the statement. "Well, as that may be, our business is to seek out and fight the servants of the Enemy wherever we may find them. In this case, we know that a satanic cult, the Brotherhood of Secret Darkness, is at work here in Nashville, and that it is somehow connected to the local Freemasons and at least one vampire."

"The Masons aren't an easy nut to crack," Hiram observed from the window.

"Nor are they a monolithic organization," Catherine added. "Each chapter has its own politics and predilections."

Wyrd rubbed his aching head. "Yes. And though Albert Pike's infusion of Luciferian mysticism into the society has rejuvenated the Freemasons in this country following the scandalous Morgan Affair, I have yet to find any *real* evidence of widespread satanic allegiances among their numbers."

"*Yet* being the kicker. There's a first time for everything," Hiram said.

"Indeed. Well, first thing tomorrow I will attempt to make contact with the local lodge. I know enough of their rituals and secrets to pass as a low-ranking brother. Hopefully this will get me an audience with someone who might be able to point us in the right direction."

Catherine crushed out her cheroot in a crystal ashtray. "And what shall the two of us do in the meantime?"

Hiram laughed. "Wait for his plan to go cockeyed and come to the rescue, as usual."

***

One good thing about the Freemasons was that, as secret societies go, they were not all that secretive. They frequently conducted their meetings in buildings located on public streets, their members proudly displayed their membership with rings, lapel pins, and watch fobs. Of course, these badges of association necessitated other levels of security to ascertain the veracity of those claiming to be Masons such as passwords and secret handshakes.

Fortunately, Professor Wyrd had among his disguise kit a Masonic ring and pin, and the education he had received from the Order included many of the secrets of organizations such as the Freemasons, the Rosicrucians, the

Oddfellows, and others. So, when he left his hotel early the next morning, he was prepared to continue his search for the Brotherhood of Secret Darkness. Or so he believed.

The first logical step was to locate the nearest Masonic Lodge or temple, but this proved problematic as the Great Hall on Church Street was no more than a suspended construction site. The building had suffered a fire in the 1850s and the reconstruction had been postponed indefinitely by the ensuing War Between the States. Apparently, as the professor was able to gather through casual conversation at local restaurants and bars, the Royal Hall had decided on a different location to represent the order's new direction in recent years, but had yet to break ground.

So, after a day of false starts, Professor Wyrd returned to his hotel somewhat dejected. He hoped that Catherine had fared better in her search at the library and courthouse, and Hiram had succeeded in gleaning something from the rougher parts of the city. Standing on the sidewalk and smoking a cigar while he pondered his next move, Wyrd paid little mind to the gasman lighting the streetlamps as the sun went down.

"Beg pardon, sir," the man said stepping close to the professor. "But are you looking for someone?"

Wyrd eyed the lamplighter suspiciously and noted the pin on his lapel. "As a matter of fact I am, sir. I am a traveler seeking his brother."

The man extended his right hand and Wyrd shook it with the ritual procedure he'd been taught. "Perhaps I can help," the lighter said.

Before the gasman had released the professor's hand, a black carriage pulled to the curb and the door opened. Inside, a man in shadow extended a short-barreled revolver and gave the command, "Get in."

Professor Wyrd glanced at the gasman who now held his lighter like a weapon. "Of course, gentlemen. No need to escalate the situation. I will come along quietly." He smiled but hoped someone had seen the abduction and would be able to put Hiram and Catherine on his trail before things got beyond his control. If they hadn't already.

The gasman took Wyrd's silver-headed cane and inspected it, partially drawing the concealed rapier within. With a scowl, he handed the walking stick and sword combination to the armed passenger.

Wyrd smiled. "One cannot be too careful these days."

As soon as the professor was alone in the carriage with the shadowy gunman, the driver cracked his whip and the team of two set off at a trot along the brick-paved street. The traffic was picking up with the after-dinner crowd as Nashville's affluent citizens and those who prospered by them took to the night for entertainment and commerce. Wyrd looked at the man as they passed a lit streetlamp, realizing he was not the assassin from the railway station. This gunman was trim and elegantly dressed with manicured nails and freshly-barbered hair and sideburns. He had the look of a banker or lawyer rather than a killer. He wore a large Masonic ring on his left hand while his right held the pocket pistol casually in his lap.

"I take it I am not welcome among the brethren of Nashville?" Wyrd asked.

The man smirked. "You are not one of us, and yet you seem very intent on discovering our secrets, sir. We've had far too much of that lately."

Wyrd narrowed his eyes. "Ah, yes. I suppose yours is a *secretive* brotherhood."

The man scowled. "I do not believe you know what you think you know, sir. It is my sincere hope, however, that before the night is over you will have an edifying enlightenment."

"Well, at least we have that in accord."

Wyrd settled back into the leather of his seat and tried to enjoy the fresh night air as the carriage rumbled away from downtown, passing over a great stone bridge and into darkened farmland. On the other side of the bridge, the paving disappeared and soon the vehicle traversed a wide dirt lane. The professor wondered if his friends would be able to track him much further into the hinterlands. He tried not to think of them finding his body floating face down in the Cumberland River tomorrow morning.

At length the carriage pulled onto a graveled drive that passed through iron gates and into an expansive yard surrounding a large, red brick mansion. The white-colonnaded house's front rooms all glowed with yellow light, and gas lamps flickered to either side of the wide front door.

"I take it this is where the chapter meets while the permanent temple is on hold?"

"All will be revealed in time, sir." The man used his weapon to motion Wyrd from the carriage as a tuxedoed porter opened the door and extended the folding step. When both were outside the vehicle, the gunman raised the professor's cane. "Please allow the porter to help you inside. I will hold onto this for the time being."

Wyrd acquiesced and leaned on the silent young man's shoulder as they mounted the mansion's wide steps and entered the house. Inside the front room, the professor sighed at sight of the carpeted stair leading to the second floor and felt the pain in his thigh grow heavy. To the right of the front door was a formal dining room, to the left an elegant parlor.

The professor was relieved when the porter guided him to the left of the stair, past the parlor and into a library on the back side of the house. The cherry-paneled room was large and masculine in nature, save for a life-size portrait above the mantle depicting a lovely young dark-haired girl in an eggshell-blue dress, smiling at her Irish Wolfhound beneath a willow tree.

"My daughter, Elizabeth." A tall heavyset man stood in the opened French doors behind the broad cherry desk. He wore a tailored suit of dark blue, and smoked a cigar while sipping from a crystal tumbler. His bright blue eyes sparkled as he watched Wyrd admire the painting.

Stepping into the library, the man motioned to one of the upholstered chairs before the desk. "Please, have a seat, Professor. I apologize for the manner of this *invitation*, but you have come to Nashville during some rather unprecedented times. Let me assure you, it is better that we got to you first." With a wave, he dismissed the silent porter.

Wyrd studied his host and captor. The man looked slightly familiar and had the bearing of a soldier and a leader. "I suppose I shall have to take your word for that, sir. You apparently have me at the disadvantage."

The man smiled. "Jonas Donelson, at your service. I am the head of the Royal Arch here in Nashville, though not uncontested." Wyrd recognized the name of the wealthy landholder and businessman, a scion of one of Nashville's founding families.

The gunman placed Wyrd's cane across the desk. "He had this."

Donelson drew the blade halfway and read the inscription above the hilt: "*Deus Vult.* You fancy yourself a modern-day crusader then, Professor?"

"My crusade, sir, is against the very real forces of evil, not misguided men."

Donelson's smile grew wider. "Very good, sir. May I offer you a cigar or a drink?"

Wyrd finally eased into the offered chair and rubbed his aching leg. He accepted a cigar from the presented humidor. "Whiskey, neat, thank you."

Donelson lit the professor's cigar as the dapper gunman prepared the drink at the sideboard. "Yes, Professor Wyrd, I know who you are and why you've come to my city. Despite what you think you found in Knoxville, I can tell you for a fact that our organization is not in league with the likes of Damon Ravenscroft."

Wyrd accepted the tumbler and took an appreciative sip. It was fine Kentucky bourbon. "Of course you would say that, wouldn't you, Mr. Donelson?"

"Yes, I would. However, I can tell you the name of the man you are actually seeking and avow that he has no real connection to my lodge. At least not anymore."

Wyrd sat up. "I am listening, sir."

"Have you ever heard of Leonidas Fell?"

Wyrd frowned, the name sounding all too familiar. "Yes... I believe I have. Wasn't he a Confederate general and an associate of Albert Pike? But I believed he was dead or fled to Europe or Mexico or some other far region."

"Correct on the former, Professor, but the latter were all rumors. At least as far as his death and flight are concerned. He is very much alive and here in Nashville." Donelson sat back in his chair and steepled his fingers above his chest. "Fell commanded a volunteer brigade from Louisiana and had a... reputation of sorts. It was said that he was a necromancer and a practitioner of dark magic learned in the swamps of his home state from priests of pagan gods; that he consulted spirits and demons for advice and intelligence reports. The darkest rumors said that his men killed in battle would rise from the field the following night and fall in beside their still-living comrades to continue the fight."

Wyrd sipped the bourbon and tried to sift these tall tales through what he actually knew to be true as far as the supernatural was concerned. "I take it General Fell is the one currently contesting your claim to the Royal Arch leadership?"

Donelson nodded. "Yes. I fought for the Union and was fortunate enough to be part of the occupying force here in Nashville. I was able to curtail most of the worst privations an enemy force can inflict on an occupied community. You see, Professor, I grew up here and I love this town and this state. It is my home, and I will defend it to my utter extremis."

"Even against members of your own order? If Fell was a close friend to Albert Pike, then he should be on the fast-track to take your title, regardless of your local connections and the differing branches."

Donelson scowled. "Or so he thought. So many of us thought. However, Fell had a falling out with Pike over some interpretation of the Scottish Rite's... ritualistic elements. I have since learned that Fell wanted to push the Rite and all North American Freemasons into the realm of *real* dark magic, whereas Pike simply wanted to invoke the symbolism and mystique of esoteric powers. To that extent, Fell has siphoned off a good portion of our brothers to follow his new splinter group."

Wyrd exhaled a ring of smoke. "The Brotherhood of Secret Darkness."

"Yes. Since the War, Fell has traveled far and wide studying mysticism and magic from cults and cabals across the globe. He has returned with a considerable library of grimoires and ancient tomes, some of which he claims were smuggled out of the Library of Alexandria before its infamous immolation. But even before he gathered this knowledge, Leonidas Fell was a powerful force to be reckoned with, Professor. He is not a man to be taken lightly. To this I can personally attest."

"Well do I believe it, Mr. Donelson. I am grateful for the warning, but I am on the side of the angels and my Great Benefactor is undefeated in these matters. However, I would ask one favor of you: could you tell me where Fell is to be found?"

Donelson leaned forward and placed his elbows on the desk, studying Professor Wyrd with his piercing eyes. "I am afraid that is the one question I cannot answer, sir. Since his rather dramatic departure from my house on the night he lost the election for my seat, I have had no word of his or his followers' whereabouts. The twenty-nine men who went with him haven't even returned to their jobs or their families. It is as if they have vanished from the city altogether."

"Perhaps they have."

"I only wish that were true. Unfortunately, in the past two weeks we've lost three of our tenth-degree brothers to rather dubious circumstances. I believe Fell and his followers are killing us off one by one until they can claim the chapter outright and reshape it into Fell's Brotherhood of Secret Darkness."

Professor Wyrd nodded in understanding. He crushed out the stub of his cigar in the crystal ashtray and finished off his whiskey. "Well, Mr. Donelson, I thank you for your hospitality and for the information. I can assure you that I will no longer pry into your business while I am here. And I promise that my companions and I will do all within our power to seek out General Fell and put a stop to him."

Donelson stood and extended his hand with a slight smirk. "The enemy of my enemy is my friend, as they say. I thank you, Professor, and wish you happy hunting." He handed Wyrd his cane and told his subordinate, "Please return the gentleman to his hotel, Aaron. And you can put the gun away as I do not think you will be needing it."

The return trip to downtown Nashville was quiet, as Aaron showed no sign of Jonas Donelson's tendency for conversation. Wyrd did not mind as it gave him time to think. He had heard the rumors of Leonidas Fell, of course, but had chalked them up to "old war stories," the sort of mythology that grows up around certain men during times of violence and conflict; the tales that help men make sense of the horrors and atrocities of combat. However, the professor also knew that some of the dark magic rumored to be practiced in the bayous of Louisiana was all too real. If Fell had mastered such arcane arts before the War and had added to these esoteric skills in the ensuing decades, the man would be a formidable foe, indeed.

"Is that Thompson?" Aaron leaned out of the carriage window and called to the driver. "Stop here."

The professor followed the young Freemason out of the carriage and onto the foggy street. It was late and the town seemed all but abandoned as a heavy mist had rolled up from the Cumberland. The thick cloud was lit in hues of amber by the burning gas lamps along the sidewalks. In that murky illumination, Wyrd saw a familiar dark shape lurching along, a lamplighter at its side.

Wyrd and Aaron reached the gasman as he stumbled against a building. Even in the wan light, the professor saw that the man was pale and his eyes glimmered like glass marbles in their darkened sockets. A thin streak of blood ran from his lip down his chin, though no other signs of violence marred his face.

"Thompson," Aaron said. "Thompson, are you all right? What's happened, man?"

Thompson the gasman swiveled his head so that his glassy eyes fixed on Professor Wyrd. An eerie grin slowly crawled across his face, revealing teeth yellow in comparison with his pallid skin. He spoke in a deep sepulchral voice that seemed to originate somewhere outside his body. "*I know your secret...*" Then his head flew back as if in convulsion and a maniacal laughter erupted from his throat.

Professor Wyrd and his companion stared in horror at the display until the gasman collapsed onto the sidewalk and was silent. As the young Freemason began to babble some mixture of prayers and esoteric rites, the professor knelt beside the dead man and searched for evidence. "Quick, get a lantern! I need light."

When Aaron returned with the lantern a moment later, the professor found what he was looking for. "A small bullet wound, just below the right armpit. Powder burns on his jacket indicate it was done at point-blank range. By the size of the hole and the absence of an exit wound, I'd say a small caliber. Easily concealable, relatively silent amid the hustle and bustle of a busy street, yet powerful enough to puncture the heart and both lungs at this range."

Rifling the dead man's pockets, the professor came away with a small black leather bag bound in what appeared to be human hair. "And this. Placed on the corpse as part of the reanimation ritual." He opened the gasman's mouth and turned the head toward the light. "Yes, and I see the edge of a coin at the back of his throat. That's what allowed the necromancer to speak though him."

The Freemason shivered. "It said... it said it knew your secret. What does that mean?"

Professor Wyrd sighed. "I am an Oxford-educated English aristocrat going by the unlikely *nom-de-guerre* of Phinehas Wyrd, owner and operator of a travelling sideshow called the World of Wonders. I hunt monsters and demons in the Americas. I'm afraid our necromancer wasn't quite specific enough for me to answer your question."

***

Catherine met him in the empty hotel lobby. Her lovely face showed a rare emotion, a hint of concern before reverting to its normal placidity. She had been sitting on one of the circular leather sofas, reading a newspaper and ignoring the scowls of the man at the desk. The concierge's scorn no doubt resulted from Catherine's attire of slacks and shirt as opposed to more feminine fashion, and the fact that she used a brass cuspidor as an ashtray for one of her black cheroots. "Look what the cat dragged in. That is the saying, is it not?"

The professor took off his top hat and gave her a tired smile. "It is. Though in this case, it was a Freemason and not a cat. Where is Hiram?"

"Out looking for you." Catherine took his arm and led him to the Otis elevator. "When you weren't back in time for supper, he was worried." She gave no hint that she shared in those concerns. "I told him you were fine, probably enjoying a steak and fine brandy at some gentlemen's club. But he would not hear of it."

The mention of steak reminded Wyrd that he hadn't eaten. "If only that were the case. As soon as he returns, I will tell you everything. Right now, I would very much like to freshen up and order some room service..."

Hiram knocked on the professor's door just as the bellman was taking away the remnants of Wyrd's late supper. "Glad you made it back. I didn't much fancy the idea of searching all the ditches and riverbanks in Nashville tomorrow morning."

The professor sat back in his wingback, opposite the Russian knife-thrower, and lit a cigar. "Based on what I learned tonight, if I had fallen afoul of our quarry, it is safe to say you wouldn't have found my body in any case. Or, more precisely, my body would have found *you*. Did you have any luck in the rowdier establishments?"

The gunfighter tossed his black Stetson onto the hat tree and stepped to the low-burning fireplace. "Some. Seems there's quite a few upper-crust types slumming lately, pretending to be river-boaters and stevedores and the like. Spending a lot of cash."

Wyrd nodded. "That makes sense. The converted Masons would have to go somewhere." He quickly outlined to Hiram and Catherine what he had learned from Donelson concerning Leonidas Fell and the Brotherhood of Secret Darkness, finishing with his encounter with the reanimated gasman. "I just don't understand why Fell has his people leaving their elevated positions and carousing with the working folk. It seems they would have a greater influence as businessmen, doctors, and lawyers. Community leaders."

Catherine crushed out her cheroot and exhaled a jet of smoke. "I think I understand. In my research at the library, I found several recent news stories describing a growing unrest among the working classes of the city. Perhaps

Fell means to incite a class struggle to further his plans. Obviously there are more have-nots than haves, among whom this Donelson apparently holds sway. Fell is counting on the strength of numbers to further his success."

"Or he's building something," Hiram offered while rolling a cigarette. "Those fancy dudes have been hiring men from the saloons and cathouses. I never got a straight answer as to what the jobs are, though. But it don't take book-learning to know businessmen and lawyers ain't the best at manual labor."

Wyrd thought on this. "The temple. Fell is building a new temple somewhere. While the Royal Arch is idle with plans to rebuild the old lodge, he plans an alternative. One with a broader membership. But if he plans to consecrate it to this Secret Darkness, he'll need more than brick and mortar. He'll need a sacrifice of some kind, of that we can be sure."

"What do you know about the Secret Darkness?" Catherine raised an eyebrow.

The professor frowned. "Almost nothing, I'm afraid. Only the little we found in Ravenscroft's journals. Though I wired my superiors within the Order before leaving Knoxville, I have yet to receive a response or guidance. Obviously 'Secret Darkness' is a euphemism for some demon or pagan god of antiquity, but without knowing its true identity we have very little to go on."

"Perhaps not." Hiram said with a smile. "One of the fellers I had a drink with this afternoon was a groundskeeper over at the big cemetery here in town. He said he'd chased a couple possible resurrection men off last night. Said they actually dug up a pair of stiffs last week and got away with 'em. Probably sold 'em to the doctors over at the university."

"The dead Freemasons," Wyrd said. "Donelson said three of his ranking lodge members had died under strange circumstances over the past two weeks. Fell is trying to recover their bodies for some reason. Considering what he did to that poor gasman, I shudder to think what he could be planning."

Catherine stood. "Then we need to get to the Mount Olivet Cemetery. I found the obituaries today. All three men were interred in the same place. No doubt Fell's henchmen will try again tonight."

The professor sighed, not relishing the thought of spending the night in a cold, damp graveyard. His leg was already giving him fits. But battles between good and evil were seldom fought by the light of a cozy hearth. "Yes, let us adjourn to Mount Olivet. I trust you both have your weapons at the ready."

"Always."

***

After meeting with the groundskeeper, and giving him a pint of whiskey in exchange for guiding them to the last unmolested Mason's grave, Professor Wyrd, Hiram Jones, and Catherine Yeltzen took up concealed positions to wait. Hiram, though well into his fifties, shinnied up a big willow tree while Catherine lurked behind a stone angel of death. Professor Wyrd admired the aptness of her choice from his position in the shadows of a mausoleum's opened door.

The river mist was thinner this far away from downtown, but not altogether absent. It was chill as it coiled among the tombstones, obelisks, crosses, and statues. Professor Wyrd had to resist the urge to stamp his feet to keep the cold at bay, knowing such a demonstration would boom and echo throughout the cemetery. He pulled his cape tighter about his arms and shoulders and quietly paced the vault as the night dragged on.

After a while, he began to fear they were wasting their time. He worried that Hiram might fall asleep and drop from his perch with disastrous results or that any one of them might catch cold and the illness would further imperil their investigation. He was about to clear his throat and call to his companions to end the vigil when he spotted a lantern coming up the hill.

He crouched deeper into the darkness and narrowed his eyes. He waited until he was certain that it was not the caretaker. Indeed it was not, for the lantern carrier was not alone. If their informant had chased away two or three men the previous night, the rascals had returned with reinforcements. Professor Wyrd clearly saw six men carrying shovels, pickaxes, and even a shotgun. Clearly they intended not to be denied this evening.

The light bearer sat the lantern on top of the big, polished headstone, and by its glow the professor saw that this man was better dressed than his companions, save for the man with the shotgun. He deduced that these two were part of Fell's splinter cabal while the other four were hired hands. Their voices, though hushed, carried clear and flat in the misty graveyard.

"All right, lads. Let's get to it," said the lantern man. The four workers nodded ascent and set to work with the pickaxes to soften the turf while the man with the shotgun kept his head on a swivel, looking for the expected approach of the groundskeeper.

Using his theatrical skills, Professor Wyrd threw his voice in the direction of the tombstone and gave a low, wailing moan. "*Who dares disturb my grave?*"

One of the diggers gave a surprisingly feminine squeal as two men dropped their tools and hurried back from their work. The shotgun swung in a wide arc as the lantern was raised above their heads. "Who's there? Who was that?"

Wyrd smiled from his hiding place and recalled the dead man's name. "*It is I, Nathan Chambers, Holder of the Tenth Degree and all the secrets contained therein. Why do you disturb my grave? Why do you invite my curse?*"

One of the workers broke and ran blindly into the night. Another quickly followed, the Lord's Prayer on his lips as he vanished into the mist. Two of the men raised their pickaxes like weapons while the man with the lantern drew a revolver. The man with the shotgun shouted, "Whoever you are, you aren't a ghost! And you're damn sure not bulletproof! Come out where we can see you and I'll prove it to you!"

The man screamed and let go of his weapon, spinning aside and clutching his hand. The shotgun struck the ground and discharged one of its two barrels in a thunderous flash. By that brief light, the professor saw one of Catherine's knives protruding from the man's bloody wrist.

The men with the pickaxes glanced at one another and turned to follow their fellow deserter. The man with the lantern and revolver snarled at them, "Don't do it or I'll plug you where you stand."

A pistol shot rang out and the man's revolver flew from his hand in a shower of sparks. He gasped and dropped the lantern. It struck the headstone, shattered and spilled flaming oil down the side of the monument and onto the damp grass. A tongue of flame lit the scene. The two well-dressed men now disarmed, the remaining workers took to their heels, leaving their picks behind.

The professor stepped from his hiding place and approached the men illuminated by fire. "I beg of you to show no further signs of hostility. It is not my intent to kill either of you, but I assure you my friends will not hesitate

to do so should the need arise."

To his surprise, the two injured men laughed. "I didn't think you'd show," the man with Catherine's blade in his hand said. "I was sure you'd be shaken to your soul by that little chat with Thompson."

The man who had wielded the pistol and the lantern smiled. "And I doubted you'd have the wits to put the clues together. But the general had faith. He knew you'd come, and so he made his plans accordingly."

Professor Wyrd suddenly felt trapped. "Fell? Where is he?"

The men laughed harder, glanced at one another and said in unison, "It's a *secret!*"

Yellow globes of light sprang up at the edge of vision in every direction. Lanterns being carried by dozens of men, no doubt armed. They began closing in, chanting a deep, somber song. The two men standing amid the dying flames joined in:

> *The sea is dark and deep,*
> *And many a secret does she keep.*
> *Our Lord doth know them all,*
> *So harken, ye, to his immortal call.*
> *The sea is dark and deep,*
> *And many a secret does she keep.*
> *Our Lord is greater still,*
> *So bindeth, ye, to his immortal will.*
> *The sea is dark and deep,*
> *And many a secret does she keep...*

Professor Wyrd slowly turned about, seeking a break in the closing circle but finding none. "Hiram! Catherine! We need to run!"

His companions were at his side. Catherine pressed one of her blades against the throat of one of the singing men. "I say we use these two as shields and force our way out."

A gunshot sounded from the left, the bullet pinging off a stone and whining into the night. Hiram looked that way as another shot rang out. "Don't seem like they care too much about friendly fire, Cat."

Professor Wyrd drew his sword. "Come, we've got to charge and hope we can break through. Just remember, our lives are in God's hands, not theirs."

Outnumbered and surrounded as they were, Wyrd and his friends had no right to expect to survive, much less escape. However, the Brotherhood of Secret Darkness was not facing three mere adventurers on this particular night in Mount Olivet Cemetery. Hiram Jones, aka Doctor Duel, and Catherine Yeltzen, better known as Catherine the Great, were what Professor Wyrd had dubbed Miracles. Conceived on the Night of Falling Stars in November of 1833, they were but two of the handful of remarkable individuals the professor had discovered and recruited into his World of Wonders. He believed they were gifts from God, sent to help in the ongoing struggle against the supernatural forces of the Adversary.

Hiram's revolvers found their target with every squeeze of the trigger, despite the darkness and the frantic conditions, as did Catherine's throwing knives. Where Hiram's reflexes and vision were honed to superhuman perfection, Catherine possessed an almost unquantifiable talent for moving in and out of time, of perceiving its flow at her own pace. Not only did this account for her deceptively youthful appearance, it also allowed her to guide her projectiles through time and space as if placing them by hand.

Though Professor Wyrd possessed no such uncanny ability, he was a skilled swordsman and a savage one when necessity dictated. As the ambush at the cemetery did dictate, he and his companions left a trail of dead and wounded in their wake as they fled Mount Olivet and escaped into the night.

***

Professor Wyrd limped across the hay-scattered space, trying to work out the stiffness in his bones and especially his misshapen thigh. It was cold in the old horse barn, though it was relatively dry, unlike the outskirts of Nashville which had seen a chill, misting rain descend upon the region overnight. The barn was one of several abandoned or foreclosed properties discovered in Catherine's research from the day before, and it had made for a convenient rallying point after the retreat from the cemetery.

At present, the professor and the knife thrower waited for Hiram to return from gathering their things at the hotel. They knew the Brotherhood would no doubt come for them there, having failed to take them at Mount Olivet.

"Your pacing is driving me insane," Catherine growled without looking up from sharpening her remaining blades. "Would you please sit down?"

Wyrd glowered at the woman and rubbed his arms. "I suppose you are not cold?"

"I am from Russia. You do not know the meaning of the word."

Wyrd conceded the point which only aggravated him more. "And are you also not worried about Hiram? He's been gone for hours."

She looked up with a frown. "The man survived on his own for quite some time in what even the Americans call the 'Wild West'. I daresay Hiram is more than capable of surviving a few hours alone in this mostly civilized city."

The professor harrumphed and continued his pacing. "But in this 'civilized city' there are organized forces of evil actively seeking his demise. Or worse."

Catherine sighed. "I think the Brotherhood of Secret Darkness suffered greater losses than we last night. I know my blades opened the veins of at least three men, not counting the one I wounded at Chambers's grave. Hiram probably killed or wounded twice that number. And you?"

Wyrd glanced at the silver handle of his sword cane. "I know I ran one man through and cut another across the shoulder. I may have struck yet more, but I cannot recall. It was all so... chaotic. I am just thankful that God surrounded us with His shielding wings last night."

Catherine lit one of her cheroots and exhaled a stream of smoke. "Which is why you should not worry about Hiram."

Wyrd nodded in acknowledgment and checked his watch. "Eight fifteen on a Sunday morning. We've been here for nearly two days and are no closer to putting an end to this cabal, nor to discovering its place in the Enemy's plan."

"Perhaps there truly is no plan. Perhaps the Order's hierarchy is correct in that the Adversary is simply creating chaos with no rhyme or reason until the End. Perhaps your notion of a global satanic conspiracy is just that, a notion and nothing more."

Wyrd shook his head. "No. I've seen too many pieces of this puzzle, seen how this one fits to that. There is a pattern forming. I just need to see what the final picture is meant to be, and I believe that Fell's organization may just be able to give me that glimpse."

"Well," Hiram said as he stepped into the barn and tossed an unconscious man to the stale straw. "I reckon this here feller might be able to put us on the right track."

Wyrd recognized the man as the lantern bearer from the cemetery. "How?"

Hiram sat on a bale of hay, removed his black Stetson and ran a gloved hand through his graying hair. "You were right. They ransacked our rooms last night, probably right after the fight at the cemetery. I reckon they left this feller and a couple others to watch for our return."

Catherine smirked. "I take it they did not see you?"

Hiram smiled. "Nope. And this one'll have a hell of a headache when he wakes up."

The professor nodded. "Well, let's hope you haven't scrambled his brains too badly. If he oversaw the grave robbery and this morning's reconnaissance, then he must be one of Fell's lieutenants. He may possess the answers to our questions."

Catherine fluttered one of her throwing knives across her knuckles with a cruel smile. "Well, if he is reluctant to give up those answers, I know how to persuade him."

Wyrd grimaced. "Let us pray it does not come to that."

Hiram chuckled. "All's fair in love and war, Professor. And if this ain't war I don't know what is."

In any event, they were not forced to resort to torture. After binding the unconscious man, Professor Wyrd and Hiram searched his pockets for clues. In the process, Hiram uncovered a relatively fresh tattoo on the underside of the man's left wrist. "Lookee here."

Professor Wyrd took a deep breath at the sight of the black crescent moon above the neat row of three black Xs. "I've seen that symbol before... I should have guessed... It all makes sense now."

"Perhaps to you," Catherine said. "Hiram and I do not have the benefit of years of occult education. What does this mark signify?"

"The 'true' name of the Secret Darkness. It symbolizes the moon god, Sin, or Suen, or Enzu, of ancient Mesopotamia. One of the pantheon's trinity representing sun, moon, and star, Sin was both rival and ally of Utu, the sun god. Both were brothers and consort to Inanna, or Ishtar, goddess of the stars. One of Sin's titles was 'Bringer of Wisdom from the Abyss'."

Hiram whistled. "Sounds like the Secret Darkness to me."

Catherine nodded. "And that song they sang last night. Referencing the sea..."

"Noah's flood. Yes, these pagan deities were demons or at the very least, Nephilim, who survived the Antediluvian World."

"And does that help us find where they are hiding?" Hiram asked as he prepared to backhand the prisoner awake.

"It does." Wyrd raised his hand to stay the blow. "If Donelson, leader of the local Freemasons, represents their idea of a sun god, then it only stands to reason that Fell, as representative of Sin, will want to take possession of his rival's temple."

Hiram scowled. "But they ain't got no temple."

Catherine raised her chin in understanding. "The old one. Though it burned, it still stands. They are hiding in plain sight."

Professor Wyrd rubbed the stubble on his chin, desperately desiring a shave and a wash. "And if Fell can keep such an operation a secret in the heart of downtown Nashville, then he is a powerful magician indeed."

The prisoner opened his eyes and grinned. "And our master has given him his favor. In this city, Professor, our Brotherhood is stronger than your faith."

"That remains to be seen."

***

After turning the prisoner over to the local police for the crime of grave robbery, Professor Wyrd and his companions adjourned to a different hotel under pseudonyms. By lunchtime, they were prepared to meet and formulate a plan of attack. They convened in a secluded booth in the hotel restaurant.

"Even given the casualties the cult suffered last night," the professor said as they ate, "the Brotherhood still has us greatly outnumbered. In light of this fact, I think it best if we clearly define our goals for tonight's operation."

Catherine took a sip of wine. "Tonight? Should we not investigation further before we enter the lair?"

Wyrd shook his head. "I am afraid we do not have the luxury of time. Tonight is the first night of the crescent moon, which we know is the symbol of Sin, the Secret Darkness. I believe they intend to perform some vile rite now that they possess all three corpses of the tenth-degree Masons. Each represents one of the Xs in the demon's symbol. We must find a way to stop this ritual before it can be completed."

Hiram chewed thoughtfully, then offered, "I say we just torch the place to the ground from outside. Finish what that fire in the fifties started."

"No. I need to know what Fell knows of the Adversary's plans. I need to know how he, the Brotherhood, Sin, and Ravenscroft all tie into it."

The gunfighter gave an ironic laugh. "Well, based on how tightlipped that sumbitch was this morning, ain't no way this Leonidas Fell is going to tell you nothing worth knowing."

The professor frowned. "Not willingly, perhaps. But he must have papers or books either in his possession or even on his person that will point me in the right direction... Besides, I would prefer not to engage in the wholesale loss of human life. Some of these men may not be beyond redemption. If it is possible, I would like to leave them that option."

Catherine sighed. "That means leaving them the option to continue to do evil."

Wyrd tilted his head. "We all have that option, my dear. It is not our duty to deny it to others. If we must slay the servants of our great enemy, let us make it an unpleasant obligation and not a matter of course."

Catherine raised an eyebrow. "You sound in accord with Nietzsche: 'Whoever fights monsters should see to it that in the process he does not become a monster.'"

The professor scowled. "On this matter, at least. Now, we'll need to look at the floorplan of the temple and determine whether or not any of the uninitiated workers are present—another reason to avoid arson. My guess is that when they begin to perform the ritual, a handful of wardens will be left to guard the ceremony while the balance of the cult participates. This is our best time to strike as this is when they are most vulnerable."

Hiram sat back and twitched his moustache. "I just can't figure out what this is all about. You said they'd need a sacrifice of some sort to dedicate their temple. What kind of sacrifice is three men who are already dead? Don't make sense to me."

Wyrd raised an eyebrow and shook his head. "Honestly, I am just as confused as—" A shadow fell across the table. Wyrd looked up to see a somewhat disheveled Jonas Donelson.

The man doffed his hat and stared at the professor with bloodshot eyes. "I've been looking for you all day, Professor. He's got her. Fell has taken my daughter."

Wyrd felt the blood rush from his face as he recalled the lovely girl in the painting. If Fell considered himself the avatar of Sin and Donelson the embodiment of Utu, then it stood to reason that poor Elizabeth would be forced to play the role of Inanna. The necromancer intended to consecrate his new temple with a mockery of holy matrimony. He would take the young girl as his dark bride and dedicate her to the Secret Darkness.

✳✳✳

Plans were hastily made and put into action in the short hours between the vile revelation and the expected hour of moonrise. Donelson, though an experienced soldier, was at his wits' end and therefore of little use in the actual operation. After settling his nerves somewhat with several glasses of whiskey, he agreed to handle the local authorities for the evening and to place his participating lodge members under direct authority of Aaron, his lieutenant. These men, taking up arms and knowing the general layout of the abandoned building, would then assist Professor Wyrd and his companions in the nighttime raid on the cult.

A gray, clammy fog had risen in the waning hours of sunlight, covering Nashville from the Cumberland to the outskirts. Professor Wyrd was thankful for this despite the havoc it wrecked on his thigh. Few locals would venture far from hearth and home on such a night, and thus the chance of collateral casualties was greatly reduced. Standing in the alley between a printer's office and a bank across the street from the burned Great Hall, he hid in the shadows with Catherine, Hiram, and half a dozen of the local Freemasons. He checked his sword in its concealed sheath.

"Are you sure this will work?" Catherine asked at his side. She wore a dark coat and a flat cap, her blonde tresses tucked beneath. "If something goes wrong, it could mean the end of that poor girl."

Wyrd bared his teeth. "Her soul may very well be doomed if we do nothing. We must risk losing her life if we hope to save that." He checked his pocket watch. "It is time. Let's go."

The professor stepped onto the deserted street and led his small force toward the lodge's front door. He hoped Aaron and his men were in place at the building's rear and would force their entrance as soon as they heard the commotion at the front. As expected, a pair of men stepped from the shadows behind the rickety fence surrounding the construction site. They wore long coats and broad-brimmed hats. The streetlights glinted on gunmetal beneath their coats.

"Catherine," the professor said without breaking stride.

Two blades sliced through the fog with expert precision. The two guardians clutched at their throats in surprise. Blood, almost black in the murky haze, spurted from the fatal wounds, glistening on the paving bricks as the men fell writhing to the ground. Wyrd said a silent prayer for their souls as he passed the dying men, hoping they would be the only fatalities of the night while seriously doubting it.

At the front door, one of the Masons stepped in front of the professor with a set of brass keys and went to work on the locks. These were surprisingly sound given the desiccated nature of the lodge itself. The door swung open, and a shotgun blast erupted from the shadows within. Wyrd staggered back as blood and tissue spattered his face and chest.

Catherine grabbed and pulled him away from the door. Hiram moved past in a strobe of gunshots. The professor saw his friend standing above the key man's near-headless corpse, a nickel-plated pistol in each hand. Two more guardians went down in that hail of bullets and Hiram motioned them forward into the smoke-filled corridor.

"Well, the element of surprise is gone," Catherine observed as she steadied Wyrd on his feet and led him in the wake of the remaining five Masons.

His ears still ringing from the thunder of Hiram's guns, the professor strained to hear what sounded like singing or chanting from within the darkened structure. "They've already begun the ceremony. We must hurry!"

The Freemasons jogged ahead in the narrow corridor leading toward a gray light. By this dim illumination, the professor could see the evidence of the decades-old fire—scorched and withered beams and blackened paneling where walls had once stood. Through the skeletal apertures, only darkness prevailed.

A scream at the end of the hall snapped Wyrd back to attention. Gunshots and cries followed as the startled Masons fell back at the mouth of a larger room. The professor followed Hiram and Catherine into the chamber to see what had caused the commotion.

The entrance corridor terminated in a rectangular vestibule opposite a set of newly hung double doors. A pair of lanterns flanked the portal, and standing before them, surrounded by a halo of gun smoke, was a pale man. He was tall and naked save for a black leather loincloth and a head-concealing hood of similar make. On his broad, bullet-riddled chest was carved a blood-less X. He held in his lifeless hands a great ax, fresh gore dripping from its keen edge and trailing to a headless corpse on the blackened floor.

The four Masons cowered in the corners, spilling cartridges from their pockets as they tried to reload their emptied weapons. Hiram raised his own weapons to draw a bead on the still guardian. "Don't know what good these'll do. Those boys done put about six shots in him to no account."

Professor Wyrd rested his cane across Hiram's extended forearms. "Don't. It is one of the dead Freemasons, reanimated by powerful black magic. Bullets are useless against it, so save them." He drew his blade and stepped forward, the necromantic fiend raising its ax to meet him.

"Professor!" Catherine shouted as two of her blades sliced over his shoulder to lodge in the hood's eye sockets.

The corpse warden staggered but showed no sign of pain. Wyrd slipped under the great ax and plunged the tip of his rapier into the center of the X. The blade passed cleanly through the bigger man so that the silver hilt met the decaying flesh of the symbolic wound. The professor grimaced, breathing the words, "In the name of God the Father, Jesus Christ the Son, and His Holy Spirit, I dispatch you to your final rest."

Black smoke sizzled from the wound and from the corpse's concealed features. The body shook for a moment, then a ghastly low moan escaped its dead vocal chords before it toppled to the floor and lay quite still.

Wyrd shook off his revulsion as he heard sounds of battle coming from behind the doors. Even more urgent, however, was the growing volume of the continuing chant.

"Come! We have no time to waste!"

The Freemasons regained their composure and set to trying to break down the doors with their shoulders and rifle stocks. Hiram holstered his pistols and fetched the guardian's ax. "Stand back, you bunch o' yay-hoos!" With that, he let fly a mighty swing that sheered through one of the portals, cleaving the wooden panel nearly to the locked handle. Another blow knocked it from its hinges, granting them entrance to the lodge's central chamber.

For a moment before crossing the threshold, Professor Wyrd caught a glimpse of madness and chaos in the large, marble-lined room. Men in black robes stood in rows beneath a raised altar, their hands lifted in supplication as their voices were in chant. Behind the altar stood a large man in a gilded black robe, his bald head exposed where his followers were hooded. In one outstretched hand, he held a ceremonial dagger, in the other a glass vial of dark liquid. A great tome was spread open on a brass bookstand beside him. Upon the altar lay a pale, naked figure, bound at wrist and ankle in golden chains: the unconscious form of Elizabeth Donelson.

Just beyond this tableau, a swarm of men in coats and hats swung blindly at one another, firing their weapons at random as they gave voice to terror. Another of the dead Masons strode amongst them dealing death and injury with its great ax. Wyrd could not understand the men's confusion and terror until he entered the room.

His eyesight vanished.

All went dark, though he still heard the battle as well as the chants of the Brotherhood. In that sudden blindness, the sounds of gunshots were all but deafening and the smell of blood and spilled bowels was choking, the cloying scent of incense and days-old death suffusing all.

"Hold tight, Professor," Hiram said at his side, his left hand grasping Wyrd's upper right arm. "I can see, but just barely. I reckon I'm the only one that can. And we got another one o' them dead fellers comin' our way."

Professor Wyrd took a deep breath to stave off the growing panic and tried not to retch. Clearing his throat, he recited from the Book of Genesis in a loud voice: "*And God said, Let there be light: and there was light. And God saw the light, and it was good; and God divided the light from the darkness.*"

The blindness fell from his eyes as the scales must have from Saint Paul's in Damascus. Just in the nick of time as a dead man loomed before him, a great ax raised over its hooded head.

Hiram fired, putting a bullet in the weapon's haft. The ax head flew across the room and clattered to the marble floor. Professor Wyrd lunged forward, again transfixing the symbolic X on the cadaverous torso. Again, he called on the power of the Holy Trinity to complete the victory.

However, as this foe fell like the one before, the professor saw that the last corpse warden was still making a slaughter of Aaron's men on the other side of the great chamber. Turning to Hiram and Catherine, he said, "I'll help those fellows. It's up to the two of you to save the girl and stop Fell's ceremony."

"Already ahead of you," Catherine said as she let loose one of her daggers.

Wyrd gasped, pausing in mid-stride as he watched the weapon's flight. He wanted to remind them that he needed the necromancer alive but knew it was too late. The blade crossed the room faster than the speed of thought, burying itself up to the hilt between the evil old man's hoary eyebrows.

Hiram Jones leveled both pistols at the crowd of suddenly silent robed men, clearly waiting for them to attack their leader's slayer. He was not disappointed as they turned in rage and drew weapons from beneath their ceremonial garments. The gunfighter's salt-and-pepper moustache spread in a wide smile as his revolvers came to deadly life.

Professor Wyrd turned from the fray and charged the last of the reanimated abominations. He reached the thing as it pulled its weapon from the crushed ribcage of a fallen man. Taking it by surprise, Wyrd impaled the corpse from behind and recited his exorcism for the third time.

A moment later and all was done.

Wyrd looked around at the carnage of the big, fire-blackened room now lit by burning braziers and sticks of glowing incense. Robed bodies lay in a sprawling heap in front of Hiram and Catherine. The remains of shattered men in modern attire were scattered in bloody stains across the marble floor. Only a handful of the local Freemasons remained on their feet. None of the Brotherhood of Secret Darkness did so.

Aaron, Donelson's second-in-command, though bleeding from an ax wound to his left shoulder, hurried to the altar. The young man's face was tight with concern and pale from his ordeal. "Elizabeth!"

Wyrd and his companions joined the young Freemason as he gallantly spread his bloody coat over the unconscious girl. He swept her dark hair back from her forehead and rubbed her pale cheek. "Oh, Elizabeth! Please speak to me. Please wake up."

The professor gently touched Aaron's shoulder. "If I may?" When the young man stepped back, Wyrd knelt at the girl's side and studied her closely. "She's alive, just severely sedated. Which may actually be for the best, if I'm entirely honest. I daresay her state of mind will be much the better for having no recollection of tonight's events."

"Professor," Catherine said. Her tone sent a cold chill down Wyrd's spine. "Look."

He turned from the girl on the altar to see the Russian knife-thrower spreading out an empty black robe with the toe of her muddy boot. Her bloodstained dagger lay beside the robe in a dark puddle, but there was no sign of Leonidas Fell.

Hiram pointed to the empty bookstand. "Looks like he got away with his grimoire, too."

Professor Wyrd slammed his rapier back into its cane sheath and looked again at the carnage and the chaos. He almost swore at this setback to his goals, but his gaze fell upon the two young people kneeling at the altar. Elizabeth had regained a groggy consciousness and smiled at her apparent hero, whose own face wore an expression of utter joy.

"Now I remember why I fight this war," he muttered to himself. To his companions, Professor Wyrd smiled and said, "Praise be to Almighty God for this night's victory."

THE GRAYSVILLE TRAIN ROBBERY

My guns were loaded that night. I'd debated that with myself for nearly three days. There wasn't supposed to be anybody at the station besides Old Will Tucker and maybe his grandson. The boy helped clean up the little building for the old man. I had no ill will against either of them, and I hated the idea of somebody getting hurt by accident. I thought maybe we could walk in after the train had left, our faces covered, shouting and waving our guns. Old Will would just give over, and the four of us would be on our way out of town as rich men.

But my cousin Andy convinced me it was better to be loaded for bear. "If what those bigwigs from the company said is true, there's gonna be Pinkertons on that train, Billy. And if somethin' goes wrong, you can bet your bottom dollar that their guns will be loaded."

So around midnight on April 21, 1897, I stood in the alley across the muddy street from the Graysville stationhouse, between Rose's Hardware and Keylon's Grocery, a Winchester in my hands and a Colt in my belt. Both were loaded, with more cartridges in my pockets. I chewed a plug of tobacco to stop my teeth chattering from the nerves and the chill. A sudden rain made the spring night unseasonably cold for southeast Tennessee.

Andy was hidden across the way, behind Thurman's barn. The brothers Felix and George Sims both hunkered down on the platform, behind crated freight offloaded earlier in the day. It had been their idea to pull the robbery, Felix overhearing some loose talk at their mother's roadhouse. Some executives from the Dayton Coal & Iron Company let slip that their payroll was going to be late, owing to some special shipment out of Texas delaying the train that picked up the cash in Chattanooga.

I reckon Felix must've been pouring pretty heavy to loosen their lips that much. The payroll shipment was normally kept on a secret, random schedule. But now we knew exactly where and when it'd be coming into town.

And they'd also let slip that since it would be arriving in the middle of the night, the local company guards wouldn't be there to pick it up until the next morning. Apparently something about not ruffling their touchy security captain's feathers.

What's more, the company men speculated that the special shipment was from the Corsicana oil field. A down payment in gold bullion to the Standard Oil Company on the construction of a refinery. Who knows how rumors like that get started, but that's why Andy expected Pinkertons.

Still, it was too good to be true, the perfect window of opportunity. Based on the number of employees in the mines on Graysville Mountain and in the foundry in Dayton, we figured there had to be close to ten or twenty thousand dollars in that strongbox. Maybe more, figuring what the executives made.

It was just too big a temptation.

I was nineteen in 1897. A poorly educated orphan, I kept a whiskey still hidden down on Sale Creek with Andy and worked parttime for Mr. Keylon. Selling shine and running groceries were my only options outside of going into the mountains that killed my daddy. George, Felix, Andy, and I sure weren't the only boys to lose fathers in those mines or in that mill, but we knew what we were planning wasn't some sort of revenge or restitution. It was about simple greed and freedom. The freedom to get out from under the noses of all those folks who looked down on us. The freedom to escape Rhea County once and for all. And if we could use the Dayton Coal & Iron Company's money to do it, so much the better.

I remember looking at my pocket watch when I heard the train's whistle coming up from the south. It was just a few minutes shy of one in the morning. I kept thinking as long as everybody keeps his head, everything will be fine.

Of course, not everyone did, and it wasn't.

Best I can figure, after the train came to a stop and the freight handlers started tossing the mail and other cargo off the train and onto the platform, Felix must have gotten itchy. Probably thinking about that rumored gold bullion from Texas. Someone spotted him, maybe one of the men guarding the DC&I strongbox, maybe Old Will or his grandson. All I know is, that's when the shooting started.

By the time Andy and I reached the platform, Felix was stretched out on the wet boards, a neat little hole between his vacant eyes. George was reloading his shotgun in a cloud of smoke. He must have emptied both barrels at close range, catching the two guards and Old Will Tucker in the blast. The freight handlers had clambered back onto the train for cover, and the engineer was making that whistle scream like a banshee. I didn't see Old Will's grandson. I hoped he was hidden someplace safe.

Andy screamed at George, calling him a fool and a murderer. "Ain't your brother what got killed," George shot back, snapping shut his reloaded weapon. I just stared at the heavy lockbox, surrounded by dead men in the rain.

The train started to roll out, headed toward Dayton. Suddenly the brakes squealed, and more steam blasted out from the engine, bringing the iron horse to a sudden stop. That's when I heard that... *howl*, or whatever it was, that I'll never forget for as long as I live. It sounded like a mountain lion's roar, only filled with the buzz of a thousand cicadas.

Except, it was inside my head.

It was dark on that platform. The rainclouds blocked out the moon and stars, and the downpour had put out most of the kerosene lanterns hanging on the posts. There was a dull yellow glow coming through the window of Old Will's office. He'd brought out a lantern to do his paperwork by, and it sat upright on a bench just under the stationhouse's eaves. That was all the light there was, aside from the dim shine of the engine's lamps some hundred feet up the line.

But I know what I saw, and I'll go to my grave swearing it is the God's honest truth.

I heard a shout, then another gunshot from near the engine. I turned that way just in time to see George spin around, a black cloud of blood spurting from his shoulder. The second shot dropped him for good.

More men with guns poured off the train. Men in dark suits and hats. Men with some of the fanciest shooting irons I'd ever see for nearly twenty years. They cut loose on us like we was prize bucks and it was open season. The air was alive with errant lead, flying splinters, and the roar of gunshots.

I'll admit I was scared. Who wouldn't be getting caught in a crossfire like that? But what terrified me—absolutely unmanned me—was what happened to Andy. And what did it to him.

I'd grabbed some floor and tried to put as much lead back toward the front of the train as possible, hoping to cut a path of escape that way. "Andy!" I hollered over the thunderous gunfire. "Follow me!"

I heard him scream. But there was something in that scream, something more than panic or pain. If you've ever wondered what sound a soul makes when it shatters, well I can tell you. It is the sound of my cousin screaming that night. The last sound he ever made.

Turning, I saw him standing in the guttering light on the platform.

I only saw *it* for a minute in that hellish gloom. It pounced on Andy and took his head off like you'd flick the lid off a pop bottle. It was no bigger than a child, with shiny gray skin, and a huge head with big black eyes like a giant bug of some kind. Looking back over the years, I reckon it must have taken advantage of our holdup. It must have been trying to do the same thing I was at that moment—find a way out and escape those men with the fancy guns.

I'm not ashamed to tell you, I think I lost my mind a little, as well as my water. I remember screaming and tearing off into the dark like a scalded dog. It's more than a wonder I didn't get hit by some of that flying lead. When I got hold of myself, I was a block away, hiding under the front porch of Free Will Baptist. I remember hearing more gunshots and screams, and then the train taking off again in a hurry.

When I screwed up my courage to go back, there was nothing on the platform but puddles of blood being washed away by the rain. No guns, no spent cartridges, no strongbox, and no bodies. Whoever those men in the suits were, they must have wrangled in that monster and cleaned up the mess before getting back on their way.

I didn't wait for the sheriff to show up. I went home, cleaned up a little, packed a bag, then went to Chattanooga and joined the Army. I searched the papers for a week to see if there was any report about the failed train robbery. Nothing, except a small story in the *Chattanooga Times* about Old Will Tucker and his grandson disappearing from Graysville Station. Another blurb mentioned something about the DC&I Company payroll getting dropped in Harriman by mistake. But that was it. Nothing about the shootout, about my friends getting killed. And absolutely nothing about that little monster.

It wasn't until I got to boot camp that I was able to put two and two together. I met a fellow from Texas, a place called Aurora. He showed me a

newspaper clipping about his hometown, said it was their new claim to fame. I remember breaking out into a cold sweat and shaking like a leaf on a tree when I read "A Windmill Demolishes It" by S.E. Haydon in the *Dallas Morning News* from April 17, 1897—just days before the fracas in Graysville:

About 6 o'clock this morning the early risers of Aurora were astonished at the sudden appearance of the airship which has been sailing through the country...

And then,

The pilot of the ship is supposed to have been the only one on board, and while his remains are badly disfigured, enough of the original has been picked up to show that he was not an inhabitant of this world.

Mr. T.J. Weems, the United States Signal Service Officer at this place and an authority on astronomy, gives it as his opinion that he was a native of the planet Mars...

"The pilot wasn't the only one on board," I remember saying when the Texan took the clipping back before I could tear it to pieces. "I've seen the other one."

I got a reputation in the platoon for being the crazy hillbilly after that, but it didn't matter. I knew what the "special shipment" from Texas really was that had delayed the payroll train, and it sure wasn't gold. I finally knew what that monstrous little thing was that killed my cousin, and who those men were with the fancy pistols. The train was taking a low-profile, roundabout route to bring it back to the bigwigs in Washington, D.C. or some top secret facility. God only knows what they've done with it... or what it's done with them since it got wherever it was going.

Many years later, I recalled that that rail line runs through what is now Oak Ridge, the Secret City where they built the atomic bomb.

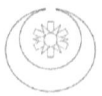

NEPHILIM PHENOMENON

Donna: *Can u meet me?*
　　Me: *When?*
　　Donna: *Now.*
Donna: *In public. Safe place.*
Me: *Call me?*
Donna: *No. Como en Casa. 20 min.*
Me: *K*

Dr. Hector Montoya looked at the cryptic text conversation again. He sat outside Como en Casa on the Av. Pres. M. Quintana, looking at the time displayed on his phone. Donna was late. He tried not to let the clandestine character of the texts stir his sometimes fertile imagination. He battled a creeping unease, sipping his latte and watching the brightly colored array of passersby, hustling to and fro in the warm April sunshine. Buenos Aires was alive and well on this lovely Tuesday afternoon, and yet he felt a chill.

It had been over thirty minutes since he had responded to Donna. He reached for his phone to text her again. To make sure she was all right. But why wouldn't she be? She was a renowned physician working for the World Health Organization, and she knew her way around the backwoods of the South American jungles like a native. What could possibly threaten her in the civilized heart of the nation's capital?

"Thanks for coming."

Hector looked up and didn't recognize her. Despite the oversized hat and sunglasses, he could tell Donna Strong was not the same woman he had seen only two months before. She was pale and thin, and looked as if she had aged nearly a decade, her auburn hair now dyed jet black. He half rose, but she gave an impatient wave and joined him at the small table. She slid a large shopping bag under the chair between them.

"Are you okay?" he whispered.

"No." Her head swiveled from side to side. She scanned the surroundings from behind the huge sunglasses. "I am not okay. Hector, I need your help."

The waitress arrived. He ordered Donna a coffee while she pretended to search for something in her purse. She kept her face hidden beneath the brim of the enormous hat.

"What is it?" He leaned forward after the girl had gone. "Are you sick? Injured?"

"No. At least not yet. You remember what I told you at the conference in Denver?"

Hector frowned, trying to recall. She had whispered something to him over late night cocktails, like a schoolgirl sharing some righteous gossip, but he hadn't really paid attention. The two wild nights they had spent together afterwards he remembered well, but so much had been going on that weekend. So much partying and drinking.

"The *children*, Hector." Her voice was an angry whisper. "You remember the theory I was working on?"

He nodded and forced a smile as Donna's unwanted coffee arrived. "Yes, I think so. Something about an anomaly in birth weights, right?"

Donna rubbed her face and cast a lingering, wary glance at the upscale kindergarten across the street. She looked as though she expected it to explode or something worse. "Turns out it isn't an anomaly at all. It's a pattern, Hector. A trend. A global one."

He blinked, not knowing what to say. He had known Donna Strong for nearly six years, and he thought of her as a friend—sometimes more. He could tell something was wrong. She was not acting like her usual carefree, put-together self. She seemed a completely different person. One being stalked by something terrible. "What are you talking about?"

She leaned forward and whispered. "Since 2001, one in every ten-thousand births has resulted in a child weighing twenty percent more than the ethnic and regional norms. I've looked at the numbers; it is a global phenomenon. What's more, I believe it's intentional.

"Someone, some organization is behind it, Hector. They're changing the DNA of the human race. They're changing the future of our species' evolution."

Hector sat back and ran a hand through his hair. "Look, Donna, I don't know what's happened to you, but you know as well as I do that when you take a sample that large, you're bound to see trends and—"

She grabbed his hand in a clammy death grip. "Listen to me! It's not just the birth weights; there's more to it. The older children are—" She stiffened and sat back. "I've uncovered something here. Something big. And *they* know it!"

Hector took her hand gently in his. It shook slightly. "Donna, you're clearly exhausted and out of sorts. I don't know what's going on, but you're talking like one of those conspiracy theorists that gets banned from the EU or something. Why don't you come home with me? I'll draw you a hot bath and cook you a good dinner. I've got your favorite Bordeaux." He smiled. "C'mon. It'll be like old times. Like London."

She almost returned the smile. Instead, she freed her hand and ran a thumb and forefinger under the lenses of the big sunglasses. "I can't, Hector. I'm already putting you in as much danger as I dare just meeting with you. In fact, I've probably said too much. I need to go."

He rose as she did. "I thought you needed my help."

Before she left, Donna gave him a weak smile. "If you don't hear from me in seventy-two hours, please mail the package in that bag."

He glanced beneath the chair. When he looked back, Donna was already striding away. He lost sight of her at the corner, and for a moment considered following. But he shook his head. She didn't want his company, or even his help. Just a favor.

He left cash on the table and picked up the shopping bag.

***

The bag sat on the foyer table in his apartment for the next two days. Hector tried to pretend it wasn't there. He tried to pretend that every time the phone rang or a text came in, he wasn't holding his breath and hoping it was Donna. He tried to pretend that when he checked his email, he wasn't looking for something from her. And he tried to pretend that he wasn't counting the hours since their brief meeting at the café.

But after midnight on the second day, after helping out in the ER, and after seeing a woman come in with a fatal gunshot wound—a woman approximately Donna's age and build—Hector couldn't pretend anymore. He locked the door and snatched up the shopping bag on his way into the kitchen. After pouring himself a big glass of wine, he sighed and looked inside the bag. There was a Jimmy Choo shoebox containing a new pair of black leather heels. And a sealed, prepaid international mailer addressed to the BBC.

Hector held the packet, gently squeezed it until he could make out the shape and size of the tiny item contained therein. "A flash drive."

He put everything back as it was, finished his glass of wine, poured another, and flopped down on the couch. He pulled out his phone and read the text messages again.

Safe Place.

Killing the wine, he sent Donna a message: *R U OK?*

When she did not respond by one a.m., Hector washed the wineglass before taking a shower, hoping he would emerge to find a message answering in the affirmative.

He did not.

He went to bed and tried to sleep, but every time he was about to doze off, his mind's eye flashed to the woman bleeding out in the ER. Only it was Donna, and not a stranger. And he couldn't save her, either. Finally, he gave up and gave in. It was after four in the morning when he said, "What have you gotten yourself into?"

Opening the packet, he hurried to his home office and loaded the flash into his laptop before he had a chance to think better of it. Though no one was specified on the address label, there was a handwritten note inside the envelope that said, "For Immediate Release," accompanied by Donna's signature and title. He could easily check the drive's content, repackage it with the note, and send it on to the BBC, with no one the wiser.

Hector closed his eyes and rubbed his face. If he had to do that, it would mean he hadn't heard from Donna in three days. It would probably mean that something had happened to her.

Again, the dead woman in the ER flashed before his eyes.

Safe Place.

The drive contained one document: Dr. Donna Strong's official report to the World Health Organization on what she called the *Nephilim Phenomenon.* Hector licked his lips at the odd word, trying to recall something from the Bible. Was it in Genesis? Something about the angels mating with human women to produce the giants, heroes, and monsters of legend?

He googled the term, Nephilim. In addition to countless references in Judeo-Christian theology, he came up with a plethora of articles and videos on conspiracy theories and pseudo-history documentaries from "giant-hunters" across the globe. Apparently, there was an emerging belief among the fringe that a race of giants had once ruled the world before the rise of humankind.

In choosing that title, was Donna seriously postulating that these beings were somehow reemerging from the human gene pool?

Returning to her report, Hector scrolled past column after column of data, showing findings in every major city of the world, as well as numerous accounts of similar results in rural settings from small towns in the United States and Canada to tiny villages in the Andes, African nomadic tribes, and even isolated communities in the Pacific Islands. Each result bore out her conclusion that there was a global trend in increased birth weight among a specific percentage of the human population. This was the first of three sections.

The second part was more outlandish, dealing with interviews and examinations of young adults born between the years 2001 and 2006. Donna's findings claimed to show the development of preternatural or psychic powers among these children.

Hector watched an imbedded video file in disbelief. It showed a sixteen-year-old Mexican girl taller than Donna lift the front end of a full-sized pickup truck off the ground with one hand. Another showed a seventeen-year-old Haitian boy smiling with closed eyes as cinder blocks and pieces of rebar danced in the air behind him. A third video was labeled "Bulletproof Boy." It looked like a bootleg copy, poor quality with digital Chinese script. It showed a large, smiling youth in a military uniform as an officer emptied an automatic pistol into him at point-blank range without any discernible effect. The camera moved through the haze of gun smoke and zoomed in on the flattened bullets lying at the young man's feet.

There were seven more videos.

Hector sat back and rubbed his face before scrolling to the third part of Donna's report. "This has got to be a hoax or something. It can't possibly be real. Has she recruited me to help her pull off some ridiculous prank or professional scam?" But he remembered how poorly she had looked at the café, how hunted...

The phone rang.

He nearly jumped out of his chair, scrambling to pick it up. He noted the time, 5:55 a.m., before registering that the number was Unknown. Still, he answered in hopes that it was Donna. "Hello?"

"Ah, Dr. Montoya?" The man spoke in English, but there was a definite Bavarian flavor to his accent. "I hope I did not wake you, but this is very important."

Hector felt cold all over. Clearing his throat, he asked, "And you are?"

"My apologies. My name is Dr. Frederick Keller of the World Health Organization, and I'm afraid I need your help."

Hector sat up. "My help? In what capacity, exactly?"

"I'm afraid we have lost one of our top researchers—Dr. Donna Strong. I believe you are acquainted?"

Hector licked his lips. "Yes. I know Donna, but I haven't seen her since... a convention in Denver a few months ago."

There was a pause. "I believe we both know that not to be true, Dr. Montoya. I'll give you some time to gather yourself before I come round. Shall we say, seven? I'll bring coffee and pastries."

The line went dead before Hector could respond. He sat in stunned silence for a few minutes before pulling himself together. He felt some of the paranoia he had seen on Donna's partially concealed face two days before, and he struggled to keep it at bay.

He tried not to think of those movies he loved so much. The ones filled with crewcut men in black blazers and sunglasses, who always carried automatic pistols with silencers and were quick to use them.

Hector swallowed, knowing he was no Liam Neeson or Harrison Ford.

He shook the thought away. He had work to do, and he hoped he had the full hour before Dr. Keller arrived. His gut told him that Donna's report, outlandish as it appeared to be, was not a hoax, and that the German's phone call was a warning of imminent danger, if not an outright threat.

***

The doorbell rang. Hector glanced at the clock on the wall: exactly 7:00 a.m. "Definitely German." He looked over the apartment one last time before opening the door.

"Dr. Montoya." The tall, thin older gentleman wore antique spectacles and a two-thousand-dollar Italian suit. He smiled and held out a drink carrier with two large coffees, and a box from the local bakery. "Breakfast, as promised."

"Thank you, Dr. Keller. Please come in."

Hector pretended not to notice Keller's slight pause when his eyes alighted on the shopping bag sitting on the foyer table. "Lovely home you have here, Dr. Montoya."

"Please, call me Hector. Not everyone buys me breakfast." He led the Bavarian into the kitchen and set two small plates and a pair of ceramic mugs on the counter opposite the refrigerator.

"Thank you." Keller mounted one of the stools and gracefully transferred his beverage from the waxed cup to the mug. "I was pleased to find an international variety at the nearby bakery. It has been so long since I've indulged in a good *stroopwafel.*"

After the first bites and first sips had been taken, Hector said, "So. Donna has gone missing? How can I help?"

Dr. Keller smiled. Hector thought the expression transformed him from a benevolent grandfather into a Nazi war criminal. "We know that she met with you two days ago, Dr. M—*Hector.* We believe she may have given you something, and a means of contacting her."

Hector shook his head. Keller had already called his bluff about not seeing Donna in months. He wasn't sure what else the man already knew. More than enough, given that he was sitting in his kitchen. "Not exactly. She did give me something, but she did not tell me where she was going. I've tried to text her since, but she still hasn't responded."

Keller sat up, his eyes darting to the foyer for an instant. "May I see what she left with you?" Hector noted how the older man's hands flexed into greedy fists before returning to his pastry and coffee mug.

"I'm sorry, Doctor, but can I see some official identification?"

Keller nodded, his smile strained. "Of course, of course." He produced a Swiss passport from his breast pocket, which verified his identity as Frederick Keller, originally of Bamberg, but now a citizen of Geneva. He also displayed a badge verifying that he was indeed employed by the World Health Organization. "Now, may I please see what Dr. Strong left in your care?"

Hector considered playing the tough guy—*And if I say no?*—but thought better of it. He shrugged and retrieved the bag. He had already planned for this, no reason to tip his hand. Or force Keller to tip his. There had to be at least one guy with a crewcut and a black blazer out in the hall at this very moment. Or maybe one on the rooftop across the street from his bathroom window, armed with a high-powered rifle. Hector tried not to think about that possibility.

"I'm guessing the shoes aren't your size?" Hector smirked to hide his nerves.

Keller gave an indulgent smile. He quickly removed the box, riffled it, and came away with the packet. "Have you opened this? Do you know what it contains?"

Hector narrowed his eyes over his coffee mug. After copying its contents to his laptop, he had replaced the drive inside a new mailer, sealed and addressed it just as the original. "It feels like a flash drive, but no. I haven't opened it. Any idea what she would want to send to the BBC?"

Keller studied the address label. "I wonder, Hector, would you mind writing down the directions to the airport from here? I do not trust GPS to be the most efficient method."

Hector's belly filled with warm water.

Keller had realized that the label was not in Donna's handwriting. Hector smiled, cleared his throat, and cursed himself for not printing the label. "Sure," he said, opening a drawer and producing a notepad and pen. "I'll try to be legible. You know, doctor's handwriting."

Again, Keller gave him that patronizing smile, but watched like a hawk as he put pen to paper. "Did you know, Hector, that two members of Dr. Strong's research team have been found dead recently?"

Hector dropped the pen. "What?"

"Yes. Dr. Craig Freeman, her assistant, was found in Mexico City last week. Unfortunately, we did not know it was him until his head was located three days ago."

Hector felt his apple fritter clawing its way back up his throat.

"And Maria Ortega, her guide and bodyguard, turned up badly mutilated in a small village in Honduras just yesterday." Keller stared at Hector. "Apparently, Dr. Strong crossed some very dangerous people in the course of whatever she was working on."

"What... exactly are you saying, Dr. Keller?"

The Nazi smile returned. "Come, come. Let us not play games. We are both intelligent and busy men, Dr. Montoya. Now, I'll ask you just one more time. Have you seen what is on this flash drive?"

Hector's heart pounded through his chest and sweat beaded his brow and upper lip. He took a deep breath. "No. What is it?"

Keller's pale eyes narrowed. "Nothing with which you need concern yourself, Dr. Montoya." Rising from his stool with a sigh of resignation, he folded the mailer and slid it inside his suit jacket. "Don't worry about the directions, I'm sure I'll find a trustworthy taxi driver."

"What are you doing? Donna left that with me. It's my responsibility."

Keller tilted his head. "You have done all that could be expected under these circumstances, Hector. Rest assured that I will see that this gets into the proper hands." He smiled, this time looking more like the grandfather Hector had met at the front door. "Do not worry, my friend. All is well, and we shall soon locate our wayward Dr. Strong."

"Are you sure?"

"Quite. Good day, Dr. Montoya."

"Thanks for breakfast, Dr. Keller. Please let me know as soon as you hear from Donna."

One last flash of the Nazi smile and the Bavarian was gone. Hector had the sudden, nauseating suspicion that the sweet pastry currently turning to bile in his gut might constitute his last meal.

Dr. Keller had known he was lying.

***

An hour later, Hector sat at a corner table with his laptop in the hospital's cafeteria—the most public and *Safe Place* he could think of at the moment. He had verified Keller's report concerning the demise of Donna's associates by trawling the international news feeds. He couldn't bring himself to do a search for Donna, or a woman matching her description. Not yet; he was too afraid. He couldn't shake the memory of the gunshot victim in the ER.

Instead, he tried to focus on the last part of Donna's report but found his eyes continually drifting to the clock displayed in the screen's lower righthand corner. His friend, Tomas Iglesias of the local INTERPOL office was late. "Where is he?"

He took another sip of cold coffee and tried to gather his thoughts. Most of the details in the report's final section eluded his distracted mind. But he had gleaned that Donna was proposing that these children with unusual birth weights and even more unusual emerging abilities were the result of a global conspiracy.

Some shadowy group of international investors was funding these unique children and their families, providing them with the best opportunities and education available in their respective locales. Worse, it seemed that Donna was narrowing down the possible suspects involved. And the names on her list were Very Important Persons with very deep pockets and very powerful friends in very high places. Hector noted the Trilateral Commission and the World Economic Forum at the top of that list.

He feared that Donna had rubbed someone on that list the wrong way. And then she had dumped this whole mess into his lap. Why had he lied to Keller? Did it even matter? Was he already the next name on their hit list?

"Hector?"

He spilled the coffee. He looked up to see Tomas staring at him with worry etched on his narrow face. "You okay, man? You look like you just crawled out of your own grave."

Hector rose and shook his friend's hand with a weak smile. He realized he had the exact same reaction when he had seen Donna less than three days before. "That bad, huh? Well, I'm afraid I've gotten myself involved in something that is way over my head. I need your help."

"Anything," Tomas said, stepping around to look at the laptop's screen. "You know, I'll always owe you for getting my Ezzy through that infection two years ago."

Hector closed the laptop and motioned to the opposite chair. "Please sit down, Tomas. You need to know what you're signing up for before you agree. I didn't get this warning, but I'll be damned if I don't give it to you."

Tomas's worry turned to genuine concern. "What is this?"

Hector rubbed his face with both hands and took a deep breath. He launched into a review of the past few days, from the moment he received the texts from Donna to his morning visit from Dr. Keller. He did not mention the specifics of Donna's report, but he did include the fate of her associates. "So, are you willing to help me? I completely understand if you say no. You do have a family."

Tomas stared at him and rubbed the worn gold band on his finger. "Like I said, I owe you, Hector. If not for you, I would not have that family. What do you need?"

Hector prayed that he was not condemning Tomas or his family to death—he kept seeing Keller's Nazi grin and the headless corpse of Craig Freeman and the mutilated body of Maria Ortega in his thoughts. Opening his messenger bag, he produced a large Ziploc containing the evidence he had gathered from his apartment: a picture of Keller taken by the GoPro camera he had hidden on top of the refrigerator, fingerprints he had lifted from the coffee mug, and even the half-eaten *stroopwafel* to retrieve dental records and DNA.

Sliding this across the table to his friend, he said, "Can you use INTER-POL resources to find out everything you can about this man? He claims to be a Dr. Frederick Keller of the World Health Organization, but I am not entirely sure of that. I haven't been able to find him on their website, or on any of their publications from the past five years."

Tomas took the bag, glanced at it, and asked, "What is this really about? What did this Dr. Strong find, Hector?"

"It's best if you don't know. For now, at least."

Tomas frowned. "I'll see what I can do, but I don't promise anything. There are some people who owe me favors..."

"Thanks, Tomas. And one last thing. You must drop this the moment I tell you, or if anything happens to me. Don't dig too deep."

Tomas looked genuinely scared when he left. Hector thought that was a good thing.

***

He sat at the same table at Como en Casa, drinking another latte and staring at the clock on his phone. It was almost exactly seventy-two hours since he had last seen Donna, and he counted the seconds. Keller had taken the original flash drive, but Hector had made ten copies. Each now in a mailer ready to send to several of the world's major news networks. He also had a zip file on his computer he intended to email to the newspapers, even the gossip rags and the conspiracy theory tabloids. All he had to do was click Send.

His phone rang. "Hello?"

"Dr. Montoya." It was not Donna. It was the superintendent of his building. "I hate to bother you, but there are men from the police here with a warrant. They are searching your apartment. There was nothing I could do."

"Warrant? Did they say what for?"

The man did not speak for a moment. When he did, it was an embarrassed whisper. "They say you have *child pornography*."

Hector inhaled sharply and closed his eyes. "Thank you, Manuel." He hung up and pulled up the live YouTube feed from the GoPro in his apartment. He could see men wearing black coats emblazoned with the white POLICIA logo across their backs, and dark sunglasses and low-brimmed caps to help conceal their faces. They wore black latex gloves as they planted magazines and DVDs in various places around his apartment before stepping back to take "evidential" photographs. One man seemed to be actively searching for something, probably his computer.

Hector closed the window just as one of the men noticed the camera. He returned to his email screen, hit the Send button, closed the computer, and gathered up his things. After his meeting with Tomas, he had gone to the bank and emptied his checking account, just to be safe.

The phone rang again. It was someone at the hospital, probably calling to tell him that the authorities were looking for him. He did not answer.

Instead, he texted Tomas: *Drop it.*

Hoping the warning had been sent in time, Hector tossed the phone into a trash can on his way down Av. Pres. M. Quintana. He would need to get a new computer somewhere along the way, as well. A new passport and a new identity. A whole new life.

Leaving the post office, Hector felt surprisingly optimistic. Right now, there were hundreds of people around the world who had seen his live YouTube feed, entitled "WHO Conspiracy," and soon there would be thousands, possibly millions more reading Donna's report in newspapers or seeing coverage on major networks. All he had to do was stay alive until the truth was exposed and the conspirators had too many fires to put out to bother with him. He had plenty of money and the smarts to make that happen.

At the bus station, he caught sight of a news report on one of the overhead televisions and his optimism vanished into an icy pit in his belly. In bold letters beneath the commentator's grim face was the caption MISSING W.H.O. DOCTOR FOUND DEAD IN CATACOMBS. Hector moved closer to hear the report. Tourists in Rome had discovered the badly mutilated body of Dr. Donna Strong earlier that morning.

She had had money and smarts to spare, too.

RAGNAROK N' ROLL

"Is that him? He sure don't look like I thought he would in real life." Carl said, shoving his shaggy head between the van's bucket seats. "Looks like he should be playing bass in a nineties metal band or something."

Ben frowned from the passenger seat and checked his camera. "If that's the guy Mike says it is, it's him." He glanced at the big ex-football player behind the wheel. "Right, Mike?"

Mike didn't take his dark eyes from the tall man in leather and denim on the opposite side of the dingy, poorly lit street. "I don't know much about nineties metal, but I *am* a licensed private investigator."

Ben nodded and put the target in frame, pressed record, and tried a bit of narration. "This is Ben Melon and crew, and we're hot on the trail of a man we believe to be an immortal. We've—"

"'And *crew*?'" Jamie said from behind Carl as she slammed an equipment box shut. "What are we, chopped liver? Your flunkies? C'mon, Ben, how about a little credit, huh?"

Ben would have snapped back if it had been Carl or even Big Mike, but Jamie was hot, and a whiz at all the tech stuff, so he let it slide. "Okay, I'll come up with a better intro in post. But right now, I want to roll while we're in the moment. So, please...?"

The blonde rolled her green eyes and shrugged. Ben tried to ignore Carl's smirk as the skinny bookworm slid into the back of the van. Mike wasn't as subtle, making a catcall and whip-cracking sound.

Ben focused on the long-haired, mustachioed man across the street and resumed his narration. "We believe we have discovered an immortal, or at least someone who has been present at various points throughout history. Possibly a time traveler or even a vampire." He turned to Carl. "This is where we'll do the montage of all the images and photos you've found of this guy from the Potato Famine to the Transcontinental Railroad to the Easter Rising, the IRA bombings in the eighties, and so on."

"He's moving," Mike said, putting the van in gear. They crept down the darkened, trash-crowded street at a crawl, keeping almost a block between them and the target. Mike pulled the van to the curb under a burnt-out streetlight when the man paused in front of an old Irish pub and whistled. After a moment, a dozen tattooed white guys stumbled out of the noisy drinking den with boisterous yells and cheers. The tall man greeted them as he was handed a beat up guitar case.

"Told you he was in a band," Carl remarked.

"Could be a gun in there," Jamie said. "I'll bet all those hooligans are packing. They kinda remind me of the gang from that old flick *The Crow.*"

Ben gave her a scowl. Everyone was already on edge; she didn't need to make things worse. "Or they're just a bunch of metalheads."

"Look." Mike drew their attention as the group of men piled into three aging rust-buckets and headed toward the freeway. "What do we do? We weren't counting on him getting together with friends. Those dudes look hardcore. I'm street, but even a brother knows not to mess with a bunch of liquored-up Paddies."

Ben licked his lips. "Keep following. We'll just see where they're going and hang back. Maybe we can catch him alone later."

"I don't like this. Not one bit," Carl said. "They could be a coven of witches or druids or something. Maybe just a run-of-the-mill satanic metal cult looking for a human sacrifice. I didn't sign up for human sacrifices, Ben. I'm a DoorDash driver, and so are you. We're not the Winchester Brothers."

"Come on, Carl. This is Detroit in the twenty-first century." Ben forced a chuckle. "You're more likely to get killed by a gangbanger in a drive-by than a cultist as a sacrifice. And that's any day ending in Y. But if we can prove this guy is legit, then we're guaranteed to land a special on the Travel Channel. Maybe even a regular series, and then all our bills are paid. So man up a little, huh?"

"Yeah, Carl." Jamie snickered. "When you're famous, you can maybe find some real friends to play D&D with. Not just kids at the local library."

Carl gave her a mean smile. "And maybe you can afford more Vagisil and

Valtrex."

"Looks like they're heading out toward the old plants," Mike said over the bickering. "The Wasteland."

Ben felt a fist tighten around his stomach. "Just keep 'em in sight and don't get too close. The cops don't like to go out there after dark, so we could be on our own if something goes down."

"*If?*" Jamie said. "Something's always going down in the Wasteland. That's why the cops don't go out there."

"I think I need to pee," Carl said.

It was the last thing spoken until Mike guided the van off the freeway and into the urban decay surrounding the rotting remains of Motor City's golden age and America's love affair with the automobile. Most of the streetlights were out and the few businesses that clung to life in this area were barred up and closed, their security lights the main source of illumination. Homeless people and drug addicts moved through the shadows like ghosts in the world's biggest haunted house. Even the dealers and the hookers weren't too keen on hanging around after the sun went down.

Ben just hoped all the gangbangers were counting their money at home or having a party at a strip club or something. As much as he wanted to be the next big thing in paranormal TV, he didn't want to face down a drive-by shooting to do it.

Mike cut the headlights and continued to follow the three cars through the Wasteland at a healthy distance. When the clunkers rolled into an abandoned lot adjacent to the old GM plant, Mike parked the van a block away with a good view.

"They're meeting someone." Ben spotted three brand new black Suburbans roll into the lot from the opposite street. "Jamie, can you get that parabolic mic out? Everybody put in your earbuds and be quiet."

They watched as the two groups got out of their respective vehicles and stepped to face each other in the glow of headlights. Ben counted a total of twenty-six big men, thirteen to a side. All were white and grim. Where the Irish looked like street hoods from a Scorsese film, the guys from the SUVs looked like well-heeled bouncers for exclusive nightclubs. The man—their "immortal"—stepped forward to face the apparent leader of the guys in the black suits.

Ben held his breath as the distant conversation came through his earbuds: "I'm surprised you showed, Loki. You have a reputation for running from a fight."

The blond man with the ponytail smiled and took off his sunglasses. "A fight, Nuada? This doesn't look like a fight to me. Is this really the best you can muster for followers these days, punks from the slums? Of course, I suppose the blood of the Tuatha has been... *diluted* somewhat over the ages."

The men in suits laughed while the Irish grumbled.

The man called Nuada raised a hand, stilling his group. Ben blinked, realizing the man's right hand flashed like silver in the headlights.

"Well, I suppose this is futile," Nuada said to Loki. "But I will ask you one last time to apologize for what you did. Do that and give me a boon, and all will be forgiven. Or don't, and I kill you here and now."

Loki laughed again, a braying sound that filled their earbuds and put Ben's teeth on edge. "Even if you somehow managed to take my life tonight, I have sewn my seed so far and wide over the centuries that you will never be rid of me. We both know I will be reborn again and again until the end of the world. My destiny is tied to Ragnarok. Can you say the same?"

Nuada shrugged and reached for his guitar case. "Who can say what the future truly holds, Æsir? All I know is tonight you pay for what you've done to me and mine." From the case, he drew a gleaming sword.

Ben and his friends cringed as the deafening roar of gunfire came through their earphones. Jamie switched off the mic while everyone cursed and stared through the windshield at the battle unfolding a block away. Automatic fire strobed against darkness. A sudden bright flash followed by a tremendous boom obliterated all sight and sound. The parked van skidded back sideways as the windshield fractured in a white spider web. For a moment, Ben and the others sat stunned in the ensuing silence.

Without thinking, Ben hopped out of the van and raised his camera to get a better shot. His ears still ringing, he barely heard Carl and the others shouting his name as if from very far away. He ignored them, his entire focus on the hi-res image coming through his viewfinder. He zoomed in to get the shot.

The six vehicles burned, and twenty-four bodies sprawled on the asphalt in the glow of lurid flames. Two towering figures stood unblemished, but greatly changed amid the carnage. Where Loki had before appeared as a high-class modern-day criminal and Nuada had worn the guise of a down-and-out rock musician, both were now revealed as the pagan gods of yore.

The Norse trickster's long red-gold hair cascaded over a bright crimson tunic edged in gold and garnets while his legs were wreathed in yellow flame. He held a sword in one hand and a net in the other. Nuada wore a black breastplate covered in silver spirals, his dark hair spilling from beneath a shining winged helm. He wielded a glowing sword in his metallic right hand and a silver-bossed black six-sided shield in his left.

"Holy crap," Ben whispered as he rushed closer. He hid behind a dumpster overturned by the explosion. From its cover, he could see and hear everything.

"You spend your followers cheap, Loki," Nuada said, eyeing the dead men at his feet.

The trickster shrugged. "Thanks to those cartoonish movies, I can find them anywhere these days. Too bad about your bullyboys, though. You Tuatha don't have any major motion picture franchises ginning up your PR, do you?"

"Once word spreads that I have taken your head for a trophy, our ranks will swell and our Pantheon will again be counted among the elite." Nuada clashed his sword across the boss of his shield, eliciting a shower of silver sparks. "We knew this fight would be determined god to god, so let us lay on and see it to its end."

"Certainly. Let me just ask you one question first."

Nuada paused with a frown. "What is it?"

"You still have Apollo's harp, don't you?"

Ben saw the Irish god's face fall. "How did you... know...?"

Loki held up his left hand, revealing a golden instrument strung with silver chords where the net had been. "Oh, because while you've been playing with this illusion, I've raided your stronghold. Just be grateful this is all I took." With that, the Norse god vanished in a shower of golden flame.

Ben cowered behind the dumpster as Nuada arched his back, spread his powerful arms wide, and roared an ancient curse into the night sky. Ben shut his eyes tight and prayed the angry god would not find him. The gravity and peril of his situation suddenly settled over him like a death shroud. He was

so overcome with sudden fear that he must have passed out...

"...Ben! Wake up! Ben!"

He opened his eyes and blinked at the bright white globe burning his retinas. "Wha—What? What is that smell?"

"It's you, buddy," Mike said, relief in his deep voice. "You just took a nap in a week's worth of wet garbage. You okay?"

Ben shook the cobwebs from his brain and climbed out of the overturned dumpster. "I'm fine... What happened?"

"We'll explain on the road," Carl said, his head jerking in every direction. "Right now, we've got to get some gone. Even if the cops hate this place, they have to come down here after all that. Even worse, those two might come back. So let's go!"

Mike and Jamie helped Ben steady himself as they hurried back to the running van. The shattered windshield had been kicked out. Piling in, they headed for the freeway and back to the relative safety of their usual stomping grounds. "Okay. So did I hallucinate all that or did you guys see it, too?"

The other three glanced at one another for a moment in silence, allowing the wail of distant sirens to be heard. Finally, Jamie cleared her throat and said, "We... we saw it, but I'm not sure what *it* was. I mean, we didn't hear what was going on because the mic was blown... Even so, that was some crazy shit."

Ben remembered his camera. He rewound his footage back to the point where he reached the dumpster and played it for Carl and Jamie, the volume loud enough so Mike could hear above the rushing wind while keeping his eyes on the road.

Carl gave a nervous laugh. "Has to be somebody's big-budget fan film. Or an indie operation. Hell, maybe Hollywood is getting back to its guerilla filmmaking roots. All I can say is, I'm buying a ticket for opening night when this thing hits the screens."

Jamie scoffed. "Did you see any film crews? Any stunt and safety coordinators? For that kind of pyro and gun work, they'd have had almost a hundred people standing by. And that doesn't include the director, camera, and sound folks."

Ben shook his head. He'd seen the looks on the two... *gods'* faces. "No. That was real. I think we got a peek into something much bigger and older than we could ever imagine. I think this sort of thing has been going on for a long, long time. Just outside of our perceived reality."

Mike laughed and slapped the steering wheel. "Well, sure beats the hell out of all them ghost hunting shows, don't it? Probably even give *Ancient Aliens* a run for its money."

Ben smiled, already counting the money now that the History Channel was on the table. "Sure does."

Then Carl stole the moment of triumph. "If they've kept it a secret this long, don't you think they want to keep it that way?"

REIGN OF THE ANNUNAKI

The alarms sound from every electronic device in the city, including my subdermal ID chip, so I put on my practiced smile and sit on the couch in front of the TV. The set comes on automatically, as does the red eye of the digital camera. Observation of the weekly sacrifices is mandatory, so I sit and watch as a hundred human beings and two hundred head of cattle are herded into the arena where I used to watch the Titans play on Sundays—what we once called the Lord's Day.

I try not to remember what a steak or a hamburger used to taste like. I try to pretend that most of those human beings are not children. I try not to feel guilty for being thankful I'm not among the herd.

I keep my smile in place and pretend to be another happy subject of the Annunaki while I say my silent prayers to the true God, asking His forgiveness, asking for His strength, and asking what, exactly, is He waiting for. I pray while the robed "priests" chant their infernal songs and the naked temple prostitutes dance and UNC soldiers usher the sacrifices into the great furnace built at the base of the giant bronze statue of Ansar (though I know his other names). I hold back tears for the millionth time and keep my smile in place as I see the men in body armor and blue helmets toss newborns into the flames, and I pray for their souls.

Before the hour is over, I have gone numb again. I'm not really seeing the orgiastic revelry of the devoted or hearing the screaming victims as they are reduced to ash. I'm not here in my apartment in the United Nations Collective, North American Region. I'm not in the year 2032, but somewhere else entirely.

When I snap out of it, the TV is black and the digital camera is off. I check my watch and see that I've zoned out for almost an hour after the broadcast's conclusion. These spells are getting longer and longer. I fear I may be going mad.

Sometimes I pray for madness or death. Any escape is welcome at this point.

I cross the small space to open a window for fresh air. At least that's what I tell myself, knowing full well that I really just want to see her. And, as usual, there she is. Selling cricket sticks from her pushcart down on the corner to those with suitable social credit scores. The afternoon sun catches in her red-gold hair and glows in her pale eyes. She smiles as always, and I wonder if it is real or practiced like mine. After all, our masters demand our joyful servitude—*Thou shalt own nothing, and thou shalt be happy.*

I almost smile for real and wave just to see what happens but decide against it. Nothing good could come of it. Not now. Either she is just as corrupt as most of the rest of the world, or she is as helpless to stand against it as I am. If the former, she could destroy me. If the latter, I could destroy her. The Annunaki and their servants are always seeking out the secret adherents of the True Faith, always looking to make an example of us.

I am already at risk. I would hate to bring that risk to her.

The chip in my hand pings and flashes yellow for a moment, letting me know that I have been preselected for next week's ritual lottery. If this wasn't at least the twentieth time this has happened, I might be worried. And if I didn't know that the regional lotteries were heavily weighted toward newborns and children, I might even panic. The reason for this is threefold: population control, the Annunaki find the terror of children more savory, and the belief in the Well of Souls—once the Well is empty He will return, and that is their greatest fear.

I frown as the chip—the Mark of the Beast—goes inert, hating myself for having accepted the cursed thing as a means of survival, of compliance. I hate myself even more because a small part of me is glad for my low priority in the lottery system. At over forty, I am too jaded for my death to offer much pleasure to the masters.

I close the window and return to my computer. I'll lose myself in my work, trying to ignore the fact that every piece of data I process is somehow in service to the Annunaki. Of course, it can't be helped as everything now done on this Earth is. They control the entire world now, and once their work in Geneva is complete, they will storm the gates of Heaven.

***

I have spent another week in seclusion, working and praying, and occasionally reading my contraband Bible. There is no need to go outside anymore, not for those divorced from this Godless world. My credit score isn't so low that I can't afford food—or the insect-based protein products that pass for food—so it is delivered. I have no friends. Everyone I used to know is either gone or has accepted the ways of the Annunaki, and I can have no part in that. I've damaged my body and soul enough as it is.

I was not selected for this week's sacrifice, so I said many prayers of thanksgiving as well as requests for forgiveness. Rereading the Book of Jeremiah, I am encouraged. Even God's chosen prophets can lose heart and feel like there is no hope for the future.

When my clandestine study is done, I hide the Bible in the air duct again. When the Annunaki first made themselves known and took power in 2024, their servants were brutal and thorough in the suppression of religion. Millions died and billions of holy texts were destroyed over the course of the next two years. And yet many copies of the Bible survived and were later disseminated among the remaining believers. When I first got my copy, I was terrified every single day for years. I just knew the UNC troops would kick in my door, search every corner and find it. And then I would be hauled off to face unimaginable tortures.

But it seems the Annunaki now suffer the consequences of the laziness and corruption they and their agents fostered among humanity for generations. After the initial zealous purge, the soldiers grew complacent in the knowledge of their complete victory and confidence in their monopoly on violence. Now their occasional raids and searches are conducted more for the purposes of intimidation and to keep the troops entertained. I was beaten quite badly two years ago, but the Bible was not found and I was not taken away. Praise God.

I hear a crashing noise and a siren honk out on the street below. I almost ignore it, but it sounds like it came from *her* corner. I'm at the window before I realize it. Below, I see a white UNC Humvee pulled onto the sidewalk, the cricket-stick cart toppled in front of its armored grill, the contents scattered across the pavement and the street. The girl is on her knees, crying as she scrambles to pick up the food. Two uniformed men exit the vehicle. I blink, actually thinking of them as men for the first time in years as they have left their blue helmets and black facemasks inside the Humvee.

I should close the blinds and walk away, but I am reminded of the Good Samaritan.

I get the fire extinguisher from beneath the kitchen sink and leave my apartment for the first time in months. My head swims with a sudden wave of vertigo when I step onto the street and breathe open air. The towering buildings of the city seem to extend up to the firmament, curving as they reach the apex. The stains on the sidewalk and asphalt coalesce and move like the patterns of a kaleidoscope. I blink to adjust my eyes and steady myself against a NO PARKING sign before I can move, lest I vomit.

By the time I have mastered myself I see the two men have hauled the screaming girl to her feet and have pressed her face down onto the hood of the vehicle. I almost can't believe what they are about to do in broad daylight on a major street. And then I remember the world in which we now live. Steeling myself, I shout and run across the street.

They turn, bemused looks battling the lurid sneers on their cruel faces. I know they are as stunned as I am. No one challenges the armed minions of the Annunaki. Not ever. But I am not acting alone. My weakness and my cowardice have been replaced by the confidence and courage of the Holy Spirit. I am a vessel and a servant.

The white foam from the extinguisher covers the men's faces and they stagger back in surprise. I swing the red canister with all my might at the nearest and feel some satisfaction at the ringing thump it makes when it connects with his foam-covered skull. He drops like dead weight to the pavement as his companion wipes at his eyes with one hand and goes for his pistol with the other. But the girl is involved now, and she is motivated. She lashes out with a powerful kick, the sole of her shoe landing hard against the side of the man's head. I hear his teeth clack as he reels away from the blow. I bring the extinguisher up in a wide arc, catching him under the chin that elicits a sharp crack. Blood and teeth fly through the air and the man's knees go lifeless.

I am shaking and breathing hard as I drop the extinguisher to the blood- and food-covered sidewalk. I don't know if I have killed the two soldiers, but a part of me hopes I have. I immediately feel guilty. "Please... forgive me, Father..."

"We need to go," the girl says, clutching my arm. "We can't stay here. They're already on the way."

I look up at her, dazed, seeing her for the first time as a person and not as an ideal or a fantasy. She isn't as young as I thought, probably in her late thirties. But she is still quite lovely, even more so considering the trauma she just endured. Her red-gold hair is a mess, and her face is flushed and tear-streaked. Her pale blue eyes lined in red. But there is a life, a fire in her that makes her beautiful.

"What?" I mutter.

She scowls and points at the dash camera in the Humvee. "They've seen everything. We have to go. Now!"

I follow as she runs into the alley, knowing that my life, such as it was, is over for good. At this I feel an unexpected sense of relief. "Where?"

"Just keep up." Easier said than done. She is quite fit, hurdling piles of trash and stacks of shipping crates, climbing chain link fences, and scaling fire escapes as she winds her way through the alleys and backstreets of the old city.

But I do manage to keep up, just barely. The Annunaki closed the gyms and health clubs when they came to power and instituted their New World Order. They don't want anyone except their chosen soldiers to be strong or overly healthy. Strong people can be difficult to rule and become strong enemies. They prefer to keep us soft and pliable, fed on weak nutrition and kept in idol lifestyles addicted to VR pornography and video games in our little apartments. But there are plenty of exercises one can do in one's bedroom without the aid of gym equipment if one is so inclined. And, as St. Paul points out, we are to make our bodies suitable temples for Christ.

I have no idea where we are when she finally comes to a halt. I see the old Interstate on the other side of a crumbling retaining wall behind a crowded row of run-down, abandoned houses. She turns and points back the way we came, and I look to see the impressive skyline of downtown. For a moment I am fear struck at the sight of a giant, white-winged Annunaki flying between the towering buildings.

A sharp, searing pain erupts in my right hand.

"Ah!" I whip my head around. The girl has buried a switchblade knife into the flesh behind my knuckle bones, impaling the subdermal chip. "What—?"

"Sorry." She grasps my wrist and uses the knife to dig out the Mark of the Beast. "Better to do it without warning. This little bugger tries to save itself if you know it's coming. Aside from being a universal ID and credit score indicator, the chip is also how they keep tabs on you. I can't have them tracking us to where I'm taking you."

I grit my teeth through the ordeal but am glad to have the thing gone when she tosses the bloody microchip to the pavement and crushes it beneath her heel. I take my jacket off and wrap it around my bleeding hand. "Thanks. I'm Jordan, by the way. Jordan Kelley."

She smiles and for a moment I see the girl I imagined for so long. "Ashley Morrow. And I'm the one who should be thanking you..." The smile vanishes into a glower as she shakes the memory from her thoughts. "But never mind, we need to keep on the move. Once the chip is removed, it sends out a GPS signal. They may have clocked it before I crushed it."

We hurry through the row of houses, climb a fence and head into a huge drainage culvert beneath the abandoned freeway. "Don't you have a chip?"

Ashley raises her right hand. "Not an official one. Mine's hacked. That's where we're going, to see the guy who did it. We'll both need to leave Nashville now. We'll need to start over, and he's the only person I know that can help us do that."

"Start over..." That is at once exhilarating and terrifying. "You mean there's places where the Annunaki don't control everything?"

"No, but they've inherited the bureaucracy of the human systems they fostered for centuries. There are cracks in their New World Order, and that's where people like us can exist. At least until He returns."

"You're a Christian?" I don't even feel the throbbing pain in my hand.

"I was raised Methodist, but I guess we're all one denomination now."

We continue through the rotting remains of Western Civilization in silence for several hours. On occasion, we duck into crumbling buildings and abandoned houses to avoid drones or patrol vehicles. A house—such an antiquated thing, the very symbol of personal property and prosperity, the badge of the American Dream. Now, in 2032, no one lives in houses, save for the hand-picked servants of the Annunaki, in their hilltop mansions and million-acre estates. We dwell in government-owned apartment high-rises until our social credit scores dictate otherwise or our number comes up on the sacrificial lottery, both of which amount to the same thing.

Finally, as the sun begins to set, we reach the edge of the urban sprawl, where asphalt meets untended forest. Ashley leads me into a stand of waist-high grass, then through a thicket of cedar and pine where we cross an old chain link fence into an overgrown cemetery. The tombstones and crosses have all been knocked over, broken, and defaced with spray paint.

"Did the Annunaki do this?"

Ashley shakes her head. "Not directly. When the world came off the rails a decade ago, a lot of folks, a lot of young people lost their way. They embraced nihilism and anarchy. They lashed out at anything that stood for legacy, tradition, and order."

The cemetery is larger than I imagined, and it takes us a while to reach the heart. The moon is rising and the stars are out when we come to a big mausoleum on a slight elevation. Ashley signals me to halt, then walks slowly toward the crypt with her hands raised like she's surrendering. Before reaching the iron gate across the heavy door, she kneels and makes the sign of the Cross. Then she waits.

A hidden speaker crackles and a tinny voice says, "What do you want?"

"Help," she says. "We are being hunted by the enemy."

"Show me your hands. Both of you."

I step forward and remove my bloody jacket to expose my wound. Ashley's hand blinks green for a second. We wait some more.

After several minutes, the door opens and the gate creaks open. A man in the shadows says, "Hurry up. Get in here." As we move toward him, I see he's armed with an AR-15, the weapon most hated by the Annunaki and their servants, a symbol of freedom and defiance.

"We're here to see AJ," Ashley says as the man closes the gate and the door. The crypt is dark and dusty, the sarcophagus defaced like the markers outside. "He helped me last time."

"AJ's gone. You'll just have to make do with me. I'm Smith." The man is older than us with long, thinning dark hair and intense eyes. "Come on, let's get underground." He picks up a flashlight and leads us to a trapdoor on the other side of the crypt. We descend into darkness on a ladder that seems to go on forever.

At the bottom, Smith leads us down a low tunnel to a square chamber, each of the three walls occupied by a heavy steel door. He uses a big metal key to open the one across from the tunnel and ushers us into what appears to be some sort of control room. The side walls have supply-laden metal racks while most of the central space is filled with computers, printing equipment, and other electronic devices. I note that most of it is antique, analog. The back wall is covered by a huge map of the United States, or what it used to be, with pins and string connecting photographs, newspaper clippings, and printouts in various locations. I recognize the faces of famous people among the photos.

Smith returns his rifle to a peg board beside the door where a variety of hanging weapons are backlit. "So, what do you need?"

"New chips," Ashley says. "Jordan here attacked two Blue Boys who assaulted me. I cut out his Mark a few blocks from the site and we've done our best to keep off the radar. But I left my pushcart behind and that will eventually point them to me."

Smith nods and opens a first-aid kit. He hands me a bottle of alcohol and a packet of antibiotics. "Clean out that wound and take these. I'll get you ready in a minute." He pulls a knife from his belt and turns to Ashley. "Sorry, but now it's your turn..."

After the unpleasantness with the chips, Smith sits at his bank of ancient computers and begins to create our new identities. "This will take a little while. Once I've generated the profiles, they'll be sent via hardline to a remote scatter-box. That'll break them up and send individual data packets to different IP addresses across the country and upload them to the Internet there through various VPNs, where eventually they will be reassembled in the UNC databases as if they had always existed."

"That's impressive." I rub the bandage now concealing my new chip. "I had no idea I wasn't alone. It seems like there are a lot of us left. Maybe we could do something..."

Smith doesn't look up from his monitor. "Not as many as you'd hope, and fewer with every passing year. More martyrs now than living members of the Church. And the only thing we can do is keep going, keep praying, and keep staying on the True Path."

Ashley wipes her tired eyes. "I just don't know how it all happened so fast. How did it come to this?"

Smith turns to face us, animation now in his eyes. "Fast? Oh no, this didn't happen fast. We've been headed here for thousands of years, and the signs always pointed to it, but we just didn't want to see it. Just like the prophets in the Old Testament, the folks who tried to warn us, to tell us what we didn't want to hear were derided, scorned, vilified, and labeled as conspiracy theorists and purveyors of misinformation."

I nod. "I remember the pandemic..."

Smith scoffs. "You mean the *Plandemic*. Not the virus, necessarily, which was just the common cold on steroids, but the reaction. A unified, global response that convinced almost all the human populace to lock themselves away, mask their individuality, and accept an untested medication into their bodies, all while putting a great worldwide economy into the toilet and laying the groundwork for a new World War. Oh yeah, I'd say that was the point where the Annunaki and their elite henchmen said, 'Okay. They're ready'."

Ashley asks, "Do you know what the Annunaki are? Where they came from? Most people believe they are aliens who created the Human Race millions of years ago and have finally returned to take dominion over their colony. I know that's garbage, but are they really demons, fallen angels in the flesh?"

Smith turns to another monitor and types something in, pulling up a diagnostic illustration of an Annunaki. The screen shows a powerful male figure with a passive face and exaggerated genitalia, a pair of great white wings on its back. A notation gives the thing's height as between nine and fifteen feet tall.

"Essentially, what we see are the Nephilim 2.0. However, these are not products of unions between angelic beings and human women. They are the product of the union of Big Pharma and Big Tech: genetically engineered superhuman bodies married to AI neural networks which serve as twenty-first century Ouija boards, doorways into the spiritual realm."

I raise an eyebrow. "You mean the Annunaki are cyborgs possessed by demons?"

Smith smiles. "In a nutshell. But these cyborgs aren't just flesh and blood and they sure don't live on food and water. Adrenochrome, which is a powerful chemical produced by the oxidation of adrenaline, runs through their veins. I guess I don't need to tell you where that comes from."

"The sacrifices."

"Bingo. But here's the kicker: they've been harvesting that stuff for centuries with their 'blood sacrifices.' That's how the Annunaki passed their essence down through bloodlines, from father to son or mother to daughter, and kept their power and plans going all this time. Remember the guy with the island that nobody wanted to talk about? He was just one of a hundred such operations, committing the worst kind of atrocities and horrors to collect the purest Adrenochrome for this." He taps the screen. "The fuel for their final form. They've reached their endgame, or almost."

"You're talking about the collider."

Ashley gives me a quizzical look and Smith nods with an appraising smile. "Yes. They've been powering that thing up for decades and I think they're almost ready to use it. How do you know about it?"

"I work in data processing. A large chunk of my workload is crunching numbers that come out of Geneva. I'd heard the rumors years ago, the jokes about how when they turned it on it screwed up our timeline and all that. I put two and two together and figured it just made sense. They want to use it to open a portal to Heaven so they can attack God."

"Maybe," Smith says. "Or maybe they just want to go home and ask His forgiveness. Either way, it means the same thing for us: total annihilation."

Ashley wraps her arms around herself and shivers. "Maybe that'll be better than what we've got right now, at least."

Smith turns to her with genuine concern. "Oh, don't lose hope. You've got to remember, it's all in His hands. No matter what happens, it will work out according to His plan. And the good news is, we know how that turns out, thanks to St. John of Patmos.

"In fact," Smith says, turning a smile on me. "I think the fact that you're here right now might be a part of that plan."

I raise an eyebrow. "How so?"

He laughs and turns on another antiquated machine. "We've been racking our brains for years, trying to figure out a backdoor into Geneva. Turns out we've been thinking too hard! We assumed that all that stuff was handled by big-government contractors, military organizations, and intelligence agencies. We never dreamed they'd actually outsource even busy work to the general populace."

"My data processing? You can use that?"

"I think so. All we have to do is plant a virus in the data you turn in, one that randomly changes equations, variables, and values in the data packs, and it could set their entire operation back months, years, or maybe even bring the whole thing down around their ears!"

I laugh. "Incorrect data. *Misinformation.* That's what I call irony."

Smith pauses then throws his head back and guffaws. "Serves 'em right."

Ashley frowns. "But that still requires a valid Mark. Jordan's is probably already red-flagged."

Smith starts typing. "Sure it is. But the data he processed this past week is probably still in the system somewhere. And I can 'ghost' his Mark for the old stuff, implant the virus, and Bob's your uncle."

"Do you think it'll work?" I am overjoyed to think that all the years I cowered in my apartment, working for the Annunaki, might actually have a divine purpose.

"It *can* work. Whether or not it does, well, that's entirely up to Him."

"But you have to try," Ashely says with a smile. "Like you said, we can't give up hope."

The lighting in the room goes red and flashes.

"Well, that's not good." Smith jumps from his chair and moves to a bank of black-and-white security monitors at another workstation. We follow to see UNC Humvees swarming into the cemetery from every direction. "Looks like this party's just about over."

"What do we do?" I look at the wall of weapons and my heart sinks. My dad was in the Army, but I've not held a gun in decades.

Smith types something on a keyboard and points to the rack on the left-hand wall. "Grab a bugout bag on the bottom shelf. Each one's got enough supplies to keep you going for about a week, maybe two if you're stingy and careful." He steps to the guns and selects a pair of snub-nosed revolvers. "And take these. They're useless against the Annunaki, but the Blue Boys haven't been shot at in so long they might just duck and cover long enough for you to get away if you send some lead their way. Here's a couple boxes of ammo."

"What are you going to do?" Ashley demands. "Aren't you coming with us?"

Smith smiles. "I've got to stay here long enough to make sure your new IDs get in the system. I don't have the bandwidth to do that and get the virus uploaded, so you'll have to make that happen when you get to Texas."

"Texas?"

The lights flicker and something crashes high above us.

"Get to San Antonio and look for Ian." Smith hands Ashley a thumb drive. "Tell him what you told me and give him this. He'll do the rest."

"How do we find him?" I ask as the lights go completely out, but the computers keep running. A generator kicks on and emergency lighting comes up.

Smith steps to the huge wall map and punches a hole in the center, revealing a hidden door. "If you're looking for him, he'll find you. Now go." He smiles. "And God's speed."

Ashley gives him a quick hug and then we're running through a narrow corridor lit with small red lights. It seems like we cross at least a couple football fields before we reach a metal ladder leading up. We race up the rusted rungs as quickly as we can. At the top, Ashley grunts and growls as she pushes against something fairly heavy. Before I can ask if we should try to trade places, she gets it to budge and starlight shines down upon us and fresh air washes over our faces.

We climb out into the cool night and almost breathe easier. But then we see and hear the most terrifying thing we've ever experienced.

We are at the base of a defunct radio tower on a hill overlooking the city, the old cemetery half a mile or more away. The entire scene is illuminated by a brilliant golden radiance and lesser blue pulses. An Annunaki, one of the biggest I've ever seen, hovers a hundred feet in the air above the big mausoleum, his great white wings languidly beating the night air. He sprays from his mouth a stream of yellow flame that turns the stone building into molten slag. The swarm of UNC troops and their vehicles form a distant perimeter around the target.

Ashley and I hold each other, barely daring to breathe as we watch the horror.

Then we see the ground surrounding the melting crypt rise gently. We hear the thump and feel the slight shockwave as the earth surrounding the mausoleum for a hundred yards in every direction collapses into a gigantic sinkhole. A few of the vehicles and men are caught in the fall while others hastily back away from the decaying ground.

We look at our hands to see the Marks blink green for a second. Smith completed the upload before sealing his own tomb. The Annunaki hovers in place a moment or two longer, surveying the destruction. It will take days to dig through the mess before anything is found, and it will require plenty of men and equipment to do so. The winged monster rises into the night sky and disappears, leaving the petty task to its minions.

Ashley looks down on the dismayed UNC troops as they try to decide their next move. She says, "To paraphrase Davy Crocket, 'I'm going to Texas. You all can go to Hell.'"

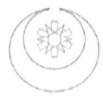

OUROBOROS

"**C**harlie! Your phone is ringing!" Sheila calls from the living room, where I left my digital leash on the end table while heeding Nature's Call. Never fails: I can have the thing in my pocket all day long, but the moment I step away to take a leak...

My slight irritation turns to despair when I see the number on the Missed Call, or rather the lack thereof: NO CALLER ID.

"Da—ang..." I catch myself, seeing the kids watching me from the couch. "He's found me again."

"Who, Daddy?" Keri asks with more seriousness than a six-year-old should possess. "Who's found you?"

"I'll bet it's his archenemy," Dillon quips. Now in fifth grade, he reads a lot of books and a lot more comics. "He found your secret identity, right? It's time for the final showdown, isn't it?"

I put the phone in my pocket as the voicemail tone sounds. "Nothing like that. Just an old college buddy I've not heard from in a while."

Sheila looks up from her iPad and frowns. "Not Andy."

I give her a sheepish smile and head to my upstairs office to see what my once-upon-a-time best friend is into these days. I'm tempted to visit the bottle of Jack I keep above the fridge for special occasions or sticky situations. But it's Sunday night and I've got a lot to do tomorrow.

The last time I heard from Andy Zicree, now a top-notch IT guru in Silicon Valley, he was digging into some seriously twisted stuff on the Dark Web. My stomach turns as I recall the vile acts he claimed to see a certain late-night TV personality committing.

I close the door to my office and play the voicemail: "*Hey, Chuck! Sorry I missed you. Or maybe you're dodging me, huh?*" (He laughs.) "*Anyway, have you ever heard of the Reptilian Conspiracy Theory? I thought it was just a bunch of hokum and would be fun to debunk. But then the EU just labeled David Icke a terrorist and banned him! Can you believe that...? Anyhow, I just wanted to give you a shout and see what you were up to and get your thoughts on this. I know you told me I needed to get back into the 'real world' or something. Well, I'm definitely not looking into that weird stuff anymore, so things are better. Anyway, I'll talk at you later."*

I delete the message and shake my head. "*Weird* stuff?"

The next day, I'm working on my sales projection report when I get a text message. I open it to find a link to a BitChute video about David Icke's theories. Beneath the link is a message from Andy: *Watch this and get back to me.*

I roll my eyes and return to work. I decide to call him on my lunch break and put a stop to this before it gets out of hand. The last time, he was calling and messaging me at all hours of the day and night with horrid stories about politicians and celebrities involving some of the worst, most inhumane and unnatural crimes imaginable. Thank goodness he didn't send any links to those findings! And that he was clever enough to misspell words like "Pizza-G8" and "Ep-steen."

I remember being into all this behind-the-curtain stuff when I was in college. Andy and I would stay up way too late, drinking beer and listening to Art Bell on the radio. We'd both grown up on *The X-Files* and had bought into the "The Truth is Out There" and the "Trust No One" mindset, fostered by the show and the whole UFO/alien/paranormal conspiracy subgenre it had spawned. Yeah, we were *those* guys back then.

Of course, getting my MBA and joining the corporate workforce made me realize it's *all* behind-the-curtain stuff. Anybody who has had to massage data for a quarterly earnings report can tell you that. The truth may be in there somewhere, but you really can't trust anyone. Not when it comes to the dollars and cents. It's all a hoax, but we willingly buy into it so we can keep the lights on and the food on the table. If we didn't, I think most of us know somewhere deep down that once somebody says, "The Emperor really has no clothes," we'll be in *Road Warrior* or *The Stand* territory inside of a week.

Being on that side of things—and settling down and starting a family—took all the fun out of the crazy "what ifs" for me. Of course, Andy got a job with one of those Big Tech über-corporations that make so much money per second that they're little more than adult daycares for their employees. Having access to all the Internet's darkest secrets with that much spare time and that much spare change, there was no way he was going to grow up and settle down. He's still playing at being a faux Fox Mulder, or at the very least an armchair Alex Jones. A keyboard conspiracy king with the keys to the castle.

I take a deep breath and make the call, part of me hoping I get his voicemail. No such luck.

"Chuck! Glad you called, man! So, what did you think of that video, huh? He's onto something, but I think he's only—"

"Hey, Andy. Look, man, I didn't watch it. I'm really busy with work and I just don't have time to get into this with you right now. With the holidays coming up, it's crunch time. I just wanted to touch base and see how you're doing. Do you need anything?"

He chuckles. "Nah, I'm good, buddy. Got everything I need. But, man, I gotta tell you this is some seriously whacked out stuff. I thought it was all a bunch of crap, but the more I dig... well, let's just say the more I *find*."

I admit to a mild curiosity prickling at the back of my brain, but then I see a vision of Sheila scowling and reminding me that I've got two kids to feed and put through grad school at some point. "Well, unless it can help me find a way to improve my numbers on this report, I don't see how I can join in the dig, my friend."

"I get it, Chuck. But before I go, let me ask you this: Did you know that virtually every single culture in this world has a hero myth attached to a Great Flood story? And almost every single one of these heroes who helps to re-build civilization is somehow associated with snakes or serpents? And the ones that don't, the serpents are the ones that caused the cataclysms. I'm just saying: look into it."

"Sure, Andy. Look, I've got a lot of work to do, but I'll try to catch up with you this weekend, okay?"

"You bet. I'll just send you an email with what I've got so far. You know, just in case you get interested."

"Thanks. Later."

I put the phone face down on the desk and look out the window at the glowering storm clouds hovering over the city. Why does talking to Andy get my mind racing in a hundred different directions? Before I try to answer that question, I force myself back to the report and bury myself in data and numbers.

And try *really* hard not to think about snakes for the rest of the day.

Or the rest of the week. I've got to present this report on Friday, and so far, things are not adding up the way I need them to. On Thursday morning, I tell Sheila I'll probably have to pull an all-nighter before heading out the door and into the cold downpour still sitting on the city.

She glares at me. "We said we would take the kids to that new superhero movie on opening night, Charlie."

"That's today?" Her frown is the only answer. I sigh and look at my watch. "We'll go to a matinee on Saturday and then take them to Dave & Buster's after. That should compensate, right?"

"Don't worry about it. I'll figure it out. You just do what you've got to do."

It's hard to concentrate on work after the caustic exchange, but somehow I soldier on. Even more amazing, by six o'clock, the numbers start to make sense and my report suddenly falls into place. I finish the project with a sigh of relief and check the time: just after seven. I call Sheila, hoping to catch her and let the kids know I can meet them for the eight o'clock show. I get her voicemail. They must already be sitting in the dark with their popcorn and sodas.

I turn out the lights of my office and sigh in acknowledgment of the Pyrrhic victory before heading out.

It's almost nine by the time I kick back in my home office with a tumbler and my bottle of Jack. I should probably find something to eat, but I'm just not in the mood. After I refill the glass for the second time, I decide to see what Andy sent in that email. I've got nothing better to do, right? Might as well kill some time until Sheila and the kids get home.

An attached PDF contains pages of hyperlinks to videos, articles, websites, and blogs, as well as clipped quotes from said articles and blogs, photos of archeological sites and artifacts, and even old black-and-white photos of people in mystic rituals. I chuckle as I take another sip of whiskey and settle in for an entertaining read.

Andy begins with David Icke's hypothesis, as set forth in his *Children of the Matrix*, which claims that the "Reptilians" are an alien race from the Alpha Draconis or Thuban star system, and that they've infiltrated the human race via tainted bloodlines among the ruling elite. No surprise that he lists the Merovingians, the Rothschilds, the British Royals, and even the Bushes as his go-to alien sympathizers.

But Andy backtracks Icke's ideas through the mystics of the late

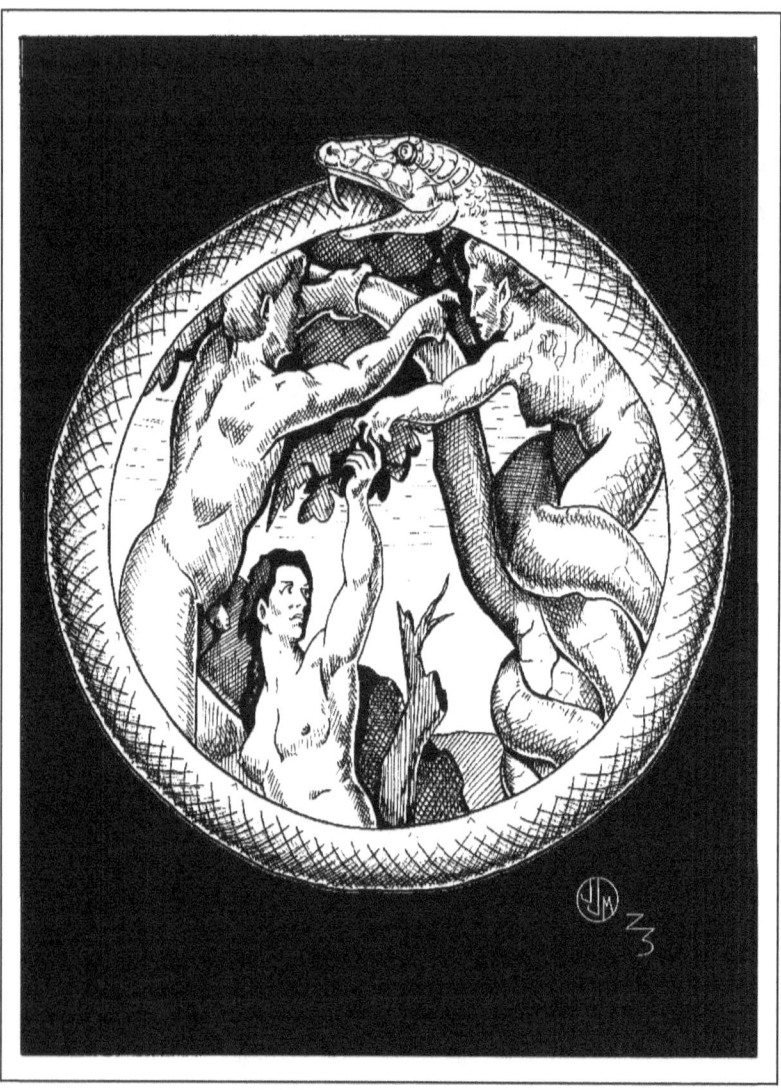

nineteenth and early twentieth centuries: the Theosophists, the Brotherhood of the White Temple, and the Hermetic Order of the Golden Dawn among others. He cites Madame Blavatsky and Maurice Doreal before going into the whole "ancient astronaut" thing. Leapfrogging across the works of Erich von Daniken, Giorgio Tsoukalos, and friends, Andy lands on the more terrestrial-themed works of Graham Hancock and Randall Carlson. From there, he winds his way through antiquity's shared flood mythology until he comes back to the Bible with Trey Smith and his *God in a Nutshell* theories.

And that's where it gets scary.

My phone rings and I nearly jump out of my skin, sloshing whiskey across the desk, barely missing the laptop. It's Sheila and it's almost midnight. She sounds tired and angry: "I thought you were pulling an all-nighter."

I close the bottle and slip it under the desk, regretting that it is considerably less full than when I got home. "I did too, but then I hit a break. I tried to call. Where are you?"

"In the driveway. The kids are asleep. Can you come help me carry them in?"

"Yeah." But she's already hung up. I take a deep breath and hope I don't smell too much like a distillery. Things are clearly bad enough.

I meet her in the driveway where she's carrying Dillon—making a point, as he's the heavier of the two kids. "I don't know whose bright idea it was to make a *three-hour* superhero movie and then release it on a school night. Clearly somebody without kids."

I give her a sheepish nod of agreement and set to extracting Keri from her harness. She stirs on my shoulder as I lock up the car. "Hey, Daddy... why do you smell like Uncle Scott?"

"Shh. Go back to sleep, honey." I'm glad Sheila didn't hear that particular reference to her freewheeling, borderline-alcoholic younger brother. I hope I can stay downwind of her until I get a chance to hit the mouthwash.

After putting the kids to bed and making a quick stop at the bathroom, I find Sheila sitting at my desk, her arms folded as she reads the PDF I left up on the screen. "What's going on?" I ask, hoping this isn't about to get ugly but knowing it is.

"Exactly what I was going to ask, Charlie." Her eyes glow in the reflected light of the laptop. "I mean, I could have used a little help tonight. But instead, you're kicking back shots and playing conspiracy theorist like a bachelor or a college kid or something."

I lean against the doorframe and sigh. "I told you, I tried to call when I finished at work. I was going to try and meet you for a later show, but I got your voicemail, so I figured you were already in the theater."

She looks at her phone. "You didn't leave a message?"

I shrug. "Didn't think I had to. Sorry."

She closes the laptop and rubs her eyes. "I'm just tired, Charlie. I've not said much about your work getting in the way of spending time with me, with the kids, with your family. But if you're going to shove us aside to get back into *this* crap... I just don't know what to say."

"I'm not getting into anything!" I struggle to keep my voice down. "Andy sent me this stuff and I figured while I had a couple hours to kill, I'd look at it and have a good laugh."

She rolls her eyes and gets up from the desk. "I wish you'd just told Andy to take a hike. We really don't need this right now. Not with the holidays coming up. You know?"

"Yeah, I know. Look, I'm sorry about tonight. Maybe we can still take the kids to Dave & Buster's this weekend." I try to put a smile on it. "If everything goes well with my report tomorrow, we might have something to celebrate. Come on, what do you say?"

She gives me a half-hearted smile and nods. "Okay."

Of course, everything does *not* go well with my report. And, of course, I have a mild hangover. I missed something in the analytics and one of my colleagues spots it five minutes into the presentation. We spend the next three hours hashing out my mistake before getting around to fixing it. The whole day is shot and so, apparently, is my weekend as I'm on the hook to redo the entire report from the ground up before Monday.

I dread calling Sheila to let her know, so when Andy's NO CALLER ID pops up on my phone, I decide to delay the inevitable by taking his call.

"Hey, man, did you get a chance to look at any of that stuff yet?"

"Yeah. Pretty interesting, but I don't know. That's a big pill to swallow." I close my office door as the last thing I need right now is my coworkers hearing me talk about lizard men in the government. "I think it's some amazing coincidences, but..."

"Yeah, coincidences." Andy scoffs. "You know what Einstein said about coincidences, right? I'm telling you, man, I've vetted this stuff and it all tracks. Even the reason Plato gives for the destruction of Atlantis jives with the Book of Genesis's reason for God destroying the world with the flood. *And* modern science has accepted the epoch of global cataclysm mentioned in every culture's mythology by calling it the Younger-Dryas era. I'm just saying, the preponderance of evidence, man."

"Yeah, well... it is a fascinating exercise in ancient history and prehistory, but like I said the other day, I've got more than enough in the modern world to keep me busy. In fact, I really need to get back to it. But thanks for tossing this one my way. Reminded me of old times."

"Sure thing, man. Keep in touch."

As soon as I end the call, I realize I was genuinely smiling for the first time in a long while. It truly did feel like the good old days. But that elation evaporates as I dial Sheila's number...

She takes the kids to her mom's for the weekend. Thursday being Thanksgiving, we were going up there anyway, so she's just decided to make a little vacation out of the holiday. I tell her I'll drive up as soon as everything at work is settled, and we can be together as a family. She doesn't sound convinced, and for the first time I wonder if we might really be in trouble.

I stop at the liquor store on the way home from the office. Ten hours of crunching numbers while trying not to think about marriage counselors, divorce attorneys, visitation rights, and all the rest has worn me thin. I need to unwind. I know my Saturday will be another slog to get those numbers to mesh, to perform the miracle of projected profits for a company that has become too big to grow the old-fashioned way, through innovation and risk.

Alone with my fresh bottle of Jack, I settle in to finish my read of Andy's findings.

Trey Smith gets into the weeds of Judeo-Christian dogma and apocrypha while drawing a relatively straight line from the Serpent in the Garden of Eden to all the modern-day occultists practicing the black magic from ancient Egypt and Sumer. From there, Andy brings in the Serpent Seed Theory, whereby the demonic blood of Satan entered the human populace through Cain, his son by Eve. Though Andy doesn't completely buy into this one, he does point out it is an interesting origin for the Rh variations in blood types which lends credence to some of Icke's claims. If, as modern science asserts, all of humanity has a common ancestor in Africa, there should be no such variation.

And then there are the Naassenes and the Ophites, Gnostic sects that revered the Biblical serpent, Naas, as a liberator and a bringer of knowledge and civilization—just like those post-Flood "heroes" Cecrops I of ancient Greece, Fu Xi of China, Tlaloc and Quetzalcoatl of Mesoamerica, and the Nagas of ancient India. One chilling note about the Naassenes, given the current state of modern society, is that they believed androgyny to be the pinnacle of perfection.

Andy's thesis, of sorts, culminates with a video clip from 2013, in which a security guard protecting the President bears a striking resemblance to a snake for a few frames. To this he has added a recent photo of an aging pop star from the 1980s side by side with an image of a serpent-headed figurine from the Ubaid period of Ancient Mesopotamia. More photos of enhanced celebrities emphasize the point. Modern plastic surgery and transhumanism seem to be emulating the hybrid snake-person look. Whether this is by design or coincidence...?

When I finish the document, I pour another glass of whiskey and check the clock. I figure Andy is still up, so I send him a text. When I don't get a reply by the time I've finished the drink and started another, I decide to give him a call.

I feel a cold chill despite the whiskey buzz when I get the recorded message: "*The number you have dialed is no longer in service. Please try again.*"

I kill the drink and send Andy an email. Almost immediately I get a delivery daemon failure notice.

I turn off my laptop and my phone and hurry to unplug the router. And then I spend the next three hours hunkered down, alone in my darkened house. Waiting for... what? *Something.* Something bad—a SWAT team raid, a drone strike, hell, maybe a pair of Men in Black to show up and wipe my memory or something worse. But eventually the paranoia gives into exhaustion, and I fall asleep in my recliner, my handgun in my lap...

I manage to pull it together and stay off the Internet and the booze for the rest of the weekend. I iron out all the kinks in the report, go over it twice on Sunday, and head into the office on Monday morning with confidence. The presentation goes off without a hitch, and even ends with a round of atta-boys. By lunchtime, the office is thinning out as most folks are getting a jump on the holiday traffic. I manage to keep myself busy with small and shop talk for the rest of the day. Somehow, I have convinced myself that

Friday night's excursion into the Twilight Zone was nothing more than a whiskey-fueled fever dream.

My life is back to normal and now I can focus on putting my family first again. I spend the night eating pizza and watching football at home. No SWAT teams pop by for a visit, and, as far as I know, neither do the Men in Black.

Tuesday morning, I load up the car and head out to join Sheila and the kids at her mom's house. I call to let her know. "Hey, I'm on my way."

"Your report went okay, then?"

"Yeah. Hey, listen. I'm so sorry about the past week. I sort of lost sight of priorities. I love you and the kids, and I don't want anything to ever get in the way of that again. I promise I'll do better. And if you ever catch me slacking off, you have my permission to slug me, okay?"

I can hear her smile. "I'll hold you to it. Now be safe and get here as soon as you can."

"Will do."

An hour later, I'm stuck in creeping bumper-to-bumper traffic on the interstate and my phone rings. I answer, expecting Sheila checking in. Instead, I hear Andy's voice. He sounds more relaxed and low-key than usual. "Hey, man. Do me a favor and delete all that stuff I sent you. No big deal, but I think I might have stepped into some copyright issues and I don't want to get sued."

"What are you talking about, Andy? I'm halfway across the state, stuck in traffic and my laptop's back at the house."

He inhales. "That's cool. You didn't show it to anybody else, did you?"

That prickly feeling at the back of my brain kicks in. "What are you saying, Andy?"

"Nothing. Don't worry about it, man. Look, I gotta go. But hey, don't forget to delete that stuff. Oh, and if you want, go ahead and wipe your hard drive. I'll foot the bill for a new one. Just let me know. Later."

The call ends and I know better than to bother calling back. Instead, I drive on, hoping and praying that my family is all right when I get there. I don't have the guts to call Sheila for fear that she won't answer.

My prayers appear to be answered when I finally arrive just after nightfall. Keri and Dillon run out to greet me and usher me into my in-laws' house. Sheila hugs and kisses me, and I finally feel like all the paranoia and craziness are gone. Her dad takes my coat and asks about the drive, and her mom hugs me before directing me to the bar. Of course, that's where I find Scott, rum and Coke in hand.

Scott beams red-faced at me, happy to have a drinking partner. "What's your poison?" He's already reaching for the Jack Daniels. We've shared a holiday foxhole before.

We slip into casual conversation about sports, movies, TV shows, and even politics. A couple drinks later, I hear myself ask Scott, "So, have you heard about David Icke and the Reptilian Conspiracy Theory?"

THE
MONTANA TRIBUNE

Vol. 19, Issue 7
16 July, 2023

Serving our community since 1978

LOCAL WIZARD'S CASTLE GOES TO MARKET

D.S. Hamilton, Staff Reporter

RAVEN FALLS, MT -

It has been over two decades since the scandal and the mystery, and few of this generation remember the name Edmund Griffiths. Just the hardcore horror fans, a handful of comics aficionados, and *Jeopardy!*-level film trivia buffs. And, of course, the natives of this sleepy little mountain town.

Edmund Griffiths, a British expatriate, became a part of the American zeitgeist in 1965 when his peculiar horror stories first appeared in such pulps as *Weird Tales*, *The Vault of Terror*, and *Room 13*. Scholars of the era have claimed it was

23 Leeds Court, staff photo

his work that kept the supernatural horror genre alive following the rising interest in little green men from outer space and giant radioactive monsters of the nuclear age. A few on the literary fringe go so far as to say that without an Edmund Griffiths, there might never have been a Stephen King. Within two years of his first story "The Horror at Hilltowne" being published in *Weird Tales*, Griffiths's yarns were being turned into illustrated comics for the Warren publications *Creepy* and *Eerie* magazines.

Continued on page A10

LOCAL WIZARD'S CASTLE...

Continued from page A1

These, of course, featured covers by such seminal genre illustrators as Frazetta, Sanjulian, and Corben. By the end of the decade, Griffiths had seven novels on bookstore shelves, and had written three episodes of Rod Serling's *Night Gallery* for NBC, one of which never cleared the censors, and has yet to be aired or included in a collection of the series.

As the 1970s got into full swing, Griffiths's level of popularity almost reached that of a rock star or film idol. At times, it seemed only Evel Knievel, this state's favored son, was more famous in the United States. It was also during this decade that the public began to learn more about the eccentric author. In addition to rubbing shoulders with popular musicians and movie moguls, Edmund Griffiths officially joined the Church of Satan in 1972. He toured the country with the organization's founder, Antoine LaVey, speaking at universities, civic centers, and TV and radio stations, promoting what he called "The Religion of the Age." As he and LaVey attempted to draw converts, Griffiths often spoke of his youth as a medic in the British Army serving in mysterious regions of North Africa during World War II, and later as a hospice nurse in England, where he claimed to have

cared for and studied under Alistair Crowley before the legendary occultist's death in 1947.

In 1975, Hammer Films commissioned a screenplay from Griffiths, but after paying the kill fee, the studio passed on the script. An unnamed source within the production company at the time said, "It's just too bloody evil, even for this gore-and-sex-fixated generation." At some point in the early 1980s, a major Hollywood studio was purported to have optioned the project, but—social mores being what they were at the time—when the script's explicit, incestuously homosexual subject matter was leaked, producers willing to put their name on the film were not to be found. Current Tinseltown rumors claim that a certain rock-musician-turned-horror-film-auteur is now in possession of the original screenplay, the title of which has still never been disclosed.

In 1989, Edmund Griffiths officially retired from the public eye, purchasing the nearly 100-year-old estate at 23 Leeds Court in the isolated mountain town of Raven Falls, Montana. The sprawling Victorian mansion was built in 1891 by shipping magnate Hiram Oreto, after the long-time sea captain returned from an ill-fated trip to the

Continued on next page

LOCAL WIZARD'S CASTLE...

Continued from page A10

South Pacific. His final voyage ended with the loss of his ship and crew. The captain was stranded alone at sea for nearly a month. There were rumors at the time that Oreto was not completely sane when he came to Raven Falls. These say he claimed to have seen some submerged horror that would "eventually drown the earth." This would explain why he built his new, high-walled home on a mountain far from any ocean. Strangely, Captain Oreto vanishes from the historical record just two years after the imposing house's completion.

The property subsequently passed through several hands and played many roles over the years before being purchased and renovated by Edmund Griffiths. These incarnations included an exclusive hotel, a health spa and retreat for the wealthy, and later a house of ill repute and a speakeasy saloon. But in spite of this checkered past, the fortified mansion's darkest chapter was yet to be written.

Although the aging Griffiths had published no new material in over a decade by 1989, it seems he still had his connections. Tales abound of processions of private planes landing at the tiny local airport, where incognito celebrities and politicians would then board limousines to make the winding trip up to Griffiths's hilltop estate for weekend parties. Over the course of the next seven years, these processions could be predicted like clockwork: the 13th and 31st of every month. Locals still believe these gatherings of the social elite and the financially powerful were in reality black masses, or witches' sabbaths, where Griffiths and his coven worshiped dark and mysterious powers.

Perhaps it was these rumors which brought the Montana State Police and the Raven Falls Police Department knocking at the mansion doors on Halloween night, 1996. Two weeks earlier, a set of newborn twins had been stolen from the Powell County Medical Center, and an anonymous tip claimed that Griffiths and his associates were planning to sacrifice the children at their satanic ceremony. Though several arrests were made that night, mostly on minor drug and weapons charges, no trials were held and no names were ever released to the public. This despite one trooper being wounded in an unspecified manner and a Raven Falls officer being confined to a state mental hospital for several months with an undisclosed condi-

Continued on next page

LOCAL WIZARD'S CASTLE...

Continued from page A11

tion. Local lore holds that an insider among the law enforcement community tipped off the coven, and that Griffiths made good his escape with a single loyal assistant and the kidnapped children. Edmund Griffiths was 74 years old in 1996, and has never been seen or heard from since. The sprawling hilltop mansion has remained vacant these many years.

Last week, the Montana State Supreme Court ruled in favor of Harold Greaves, a great-nephew of Griffiths's, awarding him possession of the abandoned estate. The estranged Greaves immediately put the decrepit manor on the market, with his legal counsel declaring that the list price is just over $6 million, as is. Of this sum, the state and federal governments will claim over $3.5

million in back taxes and fees. Greaves was unavailable for comment.

Despite the controversy and scandal that still cling to the moldering mansion, a few high profile individuals are rumored to be interested buyers. At the top of this list of big name actors, musicians, and politicians are the 27-year-old twin brothers, Alex and Mike Edmundson, the videogame wunder-kinder behind the chartbusting HorrorHouse Studios and last year's game of the year, *Nightmare Country: Infinite*. If they make the deal, one can only speculate as to what inspiration their new home might bring to HorrorHouse's next big release.

MAJESTIC DAWN

ajor Peter Staff leapt from the truck before it came to a stop. The sun rose above the Mississippi River, turning the April sky to fire and glory—what his missionary parents would have called one of God's great miracles. He might have chuckled at that prosaic notion if not for the chaos swarming over the smoke-shrouded stretch of ground. Vehicles, lit by headlights, flame, and the first crimson rays of dawn, spilled scores of soldiers, policemen, firefighters, and even a few dozen concerned locals onto the frenetic site.

Staff had seen thousands of sunrises in his thirty-six years on Earth, but the thing that had just crashed in the field outside of Cape Girardeau, Missouri—now that was a miracle.

Dressed in his olive drab field uniform, boots and leggings, Staff headed to the parked ambulance, guessing that's where his expertise would be most valuable.

A local sheriff's deputy shared a smoke with the two ambulance drivers, standing above three lumps covered in white sheets on the ground. A few feet away, another deputy spoke to a dark-clad man, possibly a country minister. Staff adjusted his glasses and produced his credentials. "Morning, gentlemen. I'm Dr. Peter Staff, United States Army Air Forces. I'd like to see what you've got here."

"You think it's a Nazi spy plane?" One of the ambulance men asked. "I mean, these sure don't look like no Germans I ever seen."

"What are you looking at?" the other driver said. "In case you hadn't noticed, these are bona fide Martians, just like in *Amazing Stories*. That ain't no Nazi plane." He waved at the shining silvery object burning several hundred yards away.

Staff ignored the speculation. Whatever this event was, the Army had given him specific orders to gather information, not to give it. He knew

someone would be dispensing government funds to hush things up once the trucks, the soldiers, the debris, and any other evidence were on their way back to Sikeston Air Field.

"Hope you've got a strong stomach, doc," the cop said, kneeling to remove the sheets.

Staff smiled, almost felt like crying at what he saw. He'd dreamed of something similar to this moment since he was a boy. He'd grown up not far from Aurora, Texas, and had been fascinated by the tale of the reported "Martian Crash of 1897." He'd even run away from home when he was ten, hopped a train and hitchhiked to get to the town. Though he hadn't found any evidence of the storied encounter or the alleged grave of the alien pilot, it had still been worth the whipping he'd gotten upon his return home. It had been his first adventure into the unknown, just like those pulp stories he loved so much. And now, almost three decades later, the government was funding a brand new installment.

"You okay, doc?" the deputy asked with an odd look. "Because I can't for the life of me think of a reason to smile at something like this."

"I'm sure you can't." Staff took a pen and pad from his pocket. "Now, if you'll see that these remains are loaded onto that Army truck over there, I'll need to get your names and statements."

"What?"

"The United States Army is now in charge of this site, officer. And we'll require a sworn statement from everyone here, as well as the confiscation of any and all photographs. I noticed a few camera flashes from the yokels on my way in. Now, if you don't mind..."

***

"Penny for your thoughts, Pete," Captain Edward Miller said. They sat in the back of one of the trucks headed back to Sikeston with the other ten men assigned to this case. All of them were military officers with scientific specialties ranging from astronomy to zoology.

Staff smiled at his best friend. They'd known each other for years, having attended Baylor at the same time. Ed majored in engineering while Staff doubled in engineering and pre-med. They had bonded over their shared love of aviation, both getting their civilian pilots' licenses before Staff had gone on to Johns Hopkins for his MD. "Can't say my thoughts are worth a penny right now, Ed."

"You had a look at the... crew yet?"

"Yep. Not a pretty sight, I'll say that. But the degree of injury and burns made it difficult to make a definitive call in the field. Won't know anything conclusive until we can get them under the knife..." Staff shook his head. "I just wonder how much the Army had to pay those folks to buy their silence."

"Probably not much. Farmers round here are still hurting from the Depression pretty bad. A little goes a long way these days."

"I guess that New Deal hasn't reached everybody just yet," Staff said. "What about you? Had a look at the hardware?"

"What's left of it. Whatever wasn't junked in the crash was all but toasted by the fire. Then the locals hosed it down pretty good, so there's quite a bit of water damage."

"Well, if it's not a Nazi spy plane and some of the smallest fascists the world has ever known, I can't imagine a little fire and water could completely erase evidence of whatever's out *there*." Staff waved at the truck's canopy.

Commander Bill Hennessey, a Navy linguistics expert and codebreaker, grunted. "You ask me, we got enough problems on this world without looking for more 'out there.' You heard Hitler signed a deal with the Japanese, right? While his goose-steppers are marching all over Europe and Africa, Tojo's guys are carving up Asia... How long you think it'll be before one or the other of 'em decide to come for us? But instead of getting ready to crack some skulls, we're chasing little green men around in the middle of nowhere."

"All very valid points, Bill," Ed said with a grin. "But my money's still on this being some kind of hoax. Probably circus performers in costumes and a rigged-up barnstormer."

Staff chuckled. "You're probably right, Ed. And once we prove it, we can get back to preparing to 'crack some skulls'."

But he had seen those bodies, and his gut told him they weren't dwarves in Halloween getups.

∗∗∗

His gut was right. Beneath the harsh glow of half a dozen lamps and the watchful eyes of two movie cameras, Staff sweated through his surgical gown and dictated his process for the reel-to-reel recorder. Of the three subjects, only one was suitable for autopsy, the one claimed to have been alive when the first witnesses had arrived at the scene. That's why the minister had been there—to administer last rites.

The first thing Staff noticed was that the subject was considerably greener than when he'd first seen it only a few hours before. At the site, it had been a greenish grey, almost pearlescent. Now, it looked like it was made of green-dyed India rubber. At least the undamaged parts of the skin did. The wounds appeared to be a soupy mess of black ash and gelatin, as though some accelerated healing or scabbing action had been suddenly arrested.

Those big, unblinking black eyes were just as wide and shiny as before. In better lighting, he could see that they were multi-faceted like those of insects, but the individual lenses were so tiny he couldn't tell if they were hexagons, octagons, or decagons. He'd have to look at a sample under the microscope.

"The reproductive organs appear to be sheathed, similar to those of a dolphin or porpoise," Dr. Wagner said. The Army zoologist was assisting in the postmortem, which only made sense as Staff was an expert in the anatomy of one species, whereas Wagner was schooled in many. "That fact and the quality of the skin makes me think it might be aquatic."

"Perhaps, but the nostrils, while not pronounced, are located on the anterior of the skull, and the skeletal structure resembles our own." In fact, the situation of limbs and joints and even the number of fingers and toes were identical to a human's. The only difference was a matter of scale. The body seemed to be roughly half the size of an adult human, while the head was almost half again the size of same.

And yet the muscular structure of the neck and shoulders did not seem augmented to deal with the disparity of weight. If anything, the entire musculature system actually appeared underdeveloped. "Perhaps a different gravitational system," Staff muttered. "That might account for the crash..."

"What?" Wagner asked.

"Nothing. Let's make the Y-incision and take a look at what's inside." He picked up the scalpel.

Nazi... Spy...

Staff looked at Wagner. "What did you say?"

The zoologist raised an eyebrow above his surgical mask. "I didn't say anything. I thought you muttered something. Might want to speak up." He nodded at the microphone hanging above the table. "This is for posterity, you know."

Staff shook his head and made the first cut. Green blood oozed from the incision.

The lights in the room flared bright, almost blinding.

Nazi... spy... looking at... case...

The bloody scalpel fell from Staff's hand. He staggered back a step. A searing white light hit him, but from behind the eyes.

"Are you all right, Pete?" Wagner said before covering his face. "Ah! That smells like ammonia... We'd better get some gas masks if we're going to finish this. And some better electrical equipment."

***

Staff sat alone in his assigned room, smoking a Lucky Strike and wondering exactly what had happened during the autopsy. As soon as he and Wagner had stepped out of the lab, they'd been met by MPs with orders to confine them to quarters until further notice. He'd seen two men in hats, dark suits and darker glasses enter the surgery as they left. They had carried large leather valises, no doubt to gather up the film and the audio recordings. Probably the test tubes filled with tissue and fluid samples as well.

There was a knock at the door just before an MP entered, followed by General Alexander Morgan. Staff stood to attention and saluted the head of the Army Air Corps Science and Research Division.

"As you were, Major," the older man said. Morgan had been a fighter ace in The Great War and had come home to rack up three PhDs while climbing the brass ladder during the ensuing years of peace. He was the reason there was an SRD. Turning to the guard, he said, "Wait outside."

When they were alone, the general sat at the small desk, motioned for Staff to take a seat on his bunk. "So, what do you think, Major?"

"I think that this is an actual alien event, sir. Without any information on the craft itself, I can't say that these beings come from somewhere other than Earth, but I can say that they are an as-yet unidentified species of sentient life. The brain alone—"

Morgan raised a hand. "Easy, Staff. I know about your... obsession with this sort of thing. In fact, that's one of the reasons you were recruited. In addition to your academic prowess in both medicine and mechanics, I thought this program could use someone who thinks outside the box. I'll admit, I never really put much stock in the whole H.G. Wells idea of beings from another world, but I guess it's a good thing you do."

"Thank you, sir."

"So tell me about the postmortem."

Staff cleared his throat. He knew that Morgan would have already seen the film, heard the tapes. Maybe even spoken to Wagner. So why would he ask Staff about what he already knew? "Did the tapes pick anything up, sir?"

Morgan pulled a pipe from inside his dress uniform and carefully loaded it. Without looking up from the process, he asked, "Like what, exactly, Major?"

Staff licked his lips and ran a hand through his hair. "Like... the words, 'Nazi spy looking at case'?"

The general lit his pipe, took a long puff on it until the tobacco glowed almost cherry red. "And you didn't say that?"

"No, sir."

"Do you think Wagner did?"

"No, sir."

"Then who did, Major?"

Staff took a deep breath. "I think... I think the subject did. With its mind."

The two men sat in silence, letting the words hang in the smoky air.

"Any idea who it could have meant?" Morgan finally asked.

"Not a clue, sir."

Morgan stood and Staff did likewise. The general picked up his hat and turned to the door. "I've got to get back to Washington, Major. If you want this division to continue as a military entity, I suggest you find out if one of your people really is playing for the other team."

"You mean I'm now in charge of this operation, sir?"

Morgan paused in the doorway. "You've got the rank, Major. And you've got my trust. Now find me that spy, and try to do it quietly. No need to involve the locals."

"Understood, sir."

***

Staff looked at the schematics spread out on Ed's desk in the heavily guarded hangar, where they were trying to reconstruct the craft. He was having a hard time reconciling his friend's sketches with the lump of twisted and scorched metal occupying the center of the cavernous building. Ed imagined that the silver, disk-like thing had once possessed wings on each side and a pair of dorsal stabilizers running across the top like twin shark fins.

"What do you think?" Ed asked, lighting a Chesterfield as he stepped to the desk.

"I think you've been watching too many Buster Crabbe serials," Staff said. It came off as short and irritable. "Sorry. Just on edge since Morgan put me in charge of this mess." He hadn't told anyone else about the spy hunt. Not even his best friend.

Ed laughed. "No problem, *Major.* Got to admit I wouldn't want to be in your shoes right now. I got my hands full trying to corral a bunch of enlisted grease monkeys into reverse-engineering a bona fide rocket ship. Can't imagine how many plates you've got spinning at the moment."

"Too damn many," Staff said, lighting a cigarette of his own. He didn't add that one of those plates—the most important one—had a big fat swastika painted on it, and he had to find it before it sent them all crashing to the floor.

"You gonna tell me about the autopsy? I know I woulda lost that bet about the midgets in the biplane, so what's the scoop? Anything you learned might make my job a little easier. I mean, if I understood how they looked and moved, I could understand how they might build their machines."

Staff smiled. "Sorry. That's classified. All I can tell you is that they had hands and feet, and all the rest pretty much like us. Only smaller." Although to be fair, Ed had a point. If an alien species had some kind of mental telepathy, wouldn't they incorporate that into their technology? Machines that ran on mental commands, rather than knobs, pedals, and levers?

"What're you thinking, Pete? I can see the gears turning behind those hornrims of yours."

Staff shook his head and tossed the butt to the ground. "I'm thinking I need to get over and see what Flannigan, our resident chemist, has come up with. He's been studying the crew's flight suits." As he headed out of the bay, Staff turned and called to his friend, "And you let me know as soon as you find a Flash Gordon Death Ray on that thing, huh?"

***

That night, Staff stood in his room, smoking too much and staring at a bulletin board he'd covered in photos and personnel files from his team. Eleven scientists from both branches of the service. All with different backgrounds, specialties, and personalities. One of them was loyal to that madman in Berlin, and it was up to Staff to find out who the traitor was.

Lt. Banks of the Navy was a mousy little astrophysicist, the quintessential absent-minded professor. If he wasn't a certified genius he'd have been busted out of the military a long time ago for uniform infractions alone. His mother was Austrian.

Commander Hennessey, the Navy linguist and codebreaker, was loud and outspoken—critical of everyone and everything. But he knew his business, which had not come into play at all on this case as they had absolutely no samples of the aliens' language or communications. But that didn't stop the man from being at everyone else's workstation at least once a day, telling them how they could better do their jobs.

Captain Wagner, the Army zoologist, was a disciple of Frank Buck of *Bring 'Em Back Alive* fame. And like his idol, he seemed wholly without political interests. In addition to sharing a surname with Hitler's favorite composer, he had travelled the world extensively both before joining the Army and after. Plenty of opportunity to come into contact with Nazi agents in the dark corners of the map.

Lt. Commander Flannigan, the Navy chemist, was Irish born with a German wife. Her brother was a known member of the Bund but had subsequently fled to Mexico when his peacetime draft number had come up. This had almost kept Flannigan out of the program altogether. But General Morgan had vouched for him after Flannigan had promised to shoot his brother-in-law in the face if he ever saw him again.

Captain Bauer, the Army archeologist, was of German descent and had crossed paths with members of Himmler's Ahnenerbe several times in the past five years. Rumors claimed he had punched or shot his way out of most of those encounters, but still...

Of the six remaining members of the team, there was a Navy astronomer and an Army geologist who had family relations who were either of German descent or German nationals.

And then there was Captain Ed Miller.

Staff was surprised when he looked over the file. He learned that Ed's surname had originally been Müller, changed by his father back in 1916. Ed's family had been some of the first German immigrants into Texas but had left their ancestral home during the Great War, moving from town to town five times between 1914 and 1918.

Staff knew this was the easiest connection to disprove, and so decided to start there. He'd clear Ed of any suspicion, and then the two of them could work the case together, bringing in the rest of the team as they were vetted.

He crushed out his last Lucky Strike, grabbed his hat and headed for the door. He glanced at his belted sidearm resting on the footlocker. Decided he wouldn't need it.

Opening the door, he didn't notice the envelope which had been slid under it sometime during his ruminations. Primarily because of Captain Wagner's pistol crashing down on the bridge of his nose, shattering his glasses, and toppling him to the floor.

"Don't move, you Nazi bastard," the zoologist said, a watery blur in Staff's vision.

"Wagner? What the hell are you doing?" Staff sputtered through the blood streaming into his mouth from his broken nose. "What are you talking about? *I'm* trying to find the spy!"

Wagner waved the pistol at the bulletin board. "That why you're going over our personnel files? More likely you're putting together a report to send to your buddy Adolf." He raised his voice and touched his chest with the muzzle of the weapon. "I know! I heard that... *thing* in my head. It said there was a Nazi spy looking at this case!"

Staff cleared his vision and was just about to try and reason with the excited scientist when an explosion outside shook the room's windows and bathed them in a bright yellow light.

When Wagner glanced in that direction, Staff swept the man's feet out from under him, pounced on him, and punched him three times until he was unconscious. Climbing to his feet, he sprinted from the room. *That came from the direction of the hangar where Ed was rebuilding the craft!*

By the time he reached the exterior of the dormitories, he could see that it was too late. The entire hangar was consumed in towering flames. Soldiers were gathering on the periphery while the emergency teams scrambled into action. Staff turned and looked, but he did not see a single member of his team among the swelling crowd.

***

Five days later, Staff and Wagner sat in General Morgan's office in Washington. Both wore their dress uniforms. Staff also wore new spectacles and a bandage across his nose—for which the battered Wagner had profusely apologized many times in the days following the tragedy at Sikeston Field. They were the only two surviving members of the team sent to investigate the crash.

"As you were, gentlemen," Morgan said as he hurried into the office and settled behind his big mahogany desk. "Let's get down to business, shall we? I presume you've got your reports in order?"

"Yes, sir," Staff said. "After a thorough investigation, we have determined that there was, in fact, no Nazi spy—or any foreign espionage agent—present during our investigation of the Cape Girardeau Incident." He opened the folder in his lap and produced two letters. One was from under his door, the other under Wagner's.

As Morgan scanned the handwritten documents, Staff summarized. "They're both from Ed—Captain Edward Miller. The one addressed to Captain Wagner is an invitation to come to the hangar in order to share a remarkable technological discovery. The letter to me describes Captain Miller's plan to lure the Nazi spy to the hangar via his invitations to all the members of the team. Miller believed that the spy would be the first to arrive, and he would be able to apprehend him...

"It goes on to describe an explosive he had rigged to the craft as a last-ditch measure to keep any intelligence from reaching Berlin."

Morgan dropped the two letters to the desk and folded his hands. "Continue."

Staff looked at Wagner, who was content to let him be the spokesperson for their findings. "We believe that the other members of the team thought Miller was the spy, and all went to the hangar with the intent of apprehending him. When confronted by such odds, with all concerned suffering from a sort of paranoia, we think that Miller enacted his failsafe plan. Killing himself and the rest of the team in the process."

"And destroying the lion's share of evidence." The general swiveled his chair to glance at the sunrise. "But why, in the wake of this... catastrophe, Major, do you insist that there was no spy? You two heard something. Apparently, the rest of the team did as well. The audio recordings even picked it up."

"Which is why I thought Major Staff was the spy, sir," Wagner volunteered. "Following the autopsy, he was acting very secretive and asking a lot of questions. I thought Captain Miller's letter was a trap, and so went my own way."

Staff licked his lips. "I have a theory, sir."

Morgan spread his hands. "I'm all ears, Major."

"When we arrived on the scene of the crash, the subject chosen for autopsy had apparently just... expired. However, it is entirely possible that it was merely slipping into a dormant phase similar to a coma. In that case, it may have still been receiving sensory stimuli."

"Yes?"

"I have gone over every detail of this encounter a hundred times, sir. I distinctly recall the two ambulance drivers using the words *Nazi, spy, looking, at,* and *case*—in that order, while standing above the subject. I believe that those words filtered into the subject's mind, and the trauma of the premature postmortem caused it to utter a telepathic cry. Just as a delirious person might repeat the last words they heard in a moment of crisis. I believe the team's proximity to the alien technology might have somehow made us more susceptible to receiving that cry."

Morgan scowled and drummed his fingers on the desk. "So we've been chasing our tails, lost a lot of good men, and the opportunity to study advanced technology all because of a... what? A Martian's insane deathbed rambling?"

Staff grimaced, thinking of his best friend. "Yes, sir. That is what we believe."

After a long silence, General Morgan took a deep breath. "Well, it is clear to me and to the higher-ups that we definitely have a lot to learn about these things. Which is why we've decided to sanction a permanent team and give it a higher level of autonomy." He opened a drawer and took out a pair of small boxes before stepping around the desk.

Staff and Wagner rose.

"Gentlemen," Morgan said as he opened the boxes, revealing new oak leaves: silver for Staff and brass for Wagner. Handing them their new rank insignias and shaking their hands, he said, "Congratulations on your promotions to lieutenant colonel and major, respectively. You two will be heading up the top-secret department now designated as Codename: Majestic.

"First order of business is to recruit a new team. And then get out there and find me some more Martian rocket ships. I have a feeling we'll be needing all the advanced technology we can get our hands on very, very soon."

"Yes, sir."

THE EXILE

"I am a good man," Harold told himself, despite the fact he was about to commit murder and treason.

He smiled for the rain-sodden crowds and put on a brave face, though his soul was greatly troubled. His actions could very well plunge all of England into a bloody civil war. This night's events could undo all he, Harold Godwinson, had accomplished. Years of hard work and battles fought to restore Saxon primacy in the land, and the much harder work of earning King Edward's trust in the wake of his father's career of intrigues under Danish rule.

Harold stood on the quay, surrounded by his best housecarls, watching the black ship make its way up the Thames. The vessel carried the sole surviving son of Edmund Ironside, the last Saxon king before Canute's short-lived dynasty. That son was the kingdom's best hope for a peaceful succession.

The best hope for England's future, and Harold was about to destroy it.

Harold cast a rueful glance at the glowering sky and the continuing rainfall, wiped a handful of water from his beard and tried to hold his smile in place. Torches sputtered and flared, struggling against the rain and the encroaching darkness. The Exile had not only chosen to return on a day of miserable weather, he had waited until dusk to do so.

"Everything is in order, milord," Ulfer said at Harold's side. The big warrior wore a bronze-trimmed helm and a coat of polished mail beneath his green cloak. "Hereward has the escort ready."

"Good." As the greeting dignitary, Harold could not afford to give the wrong impression by wearing his own war gear, so he was grateful for the presence of his best swordsman and the rest of his armored retainers. "What about the two brothers, the king's men?"

Eadgar and Cerdic were members of King Edward's own household guard, but they, like Harold and his chosen men, were also members of the Order. They acted upon the same set of instructions Harold had received from Stigand, the Archbishop of Canterbury. And yet they were not Harold's men. Could he truly count on them when it came to the sticking point?

"They seem to be trustworthy... enough, milord," Ulfer replied.

Harold did not begrudge the man his doubts. Only five years before, Eadgar and Cerdic had stood in the shield wall facing Harold and his family on this very river. Thankfully, the wise men of the Witan had ended the feud between King Edward's Norman allies and Harold's father, Earl Godwin, before England could descend into open civil war.

Since Godwin's death the following year, Harold had worked very hard not only to regain King Edward's trust but also to maintain stability in the realm. He had learned to rely upon the archbishop and the other members of the Order of Christ the King's Peace in this never-ending struggle.

"Well then, Ulfer, let us make ready to throw England into chaos in the name of God."

As the ship closed on the pier, the last rays of the August sun failed against the downpour and a dozen more sizzling torches struggled to life along the gangway. Harold watched as men hurried to secure the hawsers and make the ship fast. He could see a crowd of cloaked figures aboard the craft preparing to disembark. A sudden cheer announced that the rain-soaked mass of Londoners had also caught sight of their would-be future king.

The cheer gnawed at Harold's growing guilt.

Ever since the turmoil of the near civil war between King Edward and Earl Godwin, a worrying fear had taken root in the heart of every Englishman: who would claim the throne when the blessed Edward passed away?

The pious king was the first Saxon to rule since the mighty Canute. However, Edward had produced no offspring. Possibly of greater concern, having been exiled to Normandy in his youth as his mother had warmed the Danish king's bed, King Edward often seemed more favorable to Norman knights than to many Saxon lords. Now, with Edward drawing toward the end of his own life and showing no inclination to siring progeny—despite having a young and lovely queen in the person of Harold's own sister—all of England feared the king's eventual death would result in a bloody war of succession. Or worse, invasion.

Harold, having replaced his father as Earl of Wessex, East Anglia, and

Hereford, was easily the first choice of the pro-Saxon faction despite having no claim to the royal bloodline. But King Edward still had a small coterie of Normans in his court. It was no secret these powerful men favored the king's maternal cousin, William Duke of Normandy, to reinvigorate their control over England. It was even rumored that while Harold's family had been banished six years ago, Edward had intimated to the visiting young duke that he would name him his successor when the time came. In addition to these two factions, much of the North—the old Danelaw—still looked to Scandinavia for their next king.

Harold's smile tightened as he watched the man who promised to free England from this uncertainty step onto the pier, knowing that within a day's time the heir-apparent would be dead, or Harold would be an outlaw.

"Welcome to England, Edward Ætheling, son of King Edmund Ironside," Harold declared in a strong, clear voice. "Welcome home to the king's chosen heir."

Thunderous cheers erupted from the gathered crowd.

The Ætheling was flanked by four men in long black-hooded robes and an aging but dangerous looking Dane in mail and golden arm rings. Edward the Exile himself was tall and leanly built with a handsome face, clean shaven in the continental fashion. However, unlike the short hair favored by the French and Germans, the Exile wore his chestnut locks long and swept back from a high forehead to fall in oiled ringlets about his shoulders. His eyes, Harold noted, were a piercing blue which changed to green or grey depending on the light.

The Ætheling, though born in England over forty years ago, showed no outward kinship to his Saxon heritage. His clothes and jewelry were ornate and finely made but were a mingling of Norse and Hungarian fashion.

"Well met." The Exile's English was thick with an odd accent. "You must be Harold Godwinson, the earl of half of England and the man some call *Dux Anglorum* and *Subregulus*. The Duke of the English and the Underking."

Harold flushed as he bowed. "At your service, my lord. Those are flattering but unkind titles. I merely serve your uncle with love and loyalty as I hope to one day serve you."

The lie was bitter on his tongue.

"Now, if you will permit me, it would be my pleasure to escort you and your family out of this dreadful weather."

The Exile flashed a white smile and glanced up at the rain falling from the darkened sky. "Yes, I had heard of the delightful nature of English weather." He waved at the still cheering townsfolk as he joined stride with Harold. "The rest of the pleasantries can wait until we are indoors, I should think. Please lead the way."

Several minutes later the Exile's entourage and Harold's band of armed retainers had mounted and begun the circuitous trek to the royal palace on Thorn Island. Edward Ætheling's wife, children, and household servants crowded into one covered wagon while their belongings filled another. The Exile, however, chose to mount a horse and ride at the head of the procession with Harold, Ulfer, and Hereward. They were joined by the aging Danish warrior while the four robed and hooded men walked solemnly behind.

"Jarl Walgar has been my guardian since I was still in swaddling clothes," the Exile said to Harold, waving and smiling at the cheering commoners crowding the narrow streets. "It was he who brought my brother and me to Sweden and then guided us to Kiev and safety during the reign of Canute."

Harold nodded, casting a wary glance at the scarred veteran. "Yes, I was sorry to hear of your brother's death. As was all of England."

Edward Ætheling lowered his hooded head for a moment, then turned that white smile to Harold. "Yes, Edmund died far too young. But he lived a full life of good friends, brave battles, and true love. In the end, he married well, and his son may someday sit on the throne of Hungary."

"It would seem that you have also married well, and have a son of your own, my lord."

"It is so," the Exile said. "Edgar is just a babe, but his two sisters will force him to become a strong warrior and a cunning king. I've watched my daughters long enough to know that any boy growing up with them has his work cut out for him."

Harold smiled despite himself, thinking of his own sisters in childhood and of his two-year-old daughter, Gunhild, whose older brothers spoiled her in every way. Harold found himself liking this man, this husband and father, and wondered if the archbishop's boy prophet had not made a terrible mistake. "The men in robes," he said. "They are priests?"

The Exile's hooded head again drifted into shadow. "I have lived much of my life under the sway of Constantinople, not Rome. Despite the schism which has occurred between the two Churches, I hope that my family's ways and traditions will be welcomed here in England."

Harold nodded, realizing Edward's answer hinted at yet another un-Saxon trait, and his unease returned. If the Exile were to become king, would he force the Greek Church's doctrines upon the people of England? Stigand's current disfavor in Rome would make such a transition all the easier.

"Please forgive me for even asking this, my lord," Harold said. "But I was wondering if you would mind taking a short detour on our way to the palace. I am sure you are very tired from your long journey, but the archbishop asked if I might persuade you to stop by St. Paul's Minster to meet with him...

"We could send your household on ahead, of course," he quickly added. "I would never dream of exposing women and children to this weather for longer than absolutely necessary."

"The archbishop?" The Exile sounded hesitant, almost cautious. "What could he possibly have to say to me that cannot wait until morning?"

Harold sensed the Ætheling's odd wariness. A wariness which hinted at the credibility of Stigand's boy prophet. "I'm sure he simply wants to give you his blessing, my lord. He may also want to give you some advice on how to impress the members of the Witan and win them to your favor."

"Ah yes..." Edward the Exile made an unpleasant hissing noise. "The Witan. I had almost forgotten about that old-fashioned council. In the rest of the civilized world a royal decision is as good as a divine one. Only in England is a king's word to be questioned or even challenged by mortal men."

"In England, my lord," Harold said with as much restraint as he could muster, "even a king is not above the law. Your uncle, King Edward, had to overcome his Norman upbringing to finally understand this."

Harold feared his thinly veiled reference to the showdown between his father, Earl Godwin, and the king six years before might put Edward on his guard. But he could not stomach such a grievous affront to English tradition. Especially not from this man who, as far as Harold could tell, was as foreign as any of the Norman troublemakers he and his family had bested to secure Saxon primacy in England.

The Exile surprised Harold by laughing at the rebuke. It was a loud, sharp, and sudden sound that caused the horses to start. "Wise words, my friend...

It would seem that I am in need of such council after all. Please pass the word: I will accompany you to see the archbishop while Jarl Walgar and your men convey my family to the palace."

"I will keep four men with us as a guard," Harold replied, signaling Ulfer with a wave of his hand. "The rest will protect your family. If you would feel more comfortable with the Jarl remaining by your side, my lord...?"

The Exile waved the notion away. "Walgar will go with my family, but I will bring my priests along. I imagine they will have much to discuss with Archbishop Stigand."

They rode in silence for a time after the majority of the procession continued on to the royal palace. Harold and Edward were flanked by Ulfer, Hereward, and the brothers Eadgar and Cerdic. The four robed priests walked behind the mounted warriors.

Harold studied the Exile in the guttering torchlight as they pressed through the deluge. Edward Ætheling, he decided, was many things, but chief among them was a warrior. He wore no armor, but his sword and seax hung from his belt as if they were a part of him, and the grace of his movements denoted a man of action.

"As I think on it," the Exile said, breaking the silence, "I am glad for this opportunity to meet with Stigand. If half of what Jarl Walgar has told me is true, then the archbishop is not only the man responsible for recalling me to England and my birthright, but also the man responsible for saving mine and Edmund's lives when we were children. It would seem that I owe him a great deal."

Harold's lips tightened as Archbishop Stigand's words echoed in his mind: "The Exile is a monster, a demon sent from Hell itself, intent on the destruction of Christ's Holy Church in England and the subjugation of its people. The blessed saints have told this to Wymond, the child prophet, and he has passed their warning on to me. Therefore, it is our responsibility as the Keepers of Christ the King's Peace to insure that Edward Ætheling never ascends to the throne."

Distant thunder rumbled as they reached the minster. The sprawling building was a glorious composite of Saxon and Roman architecture with a low central structure of stone and mortar, shingled roofs, and two three-story bell towers of timber and limewashed wattle-and-daub. Half a dozen hooded monks rushed out to take the horses as soon as the party trotted into the stone-paved courtyard. A torch-bearing acolyte hurried them past the colonnaded porch and into the warmth of the brazier-lit vestibule.

After giving their wet cloaks to a pair of servants, Harold and Edward followed the acolyte through a side door and down a narrow hallway into an older part of the building. The four housecarls and the four priests followed behind in silence. They found Stigand sitting by a lit hearth in an empty parlor lined with lavish tapestries. Fresh rushes covered the stone floor while six marble columns supported the center of the expansive chamber.

The archbishop stood as they entered. The middle-aged man wore his greying blond locks and beard long and full. His black and red robes sparkled in the firelight with golden threadwork and inlaid garnets and pearls. A heavy golden cross hung from a silver chain about his neck.

"Archbishop," Edward said, a smile on his handsome face.

"Now." Stigand's command filled the room with armored men and spears. The warriors of the Order emerged from behind the tapestries to spring the trap.

Harold and the four housecarls drew their swords.

"What treachery is this?" The Exile sounded more amused than alarmed. "You summon me from the far side of Europe only to kill me like some common thief?"

"When I bade the king to summon you," Stigand said, sadness in his voice, "it was my fervent hope that you would return to England as a savior. Instead, you have come bearing the Curse of Cain." The archbishop raised a vial of holy oil from his table and uncorked it. "You have studied at the Dark One's knee in that unhallowed place of sorcery. You are an acolyte of the Scholomance. You are anathema in the sight of Almighty God and all that is holy in this world."

"I had thought to make an ally of you, Stigand." The Ætheling remained nonplussed. He glanced at Harold with a shrug. "As for you, Earl Harold... I knew I would have to kill you eventually, but I had hoped that could wait until the transfer of power was complete..."

Harold blinked as the archbishop splashed the holy oil at Edward.

In that instant the Exile vanished.

The room filled with screams and the sounds of violence.

Harold turned to see the four hooded men attack the armored spearmen with bare, claw-like hands and elongated teeth. Three housecarls were already dead, their throats torn open and necks broken.

"Their hearts!" someone shouted. "The boy prophet said to pierce their hearts!"

The first spear found its mark and one of the hooded monsters collapsed, shrieking and snarling like a dying wolf. Harold turned to see Ulfer fly across the room. The huge man hit the tapestried wall so hard that Harold heard his bones shatter.

The Exile stood before him, though transformed.

Edward's skin was corpse-pale and taut over the bones of his skull. The whites of his eyes had turned black, and the irises glowed like embers of green hellfire. His distended mouth stretched wide in a demonic grin, revealing rows of pearlescent razor-sharp fangs.

Ulfer's lifeblood stained that ghastly maw and ran down the Ætheling's chin.

Harold struck at the monster. His sword cut only air where the Exile had stood. An iron talon closed about Harold's throat and his feet left the floor. His weapon dropped from his lifeless fingers.

Two orbs of green hellfire poured hopelessness into his soul.

Drawing his seax, Harold tried to plunge it into his attacker. Edward closed his other talon around Harold's wrist, forcing the point of the blade into Harold's own thigh. He would have screamed in pain, but no air passed through his throat.

His vision darkened at the edges.

"In the name of Jesus Christ and all His saints!" Stigand roared as he caught the Exile in an arc of holy oil. "I abjure you, demon! You have no power in this sacred house!"

Harold fell gasping to the floor as Edward hissed in pain and leapt away.

"You are wrong, Stigand!" The Exile snarled, wisps of smoke curling from the places where the holy oil had struck him. "You invited me here—to all of England! The king invited me... That invitation has given me all the power I require!"

Harold's wits rushed back as Eadgar and Cerdic helped him to his feet. Hereward stood between him and the monster. Taking up his fallen sword, Harold saw that at least seven more housecarls lay dead in pools of gore on the flagstones, but all the hooded creatures were transfixed to the floor, spear shafts protruding from their bloody chests.

The Exile's hellish eyes scanned the room. "How do you hope to keep this conspiracy a secret? King Edward will not suffer this attempt on my life to go unpunished! I will see that you all are hanged for this."

In the blink of an eye, the monstrous Ætheling turned to shadow and flitted to the door through which they had entered.

"Do not let him escape!" Stigand shouted. "If it costs all of you your lives, do not let him loose!"

Harold limped after the two brothers and Hereward. Another pair of spearmen exploded in a shower of gore in the monster's wake. Eadgar and Cerdic tackled the Exile just as he reached the barred door. Before Harold and Hereward could get to them, the two brothers flew through the air to slam into the surrounding men. At least half a dozen bones broke in that impact as soldiers went down howling in pain.

Harold snatched a spear from one of the wounded men. "Please guide my hand, Dear Lord..." He hurled the weapon.

The door flew off its hinges in an explosion of shattered wood and sundered metal. The spear struck. The Exile hissed with the voice of a hundred thousand swarming locusts. He lashed and writhed like a thing possessed, abominable curses a flowing river of filth from his distended mouth.

His body went limp, and he collapsed to the body-strewn floor, finally inert.

Harold and Stigand stepped to where the Exile lay. Edward Ætheling's handsome features had returned. There was no sign of the demon that had killed half a dozen men in a matter of seconds. The banished prince appeared to sleep save for the gory shaft passing through his body.

"What do we do now?" Harold whispered, rubbing the bruises on his throat and the bleeding wound in his thigh.

"Take the body and bury it far from London." Stigand splashed the corpse with more holy oil in the pattern of The Cross. "All of them. Place them in an unmarked grave at a crossroads. We'll have to choose one of our own dead to take the Exile's place and bury him here."

Harold blinked. "But the king...?"

"I'll say the Exile chose to spend the night as my guest, and that in the morning he showed signs of illness," the archbishop replied. "I'll announce his death day after tomorrow and suggest that it was plague. That will cause the rest of his household to be isolated for at least a week to make sure they do not carry the contagion. By the time they are released, 'Edward the Ætheling' will have already been interred in royal fashion without anyone ever seeing the corpse."

Harold was chilled by Stigand's detached shrewdness and crushed by his own sense of guilt. He gripped the painful knife wound in his thigh and quietly said, "I lied to him. I betrayed his trust and led him into a trap."

"Don't be a fool," Stigand said. "You saw what this thing was, what it could do." He waved a hand at the carnage in the room. Ulfer and a dozen others were dead while the king's men, Eadgar and Cerdic, were among the severely wounded. "Is your honor so high a price to pay to keep this abomination from ruling all of England, Earl Harold? Is that honor or pride?"

Harold swallowed and accepted the rebuke. "You are right, of course."

However, he could not shake the feeling that this night's unmanly deeds would haunt him for the remainder of his life. They had destroyed a monster, but in so doing they had left the matter of royal succession still hanging dangerously in the balance.

"Where shall we take the fiends' corpses, milords?" Hereward asked as the survivors saw to the wounded and the dead.

"There is an empty field in Sussex," the archbishop said. "At the crossroads of the Dover and the Lewes Roads just above the town of Hastings. Bury them there and pray God that nothing disturbs their rest 'til Judgment Day."

THE DOOMSDAY CLUB

I know there is a global plot to end the world. And I know the group of mysterious men in the antique bookstore across the street are part of it. I just can't prove it.

Not yet.

I take a sip of warm, flat Modelo and rub the sweat from my eyes. Replacing my sunglasses, I glance at the bookshop's darkened windows and wonder just what they're doing over there. Hell, I wonder what I'm doing in *here*. Battling flies and mosquitos and sweating my ass off in a shady bar, surrounded by human traffickers, drug runners, and mercenaries on the rough side of Panama City.

Panama the country, not Florida.

I'm a politician, for crying out loud! Not a spy, a soldier, or a secret agent. That's always been Brock's shtick. I should be in Pasadena or Santa Barbara pressing the flesh and kissing babies, or smiling for photo ops at Pebble Beach and Disneyland on my run for governor. Not risking hepatitis, malaria, and kidnapping in this tropical hellhole.

Of course, if this conspiracy to end the world succeeds, I suppose it won't make much difference whether I watch the heavens open in hellfire and demonic plagues from the gubernatorial mansion in Sacramento or from a crappy hotel room here in Panama City.

At least here I won't have to see my little girl burn. At least I can tell myself that Lisa has her whole life ahead of her—high school crushes, college and grad school successes, a stellar career and happy marriage, and, of course, kids of her own someday. At least here there's a chance I can stop the end of the world. A chance I can save her and all her possible futures.

A slim one to be sure, but a chance all the same.

Even if I don't make it back, she's still got her mother. As long as I can pull this off, it will be worth all the bad things Wendy will tell Lisa about me as she grows up. That her father was a world-class loser who pissed away a promising political career to chase down crackpot conspiracy theories with his college roommate in some twisted midlife crisis. And it got him killed.

But I can't do squat by myself. If Brock doesn't show soon, it might be too late for all of us. I wish he'd just emailed the damn files when he first found them in Japan. Maybe he's getting paranoid in his old age. Maybe he's right to be.

"Still no word from the airport, Mr. Goldman."

I nod at Marcus as he mounts the barstool next to me. The pro wrestler is my bodyguard, and easily the largest addition to my personal entourage of eccentrics—what my assistant Alice has mockingly dubbed "The Doomsday Club." He's also the most loyal of the bunch, at least to my way of thinking. But when you've stood in the breach between a man and something else— something not of this world—I suppose it's only natural to expect a certain amount of loyalty from that man. I don't know what the thing was that tried to eat the big luchador in Tijuana, but I do know it wasn't bulletproof. Thank God.

On my way down the coast, I collected outsiders and oddballs the way a kid collects trading cards. Ms. Alice McBee, my longtime personal assistant, was the first of my companions. Aside from her party-time predilection for tarot cards and palm readers, her interest in the occult is almost nil. I find this an immeasurably comforting fact in light of current events. At the moment, she's plugged into the hotel's crappy Wi-Fi trying to track down artifacts, allies, and clues from around the globe and maneuver them into the hands of our little counter-conspiracy's too few agents. She doesn't know exactly why, and she doesn't ask too many questions. Which means she might be the only one not wearing a straitjacket when this is all over.

After the big earthquake in San Francisco, I found Sheldon at Stanford working on a doctorate in anthropology. The kid's name isn't really Sheldon. I just call him that because he reminds me of the goofy guy on *Big Bang Theory*. He's a walking encyclopedia of ancient languages, myths, folklore, and esoteric knowledge. A genius, even if he is a little creepy. Right now, he's holed up in his room poring over the PDF of a manuscript Brock's girlfriend, Rachel, found in Kiev. I just hope he can translate it and find something useful without getting any weirder. He hasn't bathed since he translated that variant scroll from the Egyptian *Book of the Dead*. Something about running water stealing his soul.

Then there's Mama Hazel, the wise-woman I found in Nicaragua who claims to be descended from the Mayan priests of old. The final addition to my menagerie may be a con artist just playing me as an easy mark, but if this all goes south, what difference does it make? Either she'll burn with the rest of us, her pockets full of this gringo's *dinero*, or if she is the real deal, she just may come in handy again somewhere down the line. She did help us locate the ancient Mayan calendar that pinpoints the day of the Big Event. Right now, I can only hope Hazel and the relic are both legit.

Right now, hope is about all I've got left.

The burner phone in my pocket chirps.

Only Brock and Rachel have this number. Amanda, the Mrs. O'Leary's Cow of this particular nightmare, has other ways of getting in touch with me. And God help us all if she has to do that. "Hello."

"I'm at your hotel here in Panama," Brock says. His voice is hollow and shaky. "Where are you?" I rattle off the bar's address and he grunts before hanging up. I wonder how he got into the country without being spotted at the airport, but then, he *is* a spy.

"You trust this Jackson guy, Mr. Goldman?" Marcus asks, killing his hundredth fly with lightning reflexes. I'm just glad that's all he's had to kill thus far.

"I do."

And I honestly, truly do. Like there's no one else I trust on this planet. I've known Brock Jackson almost thirty years, since we were freshmen roommates at U.C.L.A. We were called the Odd Couple, the Jewish pre-law nerd and the ROTC guy who looked like Captain America. But we were thick as thieves. It was a friendship that only grew stronger as we grew up and walked our separate paths. He's godfather to Lisa, and he's promised to name his firstborn son after me if he ever grows old and settles down like the rest of us. I'm crossing my fingers that this thing with Rachel works out. A good Jewish girl working for the Mossad might be just what he needs.

Of course if we fail, it could all be academic in a matter of weeks. Maybe days. Hell, maybe even hours for all I know. That Mayan calendar could be a fake...

I thought things were bad after 9/11 and the Coof, but what Brock showed me last month scared the shit out of me. Literally. He and Rachel had compiled a casefile identifying high-placed individuals in national governments, secret societies, big tech and big pharma companies, entertainment industries, and quasi-religions all over the world. All with ties to an ancient esoteric order with the explicit intent of bringing about the Apocalypse. Their final convincing argument had come in the person of Amanda Carnegie, the heiress to one of the largest financial empires in the United States, and a ranking member of the Church of Thelema.

Amanda had come forward, disclosing the order's secret agenda in hopes of helping us foil the global conspiracy from the inside. She showed us printouts of secret emails, copies of church documents dating back to the days of Aleister Crowley, and photos taken of world leaders and big-name industrialists and celebrities at the sect's private retreat. She then led me, Brock, and Rachel into the secret basement of her Malibu mansion. In a hidden shrine to some unpronounceable ancient deity, Amanda performed an arcane ritual which showed me that supernatural magic is all too real and absolutely terrifying.

Afterwards, when I had showered and put on clean underwear, I realized that it all made sense. The cataclysmic weather, climate change, the spiraling energy crisis, looming economic collapse, the escalating violence at home and abroad, the steady decline of morality, the upending of social priorities, and the overall "don't give a shit" attitude exhibited by your average citizen of Earth.

The world is quite literally going to Hell.

In the face of such overwhelming evidence, I had no choice but to withdraw from the governor's race and embark on this mad crusade. What else could I do? If there was only a one-percent chance that what they claimed was true, then someone had to do something. No matter how insane it seemed. *Because* of how insane it seemed. Because no one else in power would believe it. And if they did believe it, they were probably in place to make sure it happened.

When Brock enters the bar, I hardly recognize him. He looks like his own ghost—thin, pale, and wild-eyed. I wave him over and order him a shot and a beer.

"Glad you made it," I say as he gulps the tequila without a word. "How was London?"

Brock's hands shake as he reaches for the beer. Hands that have seen

action in Mogadishu, Iraq, Afghanistan, and who knows where else. "We didn't close it," he says before killing the beer in one long swallow. He motions for a refill. "Whatever else Old Jack did in Whitechapel in 1888, he made certain that particular portal would stay open forever... Amanda might have been able to close it, but it was beyond me and Rachel. Even that book of Rasputin's couldn't help us... Sheldon's notes were fine, but... I think we may have actually done more harm than good."

I nod. London might fall, but we could still save the rest, right? We have to. "And Rachel? Is she okay?"

Brock rubs his face, maybe to wipe tears from his red eyes before they fully form. "Yeah... well, as okay as I am, I guess. We spent three days in that... *other place*... before we finally gave up and came back above ground. That's when we got your messages. I decided to bring you the intel we'd gathered myself... Make sure it's all taken care of..."

"Good. Take it easy. Once we're done here, I'll have Mama Hazel take a look at you. Maybe her witch doctoring will put you back on your feet."

He shrugs and hands me the folder. I glance around the near-deserted bar to make sure no one is watching before I open it. And just like that, I have another piece of this puzzle. Inside, I see photos and surveillance reports from the Tokyo police linking the doomsday cult, *Aum Shinrikyo*, with our mysterious occult researchers across the street. It's the smoking gun I need to set the local authorities on these guys and ferret out whatever part they're playing in this Apocalypse conspiracy.

A cool, unseasonal breeze blows through the bar's open windows, and I feel a chill of despair run down my spine and settle in my gut. In an instant, the thrill I had of piecing things together and maybe stopping the end of the world is gone. I try to shake it off, but before I can, I hear Marcus say my name.

I look up from the folder a second before I hear the gunshot. Deafening and startling. Marcus's head explodes and he topples from the barstool.

My ears ringing, I blink and turn to Brock. My sunglasses are streaked with blood, bone, hair, and brains. My mouth moves but no words come out. No.

Brock points a smoking Glock at me. "I'm sorry, Jerry," he says. "But this is the best way. It's the only way... If what I saw in that other place is coming true, you'll thank me..."

"No. Brock—we're so close!"

I've got a revolver in my pocket.

"No... You're the last... I've already helped the others escape... Goodbye, old friend."

Brock raises the automatic and I close my eyes. I see my little girl's face.

"Lisa..."

I go for my gun.

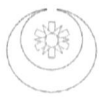

THE FEIS

Special Agent Dan Hughes stared through the windshield of the rental car they had picked up on their way out of the Tri-Cities Airport. The beautiful red, gold, and bronze tones blanketing the rolling Tennessee hills slid past a perfectly blue sky. Whomever had written "The Ballad of Davy Crockett" had obviously done so in the spring or summer. Autumn had fallen across the northeastern tip of the state, at least as far as the colors were concerned. There was still a touch of humid heat in the air, but Dan could tell it was on its way out the door.

Summer was dying.

"You're from around here, aren't you?" Special Agent Bill Biegler asked from the driver's seat. They had only met a few hours ago before boarding the flight out of Nashville. He was Dan's newest partner on the case that remained unsolved on his watch. Biegler was the third agent in six years to sign on to hunt the Sundial Slayer, the mysterious serial killer who had become Dan's private nemesis, or perhaps onus.

Dan wondered if this thin guy who looked like Clark Kent would hang around longer than the last one. The fast-talking girl from one of the Ivy Leagues up north had only stayed for six months before moving on to bigger and brighter. Word around the Bureau was that Biegler was an odd bird with weird ideas. But he had a reputation for getting inside the heads of serial killers.

Dan wasn't sure if the man was an asset or a rival.

"I went to school at Appalachian State, just over the state line in Boone, North Carolina." Dan rubbed his chin, cramming all those memories back in their dark little holes. He didn't really want to talk about the past. "So let me hear these theories of yours."

Biegler cleared his throat. "How much do you know about Celtic mythology?"

Dan smiled. "Not much. Why?"

"I don't think 'Sundial' is a correct assessment of the ritual placement of our killer's victims. I think he is making sacrifices to the ancient deity called Crom Cruach, the Crooked One of the Mound."

Dan raised an eyebrow. "And this assumption is based on what, exactly?"

Biegler glanced at him. "The situation of the stones around the body, and the presence of the jewelry and other semiprecious items. According to historians, the god Crom Cruach was represented by a golden idol surrounded by twelve smaller idols of silver or bronze. Or stones decorated with these metals."

In the past eleven years, twenty-one murders in seven southeastern states had been attributed to the Sundial Slayer. Three murders over three nights at the end of each October. Dan guessed that eventually more bodies would be found. He was certain that the killer carried out this ritual every year.

The only thing linking the victims was the way they had been discovered. Men, women, elders, and even a few children, all from different backgrounds, had been found in isolated woodland scenes. Though the bodies were always naked save for a few bits of untraceable pawn-shop gold jewelry, there was never any evidence of sexual violation or assault. The victims were all placed rather peacefully in the center of a ring of twelve stones, each capped with a piece of equally untraceable silver or bronze. Except for the single stab wound to the heart, each victim might have been sleeping.

"So, you're thinking a cult of some kind. Not a single guy? If that's the way of it, then no wonder I've never made any headway on this case."

Biegler shook his head. "No. I believe this is the act of a single, dedicated, and methodical killer. But I believe that *he* believes he is a druid, a priest of the ancient Celts. All the murders coincide with the traditional Celtic festival, or *feis*, of Samhain, what we now call Halloween. Our killer is seeking to appease an ancient god to secure the blessings for a new year."

Dan pulled the small evidence bag from his suit jacket pocket, smoothing it out on his thigh in order to read the piece of paper held within. "Well, if this anonymous tip bears any fruit, I guess we'll find out if you're right, Agent Biegler."

The note was a Xerox copy they had traced to a FedEx Office store in Murfreesboro, Tennessee. When questioned, the employees said that they had received a fax with the note and instructions to copy it, then mail it to the Bureau Headquarters in Nashville. The fax number turned out to be that of a UPS store in Memphis, where the employees had received similar instructions. By the time Dan had finished backtracking the origins of the cryptic message, he had spent a week chasing his own tail, finally locating a bogus email account logged in at a low-rent internet café in Tuscaloosa, Alabama.

But at least the note had given them a clue as to the killer's next target. It simply said:

> LOOK FOR THE "SUNDIAL" IN
> BRILEY HILL, TN.
> GOOD LUCK AND HAPPY HALLOWEEN.

"Looks like the Chamber of Commerce sent the welcome committee."

Dan looked up from the note to see the sign, WELCOME TO BRILEY HILL, TN. HOME OF THE FIGHTING IRISH, STATE CHAMPS 1997, 2011. It was decorated with the typical accoutrements of fall: miniature hay stalks, plaid-clad scarecrows, and happy-faced jack o' lanterns. Walking past the sign was a middle-aged man dressed in a cowhide hooded cloak and tunic and carrying a tall, ornately carved shillelagh. He smiled through his bushy grey beard and waved as they passed him.

"Let's find the local PD and get acquainted." Dan pulled his phone from his pocket and frowned at the single bar that kept flickering in and out on the display. "Doesn't look like Briley Hill is in any hurry to join the twenty-first century."

"Something tells me they won't be that hard to find," Biegler said.

Dan looked up just as they entered the town's main drag. Three new Ford SUVs, all painted in black and white with the BHPD logo on the doors, headed down a cross street. Blue lights flashed in the Halloween-decorated windows of the old-fashioned brick storefronts. A siren gave one long, banshee-like wail that echoed through the tiny town and the brightly colored hills enclosing it.

"Might as well offer to lend a hand." Dan returned the note and phone to his pocket. "The timing can't be a coincidence."

They followed the patrol cars out of town, where the blue lights died. A few minutes later, the procession entered the foothills, crossing an old, rickety covered bridge spanning a fast-moving stream along the way. The bituminous pavement ended just beyond the bridge and the gravel about a mile beyond that. They were deep in the woods. The sunshine was somewhere far behind them.

"Look familiar?" Dan asked.

"Like every crime scene in the file. I guess that tip was on the money. He's already here."

They pulled up behind the ring of police SUVs and were greeted by a pair of redheaded, beefy-looking bubbas in khaki uniforms. When Dan and Biegler flashed their Bureau badges, the cops glared but didn't give way. One of them touched the radio mic clipped to his shoulder and said, "Chief, we got two FBI guys here."

There was a long pause before a garbled, squawking voice said, "Send 'em through."

Dan and Biegler passed through the loose cordon and walked several dozen paces deeper into the woods. Dan couldn't help but think how calm and peaceful it was here. The thick, brightly colored canopy of oaks, maples, poplars, and hickories was dotted here and there with towering pines and sweet-smelling cedars. The undergrowth was thick and still a lush green. A stream gurgled somewhere nearby, echoing among the trees and rocks of the forest. Cicadas sang their own dirges softly in the distance, accompanied by a single bobwhite.

At the base of a massive blackjack oak, they found Chief Deidre Kelly. She was crouching over a nude body ringed by a dozen metal-capped stones. Another uniformed officer took evidence photos of the scene.

The first thing Dan noticed, before the introductions were made, was the similarity in the chief's and the victim's appearance. The dead woman covered in blue-painted knotwork and gold jewelry could have been the chief's daughter or a doppelgänger from half a lifetime ago. Both women were tall with athletic figures, pale skin, dark hair and eyes, and strong, almost Cherokee-like bone structures.

"Was she a relative of yours, Chief?" Dan asked, pocketing his ID. Agent Biegler began carefully examining the scene.

"No. Not exactly. And call me Deidre, or DD. Everybody else does, Agent Hughes."

"Dan. And what does 'not exactly' mean, DD?"

In answer, a disheveled man in grey sweats broke free of the cordon and ran to the edge of the scene before another local cop could grab him. He was tall and thick, like an aging athlete, with greying dark hair and pale blue eyes. Eyes that were filled with grief and rage. As his square features cracked and he broke into sobs, the man fell to his knees and grabbed handfuls of earth. "No. No. No. Damn it, no!"

Deidre hurried to the man's side, knelt, and put her arm around him.

The man shook her off and jumped to his feet, fixing her with a look of loathing and hatred. His voice was low and thick, spoken through clenched teeth, but Dan clearly heard him say, "This is your doing, isn't it? You couldn't let us be happy, you spiteful bitch."

Deidre said something that Dan didn't catch. Before he could interpose himself into the drama, the chief had the two beefy officers escort the distraught man away.

"What was that all about?"

The chief shook her head and ran a hand through her hair, pushing it out of her face. "That, Agent Dan, was my ex-husband, Joe Kelly. The victim here is his new bride, the lovely homecoming queen of just three short years ago, Rosalind Kelly. That's what 'not exactly' means."

Dan grimaced. "Ouch. I'm sorry. Can I buy you a coffee? Catch you up to speed on what we know at the Bureau?"

DD gave him the ghost of a smile. "Sure. So long as you're okay with making the coffee Irish."

The rest of the day was spent setting up a taskforce HQ at the Briley Hill Police Station, brainstorming a list of possible suspects, gathering files, going over evidence, and waiting on the coroner's initial findings. While Biegler handled much of the administrative duties, Dan checked them into the local motel (there was only one, just like almost everything else in Briley Hill) near the fairgrounds at the edge of town.

Dan noted the big, multi-colored banner hanging over the fairgrounds' entrance. Along with the word HALLOWEEN, it included several synonyms for a party: FESTIVAL, FEST, CELEBRATION, and even Biegler's Celtic word, FEIS.

When the coroner's report finally arrived, it brought no new information to light. The girl had been rendered unconscious, or at least insensible, by a carefully placed blow to the back of the head. The presence of a single injection site on her inner left arm indicated that she had been further sub-dued by an intravenous injection, probably of morphine or some other opiate (labs weren't in yet, but it would track with the other cases). All before being dispatched with a single stab wound to the heart. There were no indications of ligature or defensive wounds.

"Almost a peaceful death," Agent Biegler said, looking over the report. He sat at the small table in Dan's motel room. "Almost... humane. Merciful."

Dan turned from the window. He had been staring at the two huge bon-fires on the fairgrounds across the street, still burning from the previous night and waiting to be replenished when the sun set. "You crushing on this guy or what?"

Biegler dropped the page on the table and frowned. "I've worked a lot of serial killer cases, Agent Hughes. This is by far and away the least gruesome of the bunch. It's nice to see a break in the trend for once. That's all."

Dan narrowed his eyes at the man. He knew absolutely nothing about him, wondered what was really going on behind those horn-rimmed glasses. He sensed that Biegler either didn't trust him or thought him incompetent. "Right."

Biegler looked at his watch. "Well, I'm hungry. Care to join me for a bite to eat? Chief Kelly said the local place, Patty's Kitchen, makes the best fried chicken livers in the state. I'd like to put that claim to the test."

Dan shook his head, looked back to the fires. A group of white-clad men were beginning to feed more logs into the flames. "No, thanks. I'll probably just hit the vending machine and turn in early."

"Suit yourself. See you first thing," Biegler said on his way out the door.

***

When Dan answered the urgent knock at his door, it was not to discover Agent Biegler standing in the gray, early-morning light. It was a haggard-faced Chief Kelly.

"I'm sorry, Agent Dan," she said. "I'm afraid I've got some bad news."

Dan sighed. "Another Sundial murder? Well, I guess we knew it was com-ing. Please, come in."

He waved at the table, still covered with the case files and crime scene photos, as well as a greasy pizza box and three crushed Mountain Dew cans.

"Have a seat while I make myself presentable. Or you can fetch my partner."

"Dan," she said. He turned, the hairs standing on the back of his neck. "It's Agent Biegler. He's the vic."

"You're kidding…"

DD shook her head, looked at the disarray on the table. "The cross-country coach found him just after dawn while on her morning run… I'll wait in the car while you get ready."

Five minutes later they were headed back through the small town that time forgot. It was early yet, but Briley Hill being a rural community, the locals were up with the chickens. Dan stared at the old buildings built in the 1920s and 30s, some even older—the mom-and-pop haberdasheries, the Depression-era movie house, an all-brick drugstore and soda fountain, and the pre-Civil War Briley Hill Church of the Mount. If it weren't for the newer model cars parked on the streets, the town would look like something out of a history book or an episode of *The Andy Griffith Show.*

"A lovely little town," Dan said, almost to himself.

"It is." DD looked at him. "Most of the time."

"I remember hearing about a mass murder here back in the eighties," Dan said. "Something about an entire family being wiped out, butchered?"

DD frowned. "The Donnellys; they lived on a farm a few miles outside of town. The local truant officer found them when the two kids missed three straight days of school. I was a kid, myself. My dad, Fergus Riordan, was the police chief. The whole town was scared out of its mind. Dad believed it was a drifter or something, but they never caught the guy…"

"No leads at all?"

DD shrugged. "A year later, they arrested a homeless Vietnam vet down in Kingsport for torturing stray dogs. Locked him up in a state looney bin. Most folks decided to believe that he was the culprit, but it took almost a decade for the scandal to go away… And now this."

Dan decided to change the subject. "You know anything about Celtic mythology, DD?"

She put both hands on the wheel and accelerated out of town. "No."

Dan stared at the beautiful countryside as it sprang to life in the golden light of the autumnal sunshine. "Biegler had this theory. He believed that our killer fancies himself a druid, making sacrifices to some long-forgotten Celtic god. Propitiation or something."

"Interesting theory."

Dan glanced at her. "He had some doozies. Have you ever heard of the *Boyhood Deeds of Fionn?*"

"I've heard of *The Adventures of Huckleberry Finn.*" She smiled half-heartedly.

Dan looked back out the window. "It's a collection of old myths from Ireland. One of the stories tells how all the men went to the hill of Bri Eile to woo a fairy maiden. Though some versions claim she was the daughter of Crom Cruach, the very god Biegler believed our killer was courting. Naturally, like any protective father, he took exception... That version claims Crom Cruach killed the high king and a quarter of his army in a single day... Samhain..." He trailed off as they pulled up behind the line of patrol cars edging the woods.

Putting the SUV in park, DD said, "Hope you're ready for a hike."

Dan had to admit, if not for the ultimate goal of the hike, it would have been wonderful. He always loved that crisp quality of early morning air that can only be found in the Tennessee Appalachians at that particular time of year. Most of the world considered autumn the symbolic death of nature, but he'd always thought of it as a reawakening to itself. It was the one time of year that he actually enjoyed being outside, breathing fresh air and feeling real sunshine on his face.

They found Agent Bill Biegler stretched out on a bed of thick clover beside a gurgling mountain stream, surrounded by twelve stones topped with silver rings. He wore a gold chain around his neck and a gold watch on his left wrist, and nothing else save for the blue knotwork painted over his face, chest, arms, and legs. His glasses were gone, revealing a peaceful look on his narrow features.

"How's that for a break in the trend?" Dan said.

"What?" DD looked at him, brows furrowed.

Dan shook his head. "Never mind. I need to call the Bureau and let them know." He looked at his phone, unsurprised to see no coverage.

"Come on." DD touched his shoulder. "I'll drive you back into town. We'll stop for coffee on the way."

Back in the SUV, Dan said, "We've got today to catch him. That's it. He'll kill again tonight, then take another year off. Unless he sends us a tip next October, today is the last, best chance we'll ever have."

DD nodded as they drove past the sprawling Briley Hill Cemetery. "We've done everything we can. This is a small town and new faces stand out, but we've not had any visitors other than you and... Agent Biegler..."

"What about locals? Any of them travel frequently, especially this time of year?"

DD shrugged. "Lots, I guess. The high school seniors take a trip to Orlando around now. The same teachers and parents usually act as chaperones. The band sometimes attends competitions... We've got local business owners who travel for work... You know, the usual."

Dan rubbed his face. "I think we can rule out the chaperones and the band teacher. As far as I know, there've been no victims found below Georgia. And the killer will be somebody who travels alone and doesn't have a set destination." He looked at her. "But I'm certain that whoever it is, the Sundial Slayer calls Briley Hill home."

DD's face hardened. "Based on that anonymous note? That's pretty slim."

Dan looked back out the window. "I've got my reasons. Let me have a raincheck on the coffee. Take me back to the motel, and I'll grab the rest of Biegler's notes, put my thoughts in order. I'll call the Bureau. Then we can get together this afternoon and suss it all out. Hopefully by nightfall we'll have bagged ourselves a serial killer."

***

Dan stood at the window of his motel room, sipping on his sixth Mountain Dew of the day and watching a sizeable procession of kids across the street. They followed someone concealed beneath a white sheet attached to a decorated horse's skull mounted on a long stick. The sun was still up but the streetlights were already coming on, in anticipation of the early trick-or-treaters, no doubt.

"Good luck and Happy Halloween," Dan said to the empty room.

The mummer and the kids passed into the fairgrounds and made for the bonfires as Chief Kelly's SUV pulled into the parking lot.

Dan washed some amphetamines down with the last swallow of soda.

"Come in," Dan said when DD knocked. She held a good-smelling plastic bag emblazoned with the green PATTY'S KITCHEN logo in one hand and a drink carrier in the other.

"Can't solve crime on an empty stomach," DD said, setting the food on the table. "I hope you like fried chicken, pinto beans, mashed taters, and sweet tea."

Dan smiled. "Love them, thanks. What do I owe you?"

"Just the leads that are going to get this serial killer the hell out of my town." DD began setting out the foil cartons and the plastic flatware. "So what've you got?"

"Let's eat first."

They made small talk about the weather, the town's unusually large Halloween festivities, and the state of U.T. football while they enjoyed the excellent facsimile of a homecooked meal. After mopping up the last bite of mashed potatoes with a piece of cornbread, Dan pushed back from the table and sighed. "Thanks. I've missed that kind of cooking."

DD wiped her mouth and smiled. "So, how do we catch our 'Sundial Slayer,' Agent Hughes?"

Dan tried to suppress a yawn. "What if I told you that the so-called Sundial wasn't the same person responsible for the murders here in Briley Hill? At least not the most recent two."

DD raised an eyebrow. "I'm intrigued. Go on."

Dan took a long sip of tea, but it only made his mouth drier. "You ever notice how big the cemetery is compared to the town itself?"

DD raised her chin, narrowed her eyes. "So? It's an old town."

Dan rubbed his face. It was going numb. "Very old. With a surprisingly strong economy for this region. And yet, according to census records, the population hasn't fluctuated more than one percent in over two hundred years." He ended the sentence with a yawn.

DD shrugged. "Is that it? Is that all you've got?"

Dan tried to smile. "There's also the fact that this may be the only incorporated city in the State of Tennessee, maybe even the entire country, with just a single church. And that with no strong ties to any major denomination. Don't you find that odd, situated right here against the Bible Belt Buckle?"

"Spit it out. Say what you want to say, Agent. While you still can."

Dan had to work hard to make his mouth form the words. Harder to keep his eyes open. "The story I was telling you this morning... About the men of Ireland wooing Crom Cruach's daughter... It aroused the god's wrath... So the people began a tradition every Samhain... every Halloween... to commemorate and atone... Sacrifices had to be made, people had to be murdered... By an unknown person so the sacrifices wouldn't see it coming... The sacrifices had to be unwilling... To appease the Crooked One of the Mound... of Bri Eile... of Briley Hill..."

Dan tried to stand. He wanted to move to the nightstand and the pistol resting upon it. His legs had other plans. "It's you, DD... You're the killer... At least this year... You *won* Briley Hill's secret lottery... You're Crom Cruach's instrument of vengeance..."

Dan somehow found himself on the floor.

DD crouched next to his face and smiled. "I have to admit, I'm grateful that you and Agent Biegler came to town when you did. First off, I'm glad that I didn't have to kill two more locals, but I still got to take care of that little slut, Rosy...

"And now, thanks to your prepackaged scapegoat and bogeyman, the Sundial Slayer, I've got a damn good story to explain how two FBI agents got themselves killed in this sleepy little backwoods town. Without exposing our secret."

Her smile turned to a frown. "But there's still the matter of that anonymous note. I've got to figure out who sent it and make sure it never happens again."

At this, Dan laughed until he lost consciousness.

***

Dan opened his eyes and shook his throbbing head. The amphetamines and caffeine were doing yeoman's work against whatever DD had slipped him in his tea. But he was still far from a hundred percent. It took a moment or two to realize he was naked, his wrists tied behind his back, and propped against a tree trunk. He quietly mumbled a prayer of thanks that he was bound with rope and not handcuffs or a zip tie. She was observing the traditions.

He could see the silvery glow of the full moon shining through the boughs above his head. The low moaning wind was chilly, helping to spur on more wakefulness.

In addition to the moon, there was the bright blue glow of headlights. Someone walked in front of them. All else was pitch black darkness. Dan knew he was deep in the woods.

"You're awake earlier than I expected." DD crouched just outside the ring of stones surrounding the tree. By the glow of headlights, Dan could see that she was also naked and covered in the blue knotwork, a thick golden torc around her neck and gilded bracelets snaking up her forearms. She held a broad-bladed bronze dagger in her right hand. "Either you're a secret morphine junkie or you took something before I arrived."

Dan cleared his throat. "Amphetamines. Why am I still alive?"

DD reached down to a black piece of velvet, then placed the last silver ring on one of the surrounding stones. Resting on the velvet were a golden necklace, a golden bracelet, and a full syringe. "The way you laughed about that note. Got me wondering. You know who sent it, don't you?"

Dan took a deep breath and tried to clear his head. "Yes."

"You might as well tell me. You're going to die anyway. The God of the Hill must be satisfied."

Dan laughed. "Oh, believe me. I know."

"What does that mean?"

"It means I'm the one who sent the note."

DD inhaled sharply. "Liar."

Dan shook his head and chuckled. "What do you remember about the Donnelly killings?"

She edged inside the ring and knelt beside him, resting the bronze blade on his thigh. "I told you, I was just a kid. I know it was messy, brutal. They changed the rules for the lottery after that. Only leading members of the community could participate."

Dan smiled. "I was a kid, too. That's why I needed help when the lottery chose me. I'm the reason they changed the rules."

DD's eyes went wide. "You... you're Hugh Donnelly? I always wondered why four were sacrificed that year instead of three."

Dan nodded. "I asked your dad, Chief Riordan, to help me, to coach me. Little did I know that my dad was stepping out with your mom. But the chief did, which made the selection of sacrifices pretty damn clear. Since I was a kid, it was just easier to do the whole family. One stop shopping."

He laughed. "Your dad demonstrated on my old man. He took his time, enjoyed it. In the end, he was so grateful, he helped relocate me with a new name and a whole new life. But I never forgot my responsibilities to the

Crooked One of the Mound, and over the past few years, I've gotten pretty good at observing them. Of course, when you're the FBI agent in charge of investigating your own murders, it makes it kind of easy."

DD's face hardened. She raised the dagger.

Dan's right fist came up and connected with her jaw. "You know, your dad even showed me how to tie knots and how to untie them. Just like he did you."

DD sprawled on the grass inside the stone circle, stunned.

"I'm glad you're wearing gold for the ceremony, DD," Dan said as he picked up the dagger. "Praise Crom Cruach! Forgive us our sins and bless us in this New Year! *Domhnach Chrom Dubh!*"

Dan was pleased to see DD's eyes widen with realization as he buried the blade in her breast. He had finally come home, the God of the Hill had been appeased, and the Samhain Feis had been dutifully observed.

All was right with the world again.

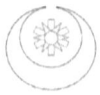

THE CHOSEN

Ryan Kurtz stood in the foyer of his thirteen-million-dollar home, sweating into the Italian cotton of his Fendi bathrobe. He sipped eighteen-year-old Yamazaki whisky from a Baccarat tumbler, and watched the two escorts flee down the walkway to the waiting Uber. The only things more obscene than the things he'd made them do were the amounts of cash, booze, and drugs with which he'd plied them.

Once upon a time, Ryan hadn't had to pay for it. Once upon a time, he hadn't had to get them high.

He watched them reach the car. The girl was ugly-face crying as she hopped in the passenger seat. The guy paused to puke yellow and red chunks on the white pavement before jumping in the backseat. Stoned as they were, Ryan knew they would race home and try to scrub his touch off every inch of their beautiful bodies. When they sobered up, they would need therapy to scrub the memory from their minds.

He'd heard through the grapevine that the last girl had killed herself a couple weeks ago. She'd scrubbed the inside with Drano and bleach, the outside with a straight razor.

When the Uber pulled out of the driveway, Ryan turned off the porch light. He blanched at the horror reflected in the window glass. Pale, jaundiced eyes stared out of a sunken, sallow face. Sweat glistened on flabby jowls and lips. His hair, little more than a straw-colored wisp, shared space on his scaly scalp with a constellation of yellow-brown liver spots. He raised the crystal tumbler to the toothless line beneath his bulbous, misshapen nose, but there was no washing the distaste from his mouth.

He looked at the Big Bang Unico King on his wrist. "Almost time to pay the piper."

Killing the whisky, Ryan turned from the revenant in the window and shuffled into the spacious, impeccably decorated living room. In spite of the air fresheners, the exotic flowers delivered daily, and the discreetly displayed Himalayan salt crystals, the place still smelled like burning medical waste. When a girl had jumped from his bed, locked herself in the bathroom and vomited all over the tiled Roman shower last month, Ryan had finally realized *he* was the source of the stench. His time was almost up. The change was coming.

A now familiar pain, growing ever stronger, swam through his body like a school of languid razorblades. He pulled a bottle of pills from the robe's pocket.

Ryan had worked from home ever since the incident with the horrified hooker. His social life had been in steady decline over the course of the past year despite the uptick in his professional success. The pretty people just couldn't stomach him anymore. He was only a screenwriter, after all, with no real power to move and shake the pillars of Hollywood. But as soon as the studio execs, producers, and directors got just the right jawlines and bustlines signed on, Ryan was the one they'd call for a script. The go-to guy for the next summer blockbuster or Oscar bait.

The leather-trimmed mahogany bar stood beneath illuminated framed posters of his two shining achievements, *Malebolge* and *The New Messiah*. Both had won Academy Awards for Best Original Screenplay. He'd won another Oscar, his first, for adapting Chambers's "The Repairer of Reputations," but he preferred to showcase his original works. Ryan was particularly proud of *Malebolge*, his retelling of Dante's *Inferno* wherein he replaced the sinners against dogmatic mediaeval religion with violators of today's mercurial social rules.

He'd heard that his aging, Army-retired father had particularly hated it. That news had made him smile.

Refilling the tumbler and downing the cocktail of oxy, Vicodin, and Quaaludes, Ryan turned and surveyed his luxurious abode. The back wall was floor-to-ceiling glass opening onto the patio and swimming pool, overlooking the bright lights of the city. After admiring the stylish living room furniture and his framed Warhols, Ryan's gaze lingered on the large collection of golden statuettes crowding the mantle above the crystal fireplace. Three Oscars, four Emmys, five Golden Globes, and even a People's Choice Award.

"Not bad for a guy slinging drinks in a Studio City lounge just twelve short years ago." He took another gulp of Japanese whisky and sighed. He had paid a high price for that success.

Or rather, he was about to. He wondered if it had been worth it.

Ryan wondered what he might say to that thirty-five-year-old struggling screenwriter-slash-bartender if he could go back to the night the doors of the universe had been opened wide to him. Would he warn his younger self? Would he tell him to run as fast as he could back to Georgia, like Lot fleeing Sodom? Or would he just tell him to make sure to savor every last second of the good times, because the bad ones were coming, and coming fast?

"What *would* I say?"

***

Ryan Kurtz whistled when the cab rounded a pine-shrouded curve and the mansion hove into view. He had expected a Marriot or maybe even a Ritz-Carlton tucked away in the snow-covered hills overlooking Tahoe. He certainly wasn't prepared for the sprawling Norman-style castle and estate hidden from the tourists, ski bunnies, and jetsetters.

"Something, ain't it?" the cab driver said. "Been here since the twenties. Built by some newspaper mogul from L.A. back in the day. Legend says he lost everything in the stock market crash. Sent the wife and kids back to the big city, locked himself in a tower room with a bottle o' Scotch and a pistol, and... *blammo!*"

Ryan looked at the backpack in the seat next to him. It was stuffed with extra socks, underwear and sweatshirts, his toothbrush and deodorant, half a dozen notebooks, two packs of new ink pens, and his laptop. "Maybe I should have packed some nicer clothes..."

When he fumbled in his pocket to tip the driver, the young man smiled into the rearview mirror. "No need, Mr. Kurtz. It's been taken care of."

The same thing happened when he tried to tip the bellman, who admittedly looked underwhelmed carrying a single JanSport, bulging as it was. He followed the yellow-jacketed man out of the crisp cold December air and through the castle's massive wooden doors.

"Ah, Mr. Kurtz," the concierge said from behind the front desk, a monument of filigreed cherry and polished marble. The resort's lobby looked like a set from *Lord of the Rings*. "So glad you could make it. You'll be staying in room 316 with Mr. Li. He's already checked in and should be settled by now. I'm sure the two of you will get along famously."

Ryan hadn't expected a roommate, but then, this whole scenario had been one hell of a gift horse, and he wasn't about to start looking it in the mouth now.

The slender, middle-aged man behind the desk smiled and handed Ryan an old-fashioned key and a thick brochure of materials. "Here's the schedule of programs, workshops, and seminars for the next two weeks, as well as the lunch and dinner menus, and the roster of evening activities and celebrations. We have a continental breakfast in the dining hall every morning from five a.m. until ten.

"Sean will show you to your room. Just past that row of shields above the grand fireplace there, you'll find the elevators."

Ryan stared at the hefty packet for a moment, noting the odd yellow symbol emblazoned above the motto: THE CHOSEN RETREAT. Slightly dazed, he turned to take in the mediaeval splendor of the place, feeling light-headed or like he was having an episode of déjà vu.

The concierge asked, "Do you have any questions, Mr. Kurtz?"

"Uhm... I was invited by a Mr.—"

"Yes, of course. He will be arriving sometime later this week or early next, depending on his busy schedule. Most of the sponsors do put in at least one appearance during these retreats. I'm sure he'll look you up when he gets here. Anything else?"

Ryan shook his head, thanked the man, and followed Sean the bellhop to the elevators and the third floor. In room 316, he met Derrick Li, caterer to the stars and aspiring leading man.

"You must be Ryan, the wordsmith." The tall, good-looking Asian-American gym rat wore a smile just this side of mischievous. "I'm Derrick. Hope you don't mind I took the bed closer to the balcony. We can switch if you want."

Ryan returned the smile and shook hands. "No. That's fine." Tossing his backpack onto the canopied double bed, he scanned the dark paneling and antique furniture, the wall tapestry depicting a mediaeval hunting scene. "Dig this place. I'll bet the top-end Disney properties don't go this all out."

Derrick pulled a gray cable-knit sweater over his black t-shirt. "I know, right? I heard this place was once owned by Howard Hughes back in the forties. Even used it as a set for one of his movies... Hey, what say we go down and have a look around? I want to see where they keep the weight room in this place, and maybe we can find some aspiring young starlets to woo—I mean, y'know... if that's your cup o' tea..."

"Yeah, it is. Let me just unpack first. See if I can get some of the wrinkles to fall out while we're gone. You know, I wasn't exactly expecting Shangri La. I figured I'd be in a Best Western with a bunch of other pencil-pushers and wannabes for a few days. Then some Hollywood bigshots would roll in, give us a pep talk, sign some autographs, then sweep out with our work in hand to polish up for their next blockbusters."

Derrick laughed while checking his hair in the mirror. "Man, you are one cynical dude. I guess you been in Hollywood a while, then?"

"About six years. Waiting tables, washing cars, bartending, even walked B-list celebrities' dogs for a while. Trying to sell a script every damn day with nothing to show for it. Then, out of nowhere, about a month ago, I'm tending bar at Seventy7 North, and I strike up a conversation with a lonesome drinker. Turns out, he's the guy who came up with the bright idea to use nerd movies as platforms for social messaging.

"He gives me his card, asks me to send him my latest screenplay. A week later, I get a packet in the mail with a plane ticket and a pass to this retreat. So, here I am... You?"

Derrick shrugged. "Same thing, pretty much. I was catering at a big L.A. shindig for the charity-of-the-month and hit on a casting director at one of the Big Five." He laughed. "Honestly, I thought she was just a tipsy MILF, and I had a shot. I didn't go home with her, but she told me to send my headshots and demos the next day. A week later, I got the same deal."

Ryan took his turn at the mirror. Running a comb through his thick chestnut hair, he checked for blemishes to his California tan or anything stuck in his pearly whites. "Weird. I never knew there was a... a 'training program' for the next wave of talent. How they've kept it a secret is beyond me. Had you ever heard of 'The Chosen' before?"

Derrick slapped him on the back and guided him to the door. "It's Hollywood, man. The CIA can't keep secrets as well as that town."

As Ryan would eventually learn, Derrick was right. The only thing to change in Hollywood since the time of Fatty Arbuckle was the industry's ability to hide the scandals.

Over the course of the next week, Ryan and Derrick became fast friends as they got down to the business of becoming the next generation of Hollywood elites. At the orientation—emceed by the super-agent responsible for half the red carpet appearances in Tinseltown—they learned that the two of them were part of a group of over seventy "Chosen," afforded the unique privilege of following in the footsteps of the entertainment industries' greatest legends. Not only were there actors and screenwriters, but also directors, composers, effects and makeup artists, fashion and costume designers, musicians, comedians, authors, and even videogame designers.

The first few days were spent in classes with four or five other Chosen in the individual's field of expertise, under the guidance of big name guests in those fields. But by the end of the first week, the groups were intermingled to put together projects, making use of their combined skills.

Every night, after dinner, there were full blown Hollywood-style parties in the lounge or the indoor pool, where the open bars were summarily abused as well as copious amounts of recreational drugs. Ryan never knew where the stuff came from, but so long as it didn't run out, he didn't care.

It was during the second night's bacchanalia that he met Amanda Grey. Fresh out of USC film school, the twenty-four-year-old auteur had Coppola and Spielberg firmly in her sights. She was one of the few attractive young people not running naked and wild around the Olympic-sized pool or cavorting in one of the six hot tubs. Wearing faded jeans and an ironically tie-dyed Punisher t-shirt, with her kinky black hair pulled back in a bushy tail, she leaned against the balcony railing and watched the debauchery. Sipping a canned PBR, she cast dark-eyed judgment on the proceedings.

When she deigned to turn those beautiful brown peepers on him, Ryan knew he was hopelessly smitten. He had just enough booze and coke in him to pass for courage, so he approached her with his best pick-up smile.

"Crazy, huh?" Ryan followed her gaze to the frolics below. "You know, I heard this place was owned by Anton LaVey and his Church of Satan back in the seventies. Maybe they left some kind of black magic that brings out the beast in folks... I'm Ryan, by the way. Ryan Kurtz."

She smiled without looking at him. "Amanda Grey. Never 'Mandy.' And you're full of shit, Ryan Kurtz. LaVey's outfit never had the capital to own a place like this. That's just a rumor that got started after the ghost stories came out in the nineties."

Ryan was intrigued. "You know the real story, then?"

Amanda cast him a sidelong glance. "You ever heard of the Ahnenerbe?"

When Ryan raised an eyebrow, she said, "The Nazi outfit Indiana Jones tussled with in the movies were based on them. They were Himmler's special archeology unit, tasked with hunting down all the supernatural relics from history... Well, back in the thirties, before the U.S. got involved in the war, the German government bought this place and used it as a headquarters for the Ahnenerbe's operations in the Americas, the Pacific, and even Antarctica. There's no telling what those fascist pricks did here or what they brought back from God knows where."

"Interesting." Ryan couldn't think of anything better to say. "So... you an aspiring actress, singer, or what?"

She frowned. "Like a woman can't be a director?"

Ryan flushed. "I didn't say that. I just thought you're hot enough to be in front of the camera. Y'know, if you wanted. But to be fair, I can't see your IQ or your CV on your face or your ass."

She smirked. "Nice. I guess you're not a dumb pretty boy like your roommate. Since he's already hit on me twice, I know he's an actor. Are you?"

Ryan laughed. "Hell no. I'm a writer."

For the first time, Amanda turned to face him. "Really. What kind of stories do you write, Ryan Kurtz?"

Ryan cleared his throat. "There's this Woodrow Wilson quote, from when he was in academia: 'The purpose of a university should be to make a son as unlike his father as possible.' I've always wanted to write stories that do that. Make movies and TV shows that get young people to stop thinking like their parents and past generations. You know, move us forward as a society."

Amanda's dark eyes sparkled when she smiled. "Want to get some fresh air?"

They spent the next couple hours walking the grounds in the cold, talking about movies, big ideas, the crafts of storytelling and filmmaking, and eventually Life Before Hollywood. They ended the evening in Amanda's room. Her roommate, a gorgeous and talented young actress, had been invited to some "special ceremony" and wouldn't be back that night.

When Ryan woke the next morning beside Amanda, he praised the name of whoever had come up with the idea for The Chosen.

The rest of the first week was an exciting blur of seminars, workshops, study groups, and, of course, parties. By the first weekend, Ryan, Amanda, and Derrick, along with a dozen other artists and technicians, were working on the most ambitious group project at the retreat.

The sponsors appeared on Saturday. The blizzard hit Sunday.

But the castle had plenty of supplies stored up, including fuel for the battery of emergency generators. Apart from the roads being closed and cell signals fading in and out, life at the Chosen Retreat went on without a hitch. The only noticeable difference was that now they were working and partying with a higher class of people.

On Tuesday of the second week, Derrick received his invitation to the "special ceremony." By now, the rumor of the "Chosen among the Chosen" had circulated through the retreat's attendants. Although everyone knew who had been called up—affording these select few the appropriate fawning awe and thinly veiled jealousy—no one had uttered a peep as to what this ceremony actually entailed. The mystique only made it all the more enticing.

Ryan wanted to be excited for his friend but couldn't get past his own envy and resentment. He lay stretched out on his bed, bouncing a stress ball against the canopy while Derrick scrambled through his wrinkled clothes, trying to find the best garments for the night's special event.

"This is just like high school," Ryan said. "They get us up here, telling us we're all *Chosen*. Then, just when we begin to feel a sense of camaraderie and egalitarianism, they start sewing dissension and enmity with this bullshit."

Derrick huffed. "C'mon, man. They've been doing this since we got here. I'm betting by the time the retreat is over, we'll all be 'Chosen of the Chosen.' It's just a big game these elites like to play. You know, like that statue of Moloch they got down in Bohemian Grove. Now, which shirt do you think I should wear?"

Ryan sighed and randomly picked one.

Derrick didn't come back to the room that night. When the group got together the next morning after breakfast, Ryan almost didn't recognize his friend. Derrick had somehow... transcended his playful, sometimes goofy former self and now exuded that leading man gravitas he'd been missing. He seemed taller, better looking, more confident. Ryan even thought his voice was deeper.

At dinner, Amanda told Ryan she was going up for the ceremony that night. He did a much better job of acting supportive for her. Primarily because he'd already decided to sneak out and see exactly what the hell was going on at these secret rites. He'd heard too many scary conspiracy theories about those Bohemian Club meetings...

That night, feigning a headache, Ryan retired from the party early and sneaked into the janitor's closet down the hall from Amanda's room. He waited for almost an hour before he saw Sean, the yellow-jacketed bellman, come to fetch her. When they boarded the elevator, he watched the numbers to see where they were headed before bolting down the stairs. He spotted them leaving the main building through a service entrance and waited a few seconds before following.

It being December in the wake of a blizzard, Ryan wasn't too keen on staying out in the open all night, but he followed anyway. Sean's flashlight beam crossed the cleared walkways to the back gardens and into the manicured patch of timber forest edging the estate. The sky had cleared following the snowstorm, so every heavenly body in the night sky shone with an uncanny brilliance, the celestial glow magnified by the banks of driven snow. Ryan wasn't the outdoorsy type, but even he would have been hard pressed to get lost with that level of illumination.

Coming to the edge of a clearing, he hunkered down behind a towering lodgepole pine to watch. Sean had led Amanda to a secluded dell edged by big stone braziers filled with yellow flames. In the center of this ring of fire stood an assembly of black-robed individuals, each robe emblazoned with the odd yellow symbol Ryan had seen on the retreat's pamphlets.

He watched as Amanda was instructed to strip in the firelight, then given a shimmering golden robe. He felt titillation and sympathy in equal measures as her dusky, lithe body shivered against the cold before sliding into the thin satin.

When Amanda had donned the ceremonial garb, the assembly began to chant in an unfamiliar language. Ryan heard the same sounds or names repeated several times: "Carcosa, Hali, Aldebaran, and Hastur, Hastur, Hastur..."

At the chant's conclusion, a tall figure in a tattered yellow robe appeared from the darkness. This shrouded individual ascended to a stone dais at the far end of the clearing. Bright amber flames erupted from the flanking braziers in true cinematic fashion. By this light, Ryan glimpsed a pearlescent or porcelain mask beneath the ragged yellow hood.

Amanda stepped forward and faced the towering figure on the dais. The two stared at one another in absolute silence for so long that Ryan feared the sound of his chattering teeth might give him away. When the preternatural quiet felt like it might last forever, Amanda nodded and said, "Yes. I accept."

Ryan blinked, wondering if he had missed something. Amanda seemed to swoon for a moment, then she turned with a wide-eyed smile as the assembly doffed their hoods and surrounded her in cheering congratulations. Ryan recognized a dozen headliners in that crowd of smiling faces, but he had lost track of the tall figure in the tattered robe.

Deciding it would not do to get caught spying, he slipped back to the castle before the backslapping ended. After taking a long, hot shower, he lay in the silent darkness of his room wondering at what he had seen. He wondered if Amanda would be as different as Derrick now. He wondered if there might not be something to all the Sunday School nonsense his dad had tried to pound into him as a kid.

"Did I just watch Amanda sell her soul to the Devil?"

At breakfast the next morning, he was joined by his sponsor. The bearded studio head in the flat-brimmed black ball cap, Chopard sunglasses, Armani suit jacket, and thousand-dollar jeans smiled like they were best friends. "How you enjoying the retreat, Ryan? Everything you'd hoped it would be?"

Ryan tried to look natural, tried to pretend like this man's face hadn't been one he'd seen in the woods the night before. "Loving it. I can't thank you enough for bringing me out here. I... I just hate that I've got to leave."

His sponsor's smile faltered. "Leave? Have they gotten the roads opened yet? Even if they did, why would you ever want to leave now? I hear your script is the driving force behind the best project coming together this session. You know, quite a few blockbusters and Oscar winners started out as retreat projects. Who knows, yours might be the next *big one.*"

Ryan swallowed, pushed his half-eaten bagel away. "It's just that, I don't know. I feel like I'm losing myself up here... Like if I don't leave now, I won't know how to get back into my own life. Does that make sense?"

The man laughed. "Absolutely, it does. But tell me, Ryan, why in hell would you ever want to go back to your own life?" He pulled an envelope from his pocket and slid it across the table. It bore the Yellow Sign. "Especially when you're so close to getting the new life you've always wanted.

Congratulations, my friend. You're up tonight."

With a wink and a Hollywood smile, Ryan's sponsor left him alone with his uneaten breakfast, cooling coffee, and his invitation to become Chosen among the Chosen.

Pocketing the unopened envelope, Ryan went to the front desk and asked the concierge about getting off the mountain. As expected, he was told, "The local authorities are clearing the primary roads at present, but our access road is regrettably not considered a priority. I will, however, let you know as soon as the situation changes, Mr. Kurtz."

Feeling trapped, Ryan reluctantly went to his group workshop. He watched as Amanda put the actors and crew through their paces as if she'd been directing for decades. Not only was she confident, bold, and precise, but she commanded the set like a beloved general. Everyone treated her as if they'd worked together for years instead of just a few days. And Derrick's work made his first days' performances look like local dinner theater.

When they broke for lunch, Amanda suggested they take their meal up to the parapet and eat in private. Though distracted and unnerved by what was happening around him, Ryan hoped she was angling for a romantic tryst.

In this he was sorely disappointed.

"How do you feel about the script?" she asked as soon as they sat on the Adirondack chairs in the chill breeze, unwrapping their steaming hoagies. "Do you think it's as strong as it could be?"

Ryan stared at her with a mouthful for a moment. Swallowing, he managed, "What do you mean? You loved the script yesterday. What's wrong with it now?"

Amanda shrugged and stared out over the exquisite view of Lake Tahoe and the surrounding mountains. "I don't know. I'm just thinking it needs a little more subtext. Maybe your message is a little too on-the-nose. Maybe we could work on a rewrite tonight?"

Ryan sighed and fished the envelope from his pocket. "I don't know. I got this from my sponsor this morning."

Amanda's eyes lit up, her manner warm again. "Oh, Ryan, that's fantabulous!" She reached over, squeezed his hand, and gave him a bedroom smile. "Don't worry about the rewrite. Go to the ceremony tonight, and tomorrow we'll figure it out. It's all good."

Ryan returned the smile and rewrapped his sandwich. "Thanks."

"You're not going to eat?"

"I'm not hungry. Nerves, I guess."

"Nothing to be nervous about. All your dreams are about to come true. I promise."

After dinner, Ryan returned to his room to find his roommate ironing his best sweatshirt. Derrick looked up with a broad, heroic smile. "I heard the good news, buddy. Thought I'd do my part to make sure you look your best for joining the Chosen among the Chosen."

Ryan returned the smile and almost gave himself away by saying, "Why bother? I'll just be naked within a few minutes of getting there." Instead, he said, "Thanks, man. I appreciate it."

By the time Sean arrived, Ryan had showered, shaved, thrown up, brushed his teeth, and dressed in his freshly pressed shirt and jeans. He was sweating like a man on his way to the gas chamber as they boarded the elevator. When they stepped out into the December night, he was thankful for the blast of refreshing cold air. Staring up into the clear starlit sky, a sudden overwhelming calm descended upon him.

"All my dreams..."

"And then some." Sean smiled as he led him to the darkened wood.

**

Leaning against the bar in his Hollywood Hills home, Ryan Kurtz sighed and took another drink of whisky, his last. He could never quite remember what exactly had happened in that flame-lit glade during his rite of passage. He understood that, like Amanda and Derrick and so many others, he had taken the Unspeakable Oath.

Like Amanda, all he had done was say, "Yes."

But the one thing he did recall, something that haunted his nightmares ever since was the personage to whom he had given that oath. The gaunt, towering form of the King in Yellow loomed large in his mind, his ever-present master.

That night, twelve years ago, Ryan knew he had stared into the face of the Pallid Mask, had seen the terrible, writhing inhuman intellect behind it, and had consigned his body and soul to it forever in exchange for... what? A shelf filled with golden tchotchkes? Bylines on movies and TV programs that would be forgotten in a decade or less? A beautiful house in the hills with a view of the City of Angels? A vintage Porsche and Ferrari that he never drove? Large but ultimately meaningless numbers on his bank statements? Closets and drawers filled with overpriced clothes and baubles?

Ryan hurled the crystal tumbler at the awards on the mantle. It didn't make it. The glass fell short, staining the pristine white carpet an ugly brown. His arm had gone limp and rubbery at the elbow, the fingers elongating into suckered tentacles.

"Dammit." Ryan shook his gelatinous head as he slouched to the patio door. He saw the bright star of Aldebaran rising on the horizon. It was time.

Sliding the door open, he thought about Derrick and Amanda. Derrick had done well for almost a decade. Until someone in his family had stumbled upon the source of his fame and had brought in an old-school witch hunter. Things had gone bad for both Derrick and the exorcist, but that particular Hollywood secret had simply gone away. Fatty Arbuckle would have approved.

Amanda still made movies, though she now wore sunglasses, big hats, and heavy clothes whenever she was on set or in public. Apparently, her skills were still of use to the master here on Earth. At least for a little while longer.

Ryan shuddered with another wave of pain as he stepped onto the concrete patio. His foot made a wet squelching sound. The robe felt constricting, scratchy, and uncomfortable, so he slid out of it. The tendrils on his belly lashed out, exulting in freedom as he breathed in the warm March air.

Staring down his bloated, squamous, naked body at the edge of the pool, Ryan Kurtz had the sudden urge to cry. That urge was washed away when his master's voice filled his thoughts. The voice called him, called him home. It was time to fulfill the bargain. It was time to become the Chosen.

The amorphous, tentacled, writhing thing that had once been Ryan Kurtz, bartender-turned-screenwriting wunderkind, slithered into the pool. It dove into the depths where a portal opened to the Lake of Hali, far beyond the stars, lying in the shadows of lost Carcosa.

As the last of Ryan's consciousness slipped away, one name filled his mind forever, "Hastur, Hastur, Hastur..."

TRANSPARENCY

Connor Mackay stepped from the cold evening drizzle into the warm cheerful chaos of The Trustworthy Pint. The big Irish-style pub and eatery and its premium parking lot dominated this particular block of downtown Chattanooga. It was a go-to eatery and nightspot for the Scenic City's locals as well as tourists. On the Friday night after Thanksgiving, the place was packed to the rafters with folks who'd had enough turkey and dressing, family time, and sales-maddened shopping crowds.

The susurrus of a hundred voices competed with John Denver's "Country Road," a soccer mom convention at the bar accompanying. The mouth-watering scent of smoked wings, fried pub grub, and alcohol blended pleasantly with the body sprays, colognes, and perfumes of the patrons. Connor missed the days when cigarette smoke was a part of the mix, but things always have a way of changing. But then again, some things never do in places like this—like being sized up by hungry cougars on the prowl and their wannabe prey fearing he might be unfair competition. He ignored both factions, just like he tended to ignore most people.

The press of so many bodies in the enclosed environment threatened to bring on a panic attack. After his experiences in New Orleans, Connor understood that not every human body housed a human soul. But he took a deep breath and counted to ten while surveying the crowd, looking for his old friend. The search was easier for Connor, standing head and shoulders above most folks, so most folks subconsciously made room for him. Connor was big and he carried himself a certain way. A professional way. A military way. A way that said, "I'm on a mission and it has nothing to do with you unless you make it."

Connor saw the beanpole profile of Aaron Dockery stand up behind the carved oaken banister of one of the elevated dining areas. His friend waved with the same big goofy smile on his homely face that had earned him the nickname "Icky"—short for Ichabod—in the days before Afghanistan. Icky's green eyes shone behind designer glasses, his black hair pulled back in a small ponytail, accentuating his resemblance to the Disney version of the iconic literary character.

Connor couldn't help but return the smile. The dull throb in his cheeks reminded him how long it had been since he'd acquainted himself with the expression. It also reminded him of the scar running from his left cheekbone to chin.

The recollection of the scar's origin almost brought the panic attack on in full force.

Connor placed a hand on the newel post of the railing. He paused to shut out the sounds of automatic gunfire, unearthly roars, and screams; the smell of blood, burnt powder, filth, and ancient evil. He remembered and exercised the techniques he'd learned while in the hospital in Baton Rouge until the horror was gone. Or at least hidden away before it could drag him into other, more recent horrors... like the horror that had taken so much from him in the bayous outside of New Orleans...

"Big Mac!" Aaron slapped him on the shoulder and guided him to the table. "Been too long, buddy. Glad you came."

"Icky." Connor nodded as they maneuvered through the crowd. Aaron Dockery had been Connor's assistant squad leader during the war. They'd been through hell and back together. But since coming home... Well, things had a way of changing people's lives and coming between friendships. Things like jobs, marriages, kids, tragedies, hospitalizations...

"Do me a favor, buddy," Aaron whispered as they drew near a table where a gorgeous smiling blonde waited. "Don't call me that in front of my fiancée, huh?"

Connor wanted to frown but found himself making the uncomfortable smile again when the blonde stood and stretched out her manicured hand. She was tall and fit, built like a volleyball player or yoga instructor; she might as well have worn a t-shirt with TROPHY GIRLFRIEND printed across her ample bust line. "Hi, I'm Helena. Aar has told me so much about you, Connor."

"I wish I could say the same." Connor felt like he should be looking for Taliban booby traps or ambushes. He gave Icky an accusing glance. "But it's nice to meet you, Helena."

Aaron slapped him on the back and pulled out a chair. "Sorry, Mac. I told you I had a surprise. Hell, *I* was surprised when Helena asked me to marry *her* last week. Chattanooga seemed like as good a place to celebrate as any. Especially with this job coming up."

Connor was saved from making small talk by the arrival of a waiter in a black t-shirt and black skinny jeans. "Guinness," he told the cheery twenty-something while the betrothed resumed their mooneyes.

Icky had invited Connor here to talk about a job. A job he'd said might require some rough stuff. Being at loose ends since his discharge from the hospital, and since he hadn't seen his old Army pal in a while, Connor had hit the Interstate to hear him out. But Connor couldn't fathom having that kind of discussion witnessed by someone who might object—or worse, could be called on to testify. Unless Helena was actually the architect, manipulating Icky into doing her dirty work.

"So..." Helena flashed her pale green eyes at Connor and sipped her martini. "Aar tells me you two were in Afghanistan together. He's told me a few stories... But what have you been up to since you got out?"

Connor had that fight-or-flight sensation again. He counted to three before Aaron answered, "Big Mac was a cop in New Orleans. A detective..." His friend's face and voice turned serious when he added, "I was awful sorry to hear what happened to—"

"Thanks." Connor looked for the waiter with his beer. He kept counting until he got to ten. "No offense... *Aar*, but I didn't think you wanted to do the high school reunion thing here. You said something about a job..."

Aaron nodded, gave Helena a knowing glance and said, "Right. Well, you remember that old family legend I told you about?"

Connor blinked. Icky had grown up in the Appalachians between Tennessee and North Carolina, half white and half Cherokee. He'd had dozens of "family legends" with which he'd regaled the team, ranging from ghost stories to possible encounters with sasquatches and skunk apes. But there was only one he cherished, one he told time and time again with gusto. "The one about the Confederate gold?"

The waiter arrived with Connor's beer. "Here you go, sir. Are you guys ready to order?"

Connor killed half the Guinness while Icky and Helena made their decisions. He ordered a burger and another Guinness, told the waiter to keep 'em coming, and waited for the kid to get out of earshot before turning back to his friend. "Please tell me I didn't cross the entire state of Tennessee, including Monteagle Mountain in a freezing rainstorm, fight my way into town in holiday traffic, and circle this block six times before finding a parking space just for you to tell me that old wives' tale again."

When Icky looked at his beer, Connor took a deep breath. "I've pretty much got it memorized from all those nights in the barracks and the overnight patrols: A Confederate detachment sent to Richmond guarding gold for the war effort got ambushed by Union Cavalry somewhere in the hills of North Carolina, but the Rebs were guided by Cherokee scouts who escaped the ambush with the gold and hid it someplace near your family's land in the Smokies, is that about right? C'mon, man. You and every other kid growing up from Asheville to Little Rock has a similar story tucked away somewhere in the family album."

Aaron looked annoyed but Helena's lovely face lit up. "It's not an old wives' tale, Connor. Aar's got proof."

Icky resumed the goofy Ichabod Crane smile as he reached inside his leather jacket, produced a manila envelope, and slid it across the table. "Take a look, my friend."

Connor killed the other half of the pint before opening the envelope. "Xeroxes? I was half hoping you'd show me a gold coin stamped with 'CSA' or something."

Aaron chuckled. "That would be easy to fake. These documents aren't. I found the originals hidden deep in the archives of the Citadel in Charleston. They'd been lost for decades... Look, this one's dated February 1865, right before the city fell to the Union. And it's signed by Jeff Davis, himself, instructing Beauregard to send 'the bullion' to Richmond at once."

He leaned across the table to direct Connor's attention to a second page. "And this is the cargo manifest of a blockade runner—the *Shenandoah*— that lists four casks of gold, weighing over eight hundred pounds, taken from a Union privateer off the coast of Cuba... And this is the harbor master's ledger, showing that the *Shenandoah* docked in Charleston in December of 1864, after slipping past the blockade."

Connor flipped to the third and fourth pages in the packet of copies. "Orders for a detachment of the 5th South Carolina Cavalry to board a train bound for Asheville..."

"We know the 5th was stationed in Charleston. The timing is right." Aaron sat back with a smug smile on his face. "See, it all fits."

Helena's eyes sparkled, her cheerleader smile widened. "Eight hundred pounds of gold. Today, that's about fifteen million dollars."

Connor smiled indulgently, understanding now why Helena was so smitten with his goofy-looking friend. He didn't want Icky to get hurt, but he was a big boy and had come out of worse scrapes than a gold-digging woman... mostly intact. Still, if there was a chance Connor could make sure she was on the up-and-up and not just looking to take Icky for all he was worth, then he needed to take that chance. "So, how did you guys meet?"

Helena blinked at the unexpected question, but Icky chuckled and put his hand on hers. "Serendipity, dude. I was looking into this when we just happened to run into each other at a bar in Gatlinburg. Helena was a park ranger in the Smokies for four years. She knows them like the back of her hand."

"Was?" Connor's instincts told him the timing seemed a little too convenient.

"Budget cuts," Helena said with a rare frown. "That's why I was there that night, drowning my sorrows. Like Aar says, it was serendipity that brought us together." She batted her green eyes at Icky who rewarded the gesture with a kiss on her knuckles.

Connor forced a smile, risking a cramp. *Serendipity, right. And fifteen million dollars of Confederate gold hidden somewhere in the Great Smoky Mountains wouldn't have anything to do with it at all...*

Carefully returning the papers to the envelope, Connor slid it back to Icky just as the second round arrived. "Okay, you've got my attention. Let's hear it..."

Two hours later, Connor bid the couple good night, standing in the chill drizzle outside the restaurant. The beer, the food, the pleasant atmosphere, and seeing his old friend again had made Connor susceptible to the harebrained scheme. But it wasn't like he had anything better to do at the moment, and his dwindling savings account wouldn't be getting any much needed infusions anytime soon. Plus, Icky had told him he'd also rounded up four other members of their squad—the last survivors not sporting government-issue replacement parts after their run in with that nightmare in Afghanistan. It would be good to see Hicks, Goldman, Hernandez, and Jackson again.

"See you Sunday in Pigeon Forge, Mac," Icky called as Helena led him to the waiting Uber. "We'll make some dreams come true!"

Connor shook his head at the drunken declaration, waved goodbye before turning to head for Gloria. He'd paid up to keep the black '68 Camaro SS safe in a monitored lot half a block away. Being the only tangible remnant of his once normal life, it was worth it. A few extra bucks were a calculated defense against some jealous asshole deciding to key or otherwise vandalize the classic muscle car.

The world, it seemed, was full of assholes, and not all of them were of the human variety. Connor had learned this lesson the hard way. On two separate occasions.

Rolling his broad shoulders and raising the collar of his pea coat against the drizzle, Connor wondered what he was getting himself into. He'd already said yes to Icky's proposal, so there was no backing out now. Not in his mind.

He mumbled to himself—another bad habit he'd picked up after the bad times in New Orleans—as he walked along the deserted sidewalk. "If he's right about where the gold is, we're risking some serious hard time if we're caught... Smack dab in the middle of the Great Smoky Mountain National Park... Possession being nine-tenths, it's the same as trying to rob Fort Knox... Helena may be a former ranger, but that doesn't mean she's a good fit for the team... much less Icky..."

Connor ran a hand through his wet crew cut, wishing he still smoked. "But then, going in during the winter is a good idea... all the tourists will be holed up in Gatlinburg and Pigeon Forge... and maybe even the rangers will be staying indoors, trying to keep warm and dry..." He shook his head. "But after all I've been through... do I really want to risk going to prison? For *lost Confederate gold?*"

His skin crawled, his senses instantly alert. Someone followed him.

Connor cleared his thoughts and focused on his breathing. He had to be sure he wasn't having one of the episodes that had landed him in that V.A. hospital in Louisiana. His counselor had told him that not every shadow hides a threat, and not every threat is a monster. Over the past few months, Connor had actually convinced himself he believed that. For the most part. But all that logic and therapy melted like so much sugar in warm water at the sound of a shuffling gate on the sidewalk behind him.

Connor stepped into an alley between a cigar shop and a music store, both closed for hours. He pressed himself against the cold, wet bricks, held his breath and waited. The shuffling step grew louder, seemed to pick up speed. Connor tensed, flexed his hands, ready to strike.

A tall, hooded figure stepped into the shadows of the alley.

Connor grabbed the man by the front of his sweatshirt, drove him into the opposite wall. The smell of alcohol and vomit breath expelled from the man's lungs on impact. Blue, bloodshot eyes widened beneath the hood's shadow. Connor blinked, barely recognizing those eyes and the thin face under the pale orange stubble. "Hicks?"

"Big Mac..." A weak smile played across the sallow features. Hicks chuckled, coughed, and wheezed. "Still got the edge, huh, Sarge?"

Connor backed off, released his old squad member. "What the hell are you doing, sneaking up on me like that?"

Hicks fished a crumpled pack of Marlboro Reds out of the hoodie's pocket with shaking hands. Connor had never seen the man like this. During the war, Hicks was the one with nerves of steel and ice water in his veins: zero conscience. The perfect combo for a sniper assigned to an S&D unit. "Sorry... I just..." He looked around, head swiveling to take in both ends of the alley. "I just wanted to give you a heads-up..."

Connor rolled his shoulders. "About what? Icky's job? His new girl? What?"

Lighting the cigarette on the second try, Hicks licked his cracked lips and took a deep, calming drag. Connor envied the man at that moment, despite his seriously deteriorated condition. Blowing a jet of smoke into the alley, Hicks said, "Yeah. The job... but you don't need to worry about the feds. There's something in those hills much, much worse than armed park rangers. You ever hear of something called the Black Council?"

Connor shook his head and thought about bumming a smoke. "Doesn't ring a bell. They some kind of political protest group?"

"Not even close." Hicks chuckled and drained the cigarette of its remaining life in one more pull. "More like an ancient secret society... Well, they got a secret they want kept. And I don't think it's just about Icky's gold, either. You go deep enough into those hills, you won't come out again... I reckon there's something worse up there than what we found in that cave near the Dorah Pass."

Connor tensed, unconsciously touched the scar on his cheek as he remembered the men killed and partially devoured in that fight. "What are you talking about, Hicks?"

Hicks smiled, a tired, crazy smile. A smile that announced he'd pretty much given up on the world making any kind of sense. He opened his mouth to answer. Connor heard a sound like a cough at the far end of the alley. Hicks's eyes rolled back in his head as the brick wall behind him turned a darker shade. He went limp, dropping to the asphalt like his bones had just evaporated.

Connor turned in time to see a shadow disappear at the far end of the alley. "Hey!"

He ran, but whoever had killed Hicks was faster. Or possessed some other means of obfuscation or escape. Connor's skin went cold and the burger he'd enjoyed an hour earlier threatened to turn on him. "Just what in the hell have I gotten myself into now?"

He went back to his friend's body and knelt to examine the small-caliber hole in the side of Hicks's head. Connor sighed and rubbed his eyes. Hicks's face was surprisingly peaceful, glowing pale in the light spilling into the alley from the street. "Hell of a way to go after all we've seen, brother... At least you didn't suffer."

Connor reached for his phone to call the police.

***

Connor rolled the cramping pain around his shoulders as he started the pump. Gas fumes tainted the fresh scent of rain permeating the chill November air. He'd been on the road for more than four hours, half of that time stuck in Knoxville's ubiquitous traffic. As soon as he'd cleared the city's environs, he knew it was time to stretch his legs and feed Gloria.

Ignoring the sign warning against cell phone usage, Connor called Icky while the numbers raced higher and higher on the pump. "Hey, I'm on my way... Yeah, I know I'm running late, but I got hung up in Chattanooga. Don't leave Pigeon Forge without me. We've got things to discuss... I'll tell you when I get there."

Ending the call, Connor shook his head and paced around the black Camaro in an attempt to vent some frustration as well as improve circulation. The Chattanooga PD had dragged him into their investigation of Hicks's murder. As soon as records connected Connor's military career to Hicks's, the lead detective had decided to detain Connor for two days under suspicion of domestic terrorism, owing to some poor choices Hicks had made since coming home. Connor had ridden the cell time out in silence, sticking to the same half-true story he'd given them at the scene: "I stopped in town to pay Hicks a visit, we went for a walk, and somebody took a shot at us. Didn't see the shooter. That's it."

The Chattanooga PD didn't buy it—primarily because Hicks's last known residence was in Virginia—but the DA wasn't in the mood to bury a "hero cop" and a veteran of Afghanistan under any more red tape or unfounded accusations. Too much bad PR to be kicked up what with things the way they were in the world at the moment. So, Connor had finally been cut loose first thing this Monday morning, and in defiance of the head detective's instruction not to leave town, he'd made a beeline for the Smokies. Based on Hicks's warning, it looked like Icky was in danger from more than just a gold digger and federal law.

"Hey!"

Connor turned at the sharp, nasally voice. A rail-thin old woman in a pink plastic rain cap over her tight pail curls crossed the parking lot, headed his way. She wore a bright floral rain slicker from a 1970s Sears catalog over plaid bellbottoms and carried a pair of heavy plastic bags laden with convenience-store purchases. "Hey there, big feller, care to give an old lady a ride?"

Connor raised an eyebrow as the pump clicked off. "Uhm..."

"Thanks," the old lady said as she opened Gloria's passenger door. "I thought you looked like the chivalrous type." Before Connor could formulate an objection, or wonder why the passenger door wasn't locked, she'd settled into the front seat and closed the door.

Shaking his head, Connor finished the fill-up, took his receipt, and slid behind the wheel. He eyed the old lady, hoping she was as harmless as she looked. The fact that it was still daylight was a point in her favor. The fact that his hackles weren't up was another, but still...

"I'm Bernice," she said with a denture-displaying smile. "Bernice Stubblefield. Some might call me a witch, but I ain't no haint nor spook of any kind. And I don't truck with demons nor devils. You got nothing to fear from me, Connor Mackay."

Connor's jaw dropped. He didn't know whether to laugh, jump out of the car, or reach for the knife tucked under the seat. "How—?"

Bernice donned a pair of big, rose-tinted glasses and stared through the windshield. "I told you, some call me a witch. I know things, boy. All kinds of things. Things you might need to know before you go on this fool's errand you've got yourself into. Now, if you'll drive me home, I'll tell you what you need to know."

Connor was curious. He realized he didn't feel threatened at all. There was no sensation of a pending panic attack. He started the engine and put Gloria into gear. "Okay. Where to?"

"Dandridge. I know you think that's out of your way, but it really ain't. I'll tell you a shortcut that'll save you fighting all that traffic in Sevierville and Pigeon Forge. I swear, as soon as Thanksgiving's over, everybody loses their ever lovin' minds and has to run out and spend all their money on all kinds of junk nobody needs. It's like they've forgotten what Christmas is really supposed to be about."

"You don't sound like a witch to me." Connor flicked on the windshield wipers and pulled back into I-40 East traffic.

"I said some folks think I am. And like I said, I don't truck with no demons or devils. Of that you can be sure."

"So how'd you know I'd stop at that particular gas station? Were you looking for me specifically or just any gullible idiot on a *fool's errand*?"

"I had a dream about you, Connor Mackay. I knew I'd find you there today, and I know what you're heading into the Smokies to do." Bernice looked at him. "And I know that you'll go even after I tell you not to. Gold can make fools of the wisest men. Unmarked graves all around the world attest to that."

"I was wrong," Connor said. "You do sound like a witch. So why me? I'm guessing lots of folks travelling this way are headed into danger. Lots of car wrecks and suicides this time of year, lots of domestic violence and armed robberies. Lots of doomed fortune seekers of one kind or another."

"You sound like a cop." Bernice wiped her nose with a tissue before tucking it back into a pocket. "But to answer your question, those dangers are, by-and-large, manmade—natural parts of this world, this life. The danger you're heading into ain't."

Connor felt cold all over and almost reached to adjust Gloria's heater. He took a deep breath. Now the panic attack was marshaling its forces. "Why does this stuff keep happening to me?"

Bernice looked at him and smiled. It was a kind, sympathetic smile. "Who knows? Maybe you were born under a bad sign, maybe something happened in your life that marked you, made you a touchstone for the other world, or maybe the forces of evil just don't like the way you look. It doesn't matter. The real question is, what do you aim to do about it?"

Connor glanced sidelong at her. What did she really know about him—aside from his name, and apparently his reason for traveling in East Tennessee? His life had been pretty normal until that man-eating giant killed or crippled half his squad in the Afghani mountains. But ever since, things in his life had just gotten weirder and weirder. He'd moved into a haunted house in New Orleans, but given the city's reputation, that wasn't anything too extraordinary. The investigation which had ended his police career—and so much more—however...

Connor fought down the rising panic attack. "Okay, so what have you got to tell me, Bernice Stubblefield? What have the Fates or the spirits or the stars or whatever decreed about my little venture into the Great Smoky Mountains?"

Bernice frowned. "If you ain't going to take this seriously, just pull over and let me out right here."

Passing the Sevierville exit, Connor saw Bernice had at least been right about the traffic. Cars were sitting on the shoulder, waiting their turn to mount the off-ramp. He felt sorry for the poor schmucks just trying to get to work only to be stuck in traffic with all the holiday shoppers and vacationers. This kind of jam didn't foster the Christmas Spirit or the Milk of Human Kindness in anybody. "We're on the Interstate in the middle of a rainstorm. You'll have pneumonia inside of twenty minutes. And I doubt very much that anybody will stop to pick you up before you die."

"Then listen up, Connor Mackay, because this is important." She closed her eyes and took a long, deep breath. When she spoke, her voice was noticeably lower. "I see ancient death, coiled and waiting in those hills. Gallons of poison, gallons of blood, piles of bones. I see a diamond, a fiery diamond filled with power, power fueled by centuries of death..."

Connor glanced at the old woman as the wiper blades thunked methodically against the wind and rain. A diamond? Maybe it was symbolic of the treasure Icky sought. He'd said the gold was taken from a privateer near

Cuba. Could it be cursed pirate treasure? A dead man's chest? Ancient death... maybe the scouts had been wounded when they hid the gold, had died nearby. Maybe they had turned on each other and killed themselves for the gold. But *coiled* and *poison* conjured images of snakes. Timber rattlers made their home in the Smokies, but it was the onset of winter, so surely there was nothing to fear from snakes...

"What do you know about the Black Council?" He surprised himself with the question.

Bernice blinked as she came out of whatever trance had taken her. She cleared her throat and wiped her nose again. "The Black Council? I've not heard that phrase in quite some time... According to myth, the Black Council was a cult of witches that enslaved the local Indian populations in these parts. They were cruel and hedonistic, abusing their power and harming the land. But they were challenged by a group of Cherokee medicine men who came into the area to free the people and restore balance. These shaman became known as the White Lodge, and they fought a great war with the Black Council, eventually destroying their power and wiping them out. Or so the story goes."

Connor grunted. Hicks's death and final words indicated the White Lodge hadn't quite finished the job. He thought about mentioning this, but the Dandridge exit loomed just ahead.

Bernice gave him quick directions and soon they were passing into rain-swept forest with tall pines and cedars blocking out the dim overcast sky. A few miles later, the county-maintained asphalt turned to crumbling crush-and-run. Bernice directed him to a gravel driveway on the left. A hand-painted sign declared: FORTUNE TELLER AND PSYCHIC, B. STUB-BLEFIELD. Crescent moons, stars, and crosses adorned the edges of the sign.

Connor smirked as he pulled onto the driveway. "You get a lot of customers coming this far off the beaten path?"

"More than you'd think." Bernice gathered her bags as they pulled up to a tidy, single-wide trailer in the midst of a lush green lawn edged by flower-beds. She pulled a canned chocolate protein shake from one of the bags and handed it to Connor. "Not a lot of places to stop for food between here and Pigeon Forge if you take the back way. You look like you might be hungry."

Connor smiled without his scar hurting. "Thanks. And thanks for the info."

Bernice nodded and patted his hand. "You take care of yourself up there, Connor Mackay. If you're mixing it up with the Black Council, you'd best not trust anyone from this point on. But then, I reckon you know that." With that, she was out of the car and running for the trailer's front door.

Connor waved as she disappeared inside, then put Gloria in reverse and headed for the Smokies. He didn't remember Bernice giving him directions, but somehow he knew the way. As he pulled onto the narrow country road, he noticed something peeking out from under the passenger seat. He reached down and fished the item out of the floorboard.

Connor was surprised when he recognized it as a Vietnam-era Army gas mask. The name CPL R STUBBLEFIELD was written in fading black marker across the back strap.

***

Icky and Helena had procured a vacation cabin in Weirs Valley as the operation's HQ. The rest of the team had assembled by the time Connor guided Gloria up the steep, switchback gravel drive leading to the posh getaway. A late-model black Nissan Armada, emblazoned with the logo JACKSON'S ELECTRONICS, and a brand new white Chevy Suburban flanked a decades-old tan Toyota Tundra with Arizona plates outside the big, three-story cabin. Classic country music blared from somewhere inside the well-lit building. The chill rain had reduced to a fine mist and the sun threatened to come out of hiding.

Connor parked behind the Suburban, unable to suppress a smile as he stepped out. The remaining members of his old team stood on the covered balcony, smoking cigars and drinking beer. They looked a bit older, but still in fighting trim for the most part. They all turned, smiling, waving, and cat-calling at the sight of him. Icky had been holding court, Helena at his side, but his face lit up when he saw Connor. Marcus Jackson: the radio man's bright teeth flashed in his dark face, half concealed by an Atlanta Braves ball cap. Peter Hernandez, the short and stocky medic, waved the most aggressively as if to make sure he could be seen standing beside the hulking form of David Goldman, the squad's surfer-turned-machine-gunner.

"Hey, you made it," Icky called from the bannister. "Now we're just waiting on Hicks."

Connor's smile vanished. He hauled his duffle bag out of the backseat. "He ain't coming." The announcement brought the party to an abrupt end.

Connor's eyes widened and his jaw set as soon as he entered the cabin's big main room. Weapons, magazines, and boxes of ammunition, as well as camping gear, survival electronics, cases of MREs, and medical kits covered the dining room table, the kitchen counter, and half of the big faux-leather sectional. A glance told him the rifles weren't ATF approved. It was just plain stupid to hit the booze with that much hardware lying around, even if it hadn't been illegal.

The sight of two strangers playing a videogame of digital war on the big screen TV made Connor pause in the doorway, his eyes narrowed at the two Native American men. One was thin and lanky with a baby face. The other one looked like he'd been carved from old wood, all hard edges and thick muscle. Both wore their black hair long and free down their backs.

Icky led the revelers in from the patio as Helena turned off the stereo. "What do you mean Hicks ain't coming?"

Connor didn't drop his gear or take his eyes off the two strangers as they paused their game and stood. "He's dead. Who are they?"

Icky frowned, glanced at the two men. "My cousin, Jimmy, and his cousin, Frank. Frank's our guide. Now, what are you talking about? Hicks is dead?"

"Guide? I thought Helena knew the forest like the back of her hand."

Helena frowned. "I do know the park. But we think the gold is actually in that iffy area between federal and Cherokee tribal land. Frank knows the ins and outs."

Connor didn't like the answer. Going on this misadventure with his old team was one thing. Traipsing through a national forest *and* tribal lands with three strangers was another. Even if they did find the gold, eight hundred pounds was a lot to pack out of rough terrain. He knew his men could do it, but these newcomers...?

Connor tossed his duffle onto a recliner and stepped to the refrigerator in search of a beer. "Somebody killed Hicks in Chattanooga. He followed me from the restaurant Friday night, tried to warn me not to come up here. He said something about a *Black Council* right before somebody put a bullet in his head. Somebody quick and professional." He opened the beer and took a long pull before leaning back against the kitchen sink. "Now, what exactly do you know about that, Icky?"

"What's he talking about, Icky?" Jackson demanded. "You said this would be like taking candy from a baby. Just a bunch of bored park rangers hiding out in their cabins."

Icky ran a hand through his hair and licked his lips. Helena stepped close and put her hand in his. Clearing his throat, Icky forced a laugh. "I honestly don't know, guys. Look, Hicks had gotten messed up with some shady characters since coming back... I was tempted to leave him out of this, but he really needed the money... Maybe he crossed somebody and they caught up with him."

Connor finished the beer. "Right. At the exact moment you tap him to help with this job. Now what do you know about the Black Council?"

"The Black Council..." Frank the guide's deep voice filled the room. At closer glance, Connor could see the man was older than he'd first thought, nearer to his own age than that of the twenty-something Jimmy. "It is a fairytale among the Cherokee. A myth, a legend, and nothing more. Boogeymen mothers tell their children about to keep them out of trouble. Like the stoneskin giant, the raven-mocker witch, and the horned serpent."

"Well..." Connor knew not all myths and legends were just that. He stared hard at the stranger. "My friend died to warn me about it. So, that makes this Black Council something more than a fairytale to me. What else?"

Frank looked at him without expression and said nothing.

Jimmy shuffled his feet and laughed nervously. "Just a ghost story, man. Come on."

"Look," Icky said, valiantly trying to lighten the mood. "You've had a rough weekend, Mac, and we're all sorry to hear about Hicks... Let's get you settled in, you can take a shower, and we'll get some grub started. Then, once everybody's a bit more comfortable, we can sit down and hash this all out over burgers and beer. What do you say?"

Connor gauged the room. His squad mates were stunned by the news about Hicks, but he could tell they were banking on this job. Icky's lifelong dream was suddenly on very shaky ground at the exact moment he was so close to finally achieving it. Helena seemed genuine in her affections and reassurances, but Bernice's advice not to trust anyone only reinforced Connor's already dubious assessment of the former park ranger. And he didn't know Jimmy or Frank, so he didn't trust either of them half as far as he could throw them. "Okay, fine. I'm tired and hungry, and I smell like a jail cell. So you've got exactly one dinner to convince me to go on this caper or I'm out."

Icky's smile widened. "Then I guess I'd better make these burgers good."

Hernandez picked up Connor's pack. "Let me show you to your room, Sarge." Connor followed him down a corridor to a short stair leading to the building's bottom floor. The medic paused as they reached the foot of the stair. "Not the best view, but I guess you got a private room, now..." He lowered his voice as he handed Connor the duffle. "What do you think about all this? You really think we're going up against some whacked-out cult or Cherokee militia or something up in these hills? Icky's cousin is just a kid. Maybe he's blabbed to somebody..."

Connor shook his head as he took in the digs. "I'm not sure yet, Pete. I just know I've got a bad feeling. Hopefully this shower will wash it off."

Hernandez gave him a smile and slapped him on the shoulder. "I hope so. I'd hate for a bad feeling to keep you out of millions in gold."

Connor nodded as his friend headed back upstairs. Hernandez's comment indicated he was staying with Icky, no matter what Connor decided. Pete's hands were scarred and calloused and his skin was sun-dark from long hours of manual labor. His clothes were new and clean, but they were clearly from Walmart. If he had to guess, Connor would say Jackson and Goldman were in similar boats if they were entertaining this scheme. Plenty of folks are willing to do a lot for a million bucks.

Being all but broke himself, Connor couldn't fault his men for signing on to the bitter end. Especially after listening to Icky spin his yarn in this secluded vacation abode. It was the perfect setting to convince a group of men who'd sacrificed so much that they were owed an opportunity like this, they were owed this kind of payday. Connor had heard Icky's spiel over dinner in Chattanooga: How the Trail of Tears justified taking the gold, how the debacle in Afghanistan justified it, and how the National Park would even see a spike in tourism once word got out that, "There's gold in them thar hills!"

"A fool's errand," Connor muttered as he headed for the shower.

***

The burgers were pretty good. Between the shower and the meal, Connor mellowed somewhat. He still kept an eye on the two Cherokee strangers, limiting his beer intake to a cordial minimum. He also noted how Helena seemed to hang on Icky's every word, laughed at all his jokes, and touched him when she didn't need to. Either the guy had found a genie lamp somewhere or the woman was just too good to be true.

Or Connor had simply grown too cynical for this world.

Volunteering to clean up while the rest of the guys broke out the cards and poker chips, Connor found himself alone with Helena in the kitchen. She loaded the dishwasher as he put away the leftovers. He gave her his pained smile, not really knowing how to start a conversation. He couldn't just come out and ask if she was a gold-digger or a con artist.

She saved him the effort. "You know Aar really needs you on this one."

Connor nodded. "Eight hundred pounds. That takes a lot of muscle to haul across rough ground. He never was much for the weight room."

Helena smirked. "You know that's not what I mean. He could have hired half a dozen goons if all he wanted was muscle." She turned to face him. "He wanted to get his team back together. His friends... Look, I know you guys drifted apart when you got home. I take it things weren't easy for any of you, but I know Aar's had a pretty rough go of it. Did you know his mom died of cancer last year?"

Connor didn't. Of course, he'd had tragedy enough of his own to keep him busy.

Helena smiled and placed her hand on Connor's arm. He noted the Breitling Emergency tactical watch, almost too big for her slender wrist. He guessed it was one of many expensive tokens of Icky's affection.

"If the money's not that important to you, I think Icky is." Helena winked conspiratorially when she used the nickname. "Please come with us. Even if there is no Confederate gold, have one last adventure with your friend."

Connor nodded, forced the smile as she went to join the poker game. He shook his head and muttered to himself, "She's smooth. That's for sure..."

***

The rain was back the next day, falling across the mountains in near-freezing sheets. Gloria's wipers battled valiantly as Connor guided the Camaro into North Carolina. Icky had wanted everyone to ride together in his new Suburban, but Connor wasn't about to leave Gloria alone and untended at the cabin while he traipsed through the woods a hundred miles away. Plus, it made more sense for him to flush out any troopers rather than risk everyone being caught in a vehicle loaded with unlicensed automatic weapons over a possible traffic stop.

He had been on the road for almost two hours, retelling Hicks's stories with his two passengers. Goldman had told the one where Hicks had dusted a Taliban fighter armed with an RPG from over twelve hundred yards, causing the man to fire the weapon into his fellow ambushers. Jackson had reminded them of the time Hicks had stampeded a herd of goats into a thicket to flush out a group of hidden enemies. Connor's tale was about Hicks overselling their heroics at every airport bar on the way back home in order to score free rounds—and Hicks scoring back room rendezvous with the cute bartenders and servers in the process.

Hernandez rode in the Suburban with Icky, Helena, Jimmy, and Frank. The medic-turned-roofer was totally committed to the treasure hunt, owing to a near-poverty level existence in Arizona since his return as the "conquering hero." He'd claimed it was racism that kept him from getting a good EMT job in every town between Flagstaff and Phoenix, but Connor had noticed Hernandez popping some pills on the sly after dinner. Not everyone's demons were of the supernatural kind.

"You got anything in here that was recorded in *this* century, Sarge?" Goldman smirked as he flipped through the leather CD case. "Any metal or hard rock?"

Connor glanced at the Californian. Goldman, out of all of them, appeared to be living the life of Riley, being an actor and producer in the adult film industry. But given his presence in the car, Connor knew the big man's life couldn't be all sunshine and rainbows. "I've got enough rotting my brain without adding modern junk music to the mix. Put on some Zeppelin or CCR."

"You haven't changed much, you know that, Mac?" Jackson said from under his ball cap, stretched out on the backseat. He'd closed his electronics repair service for the week, telling his wife he was going on a hunting trip with his old Army buddies. He'd confessed after a few shots the night before that he hoped this expedition would save both the business and the marriage. "Still set in your ways."

Connor flicked him a glance in the rearview, knowing that wasn't true.

He'd changed. A lot. "You reckon so?"

Jackson yawned and sat up. "Nah, I guess we've all changed. Not like you can survive seeing something like a friggin' giant eating half your team without being changed forever. I mean, just look at us. We've all dropped everything, jobs and families, to go all-in on Icky's midlife crisis."

Connor didn't point out that he no longer had a job or a family.

Goldman laughed. "I'd like to go *all-in* on Icky's midlife crisis."

Jackson swatted him on the back of the head. "That's his fiancée, man."

Connor cleared his throat and turned the volume down. "So, what do you guys think of her?" He glanced at Goldman. "Aside from the obvious."

"She's quiet," the Californian said with a shrug. "Unusual for a chick that hot. They know they're the belle of the ball and revel in it. Seemed like she was just happy to bask in Icky's glow." He batted his eyes with a mocking laugh.

"Which is odd in itself," Jackson volunteered. "You know that dude never had no luck with the ladies unless it came with a price tag."

Connor nodded. "She... I don't know... She rubs me the wrong way."

Goldman laughed. "I don't think she *could* rub me the wrong way."

"You're a degenerate, Goldie." Jackson sighed and flopped back on the backseat. "You know what rubs me the wrong way? Watching all our hard work, blood, sweat, and tears go up in smoke over there."

Goldman grunted. "Afghanistan: where empires go to die. I guess it's like Communism. The know-it-all academics keep telling themselves and everybody else who'll listen, 'It'll work *this* time'."

The three men shared a bitter chuckle before letting Led Zeppelin fill the ensuing silence.

***

Connor followed Frank through the forest, the rest of the group trailing out behind like an L.L. Bean or The North Face ad in *Guns N' Ammo Magazine*. He'd have preferred standard camo BDUs and G.I. gear, but Icky and Helena had decided they'd raise less suspicion if they looked like dumb tourist adventurers. Never mind the full-auto M4s.

Connor was certain he was the only one in the group toting a vintage gas mask tucked inside his new designer jacket.

The rain continued to fall and the temperature continued to drop, which was good for keeping other hikers and unambitious rangers out of their way. It wasn't so good for the members of the group who had either gotten out of the habit of forced marches or had never gotten into it. Helena didn't complain near as much as Icky's cousin, Jimmy, but her occasional comments always resulted in Icky calling an immediate halt for rest.

This had been accepted without objection on the first day after leaving the vehicles hidden just inside the North-Carolinian forest, but by noon on the second day, even the easy-going Goldman was getting snarky. "Dude," the big Californian said when Icky called a halt at the base of a steep ridge. "I'd like to find this treasure before I need a blue pill to do my next flick."

"Yeah." Jackson stepped beside Goldman. "I've only got a week, and we've already burned through three days of that. Either we find this gold by tomorrow night, or I'm Elvis."

Icky scowled at the two men, the first time anything other than a placating, goofy smile had crossed his features. "We're close, okay? It just don't make much sense killing ourselves before we get there. Do you have any idea how heavy gold is? We gotta save something for carrying it back out of here." He turned to Connor for support. "Ain't that right, Mac?"

Connor shrugged and studied the rain falling through the creaking pines, hearing the patter on the forest floor, the gentle rush of nearby streams. "I'd rather have able bodies to help carry the payload than gimpy bodies that need to be carried... Take five here, then cross this ridge. Me and Frank will go ahead and scout. I think there's a stream nearby we'll need to cross, so we'll find a good spot."

Connor heard Jimmy groan in exaggerated appreciation as the others settled in for a rest. Connor shook his head, wondering what Icky was thinking in bringing the tenderfoot kid. He quickened his pace to catch up to the scout. Frank had kept pretty quiet during the sojourn thus far, only occasionally talking to Icky or Jimmy about the terrain, giving a rough estimate of what to expect as they followed Icky's "head map" to the supposed treasure.

Frank paused at the crest of the ridge, kneeling beside a tall spruce and scanning the misty valley below. Connor stepped beside the man, slung his rifle, and took a sip from his canteen. The visibility was almost nothing, even at midday. The Great Smoky Mountains were living up to their name, sheets of rain and clouds giving the impression of an ever-burning fire deep within the forested hills. Even in this "bad" weather, Connor had to admire the primordial beauty, understanding why so many of his Scots-Irish ancestors had made this area their home.

"It was ours first," Frank said as if reading his thoughts. "It will be again, you know."

"I've heard there were other tribes here before the Cherokee." Connor put the canteen away. He thought about all the men he'd killed, who'd tried to kill him, all over the ownership of real estate or an ingrained sense of identity. "Ours, yours, theirs... Until we figure out we're all one people, it'll always be up for grabs."

Frank stood and looked at him. "You don't sound like a warrior."

Connor narrowed his eyes. "Thanks... So, what do you think about this treasure? You think Icky's story is real?"

Frank shrugged and gazed out over the mist-shrouded mountains. "As real as that, I suppose. I've heard that story, or variations of it my whole life. But then, I've heard a lot of stories about these hills. Stories that even our elders don't believe anymore."

"Then why are you doing this? If we get caught, it could mean some serious prison time, and all you're being paid in is promises right now."

Frank smiled and headed down the hill. "I want to buy myself a casino so I can get rich off of degenerate white folks."

Connor grinned and was about to follow. The muffled *rat-a-tat* of distant gunfire echoed in the distance. Quick and sporadic, then nothing. "What was that?"

Frank kept walking. "Probably poachers. Maybe a gun nut doing some target practice. Sound travels weird in these hills. Especially in weather like this."

Connor frowned. It had sounded like automatic weapons fire, not civilian firearms. And the fact that it ended so abruptly did not bode well for either the shooter or the target. The bad feeling he thought he'd washed off at the cabin was back and stronger than ever.

The group joined them at the foot of the opposite side of the ridge. They forded a fast-rushing stream about a mile deeper into the valley. Connor casually asked the members of his team, one at a time, whether they'd heard the gunfire. No one had. Acoustics in the wooded hills being what they were, and everyone chatting during their break, this was not unexpected.

The big disappointment was that the trained soldiers of his team hadn't been on their toes.

Two hours later, Jimmy was complaining of a bleeding blister on his left heel. Connor fell back to where the youth sat on a moss-covered boulder, easing his foot out of his wet boot. Jimmy's face was taut with suppressed pain. The blister had popped and there was indeed a bit of blood, but nothing to write home about. But then Connor reminded himself the kid was from the most pampered generation in the history of the human race.

"You think you can make it, or do we need to put you out of your misery?" Connor forced a smile to soften his frustration.

Jimmy put on a war face, or whatever he thought was a close approximation. "I'm fine. Just give me a second to adjust my sock."

"Pete," Connor called. "Have a look at this, will ya? Can't have him going lame with an infection."

The medic swallowed something and washed it down with a swig from his canteen. "Sure, Mac. I got this."

Connor eyed him for a moment, then with a curt nod headed back to the front of the halted column. "Come on, they'll catch up."

Hernandez hung back to dress the wound while everyone else forged ahead to find a good place to camp for the night. The rain tapered off around four o'clock and the clouds thinned out just in time for a halfway decent sunset. Connor had kept his ears open for more gunshots all afternoon, but never heard them again.

The tents were set up and Jackson had a very smoky fire going by the time Hernandez helped a hobbling Jimmy into the clearing. Icky and Helena conferred over a laminated map while Goldman huddled in his open tent, oiling down his M4. Frank walked the perimeter gathering wet firewood. Connor opened a box of MREs, wishing he'd never have to taste another government-issue interpretation of Chicken a la King as long as he lived.

"Need some help with that, Sarge?" Hernandez said after settling Jimmy into his tent.

"Sure. How's the kid?"

The medic chuckled as he started digging out the green plastic packets. "He'll live, though you wouldn't know it by his bitching. That Indian has spent more time on a PlayStation than on a hunting trail. Damn good thing we ain't run into any rangers yet."

Connor wondered again about the gunshots he'd heard. He glanced around to make certain nobody was in earshot. "What about you, Pete? You staying frosty?"

Hernandez dropped a packet of stroganoff. "Me? Yeah, of course. Why you ask?"

"The pills, Pete. I've seen you popping. What are they?"

The medic cleared his throat and stared into the box of Meals Ready to Eat. "I got... a condition. They help level me out."

"What kind of condition?"

Hernandez licked his lips. "Why the third degree, huh? I heard you got locked up in a nut hutch in New Orleans. You don't see me digging you on that, do you?"

"It was Baton Rouge. And we're not talking about me. I got a clean bill of health from the V.A. Whose name is on that prescription, Pete? Who's your doctor?"

"Screw you, man." Hernandez tossed the packets back into the box and stalked out of camp just as Jackson walked up.

"What's eating him?" Jackson squatted to open a packet of almost-spaghetti.

Connor shrugged. "The same thing eating all of us, I reckon."

That night, after dinner, they sat around the campfire enjoying a reprieve from chilling rain as they let the golden flames dry their clothes and warm their bones. Connor sat on his sleeping bag thrown over a good-sized rock, sharpening his Ka-Bar while the others chatted. There was some discussion about whether to tell ghost stories or sing camp songs. Having heard most of this group attempt to harmonize on occasion, Connor silently voted for the ghost stories.

Eventually, as the sun vanished and the forest descended into darkness, and the others tired of their own limited voices and repertoires, the campfire tales came out. By the time Connor had oiled his handgun and rifle, all the standbys had been retold—The Golden Arm, The Hooked Killer, The Girl in White, and Rawhead and Bloody Bones. He was just about to turn in when Icky invited Frank to tell them a story from Cherokee myth and legend.

The guide frowned at being put on the spot, but after taking a deep breath, he began. "When the world was newborn, the Sun became angry with the People and sent a pestilence to destroy them. However, the Little Men had grown fond of the People and so wished to save them from the Sun's wrath. They used their magic to change a priest of the People named Uktena, which means 'Keen Eyed,' into a gigantic snake and sent him to kill the Sun.

"When Uktena failed in this, the Little Men sent Rattlesnake to reason with her instead. And when the Sun made peace with Rattlesnake on behalf of the Little Men and the People, Uktena grew jealous and vengeful. He grew so angry and violent that he sprouted great horns like the stag and the fire of his rage burned like a great diamond between his eyes. The People feared him so much that the Little Men took him to Galunlati to live with the rest of the dangerous things."

Frank's deep voice dropped, his dark eyes glowing in the firelight. "But Uktena did not go willingly. He left his offspring behind to carry out his vengeance. Though not as big as the first horned serpent, these Uktena are still gigantic and wield all his powers of strength and poison. They dwell in the deep pools of the rivers and in the lonely passes of the high mountains, and the People know to avoid these places.

"But as dangerous as these monsters are, there are some brave or foolish enough to seek them out. They do this because of the Ulun'suti, the blazing diamond crest of the Uktena. This diamond, called 'Transparency' in the white man's tongue, will bestow great power upon the one able to take it from the Uktena. Only one man has ever succeeded in taking an Ulun'suti since the beginning of time, because to see the Uktena is to find death. Not only for oneself but also for one's family."

When Frank was finished, a long silence descended on the camp.

Goldman chuckled. "A little late in the game for cautionary tales about treasure hunting, don't you think?"

The others laughed but without enthusiasm. Frank shrugged and poked at the fire. "We're all still alive right now. But nobody knows what tomorrow might bring."

"I think it'll bring about fifteen million bucks in gold," Icky said. "So let's all turn in and get a good night's sleep, huh?"

The party broke up, but Connor kept his eyes on the Cherokee guide. Frank's story jived too much with Bernice's soothsaying to be mere coincidence. Contrary to Icky's suggestion, Connor would not be getting a good night's sleep. Instead, he'd be watching Frank like a hawk until sunrise.

As it turned out, he didn't have to wait that long.

***

Just after midnight, when Connor had begun to think he was being paranoid, when the comfort of his sleeping bag seemed like a five-star hotel suite, he finally saw Frank's tent flap open. Connor drew his 1911A1 from its holster and watched as the guide slipped out of the camp as quietly as a shadow.

Tired and sore as he was, Connor moved just as quickly and quietly in his pursuit. With the campfire burned down to embers, the forest was almost as dark as midnight at the bottom of a well. But Connor's eyes had grown accustomed to the gloom in the hours of waiting and watching. And the fact that the ground was saturated from so many days of rain meant that leaves and twigs were more likely to squish than snap or crackle.

Catching sight of Frank coming to a stop at the base of a towering pine some thirty yards from camp, Connor almost rebuked himself. *He's just answering nature's call.* But when a second shadow emerged from the other side of the tree, Connor's blood ran cold, and all his senses went to red alert.

This second shadow had a rifle.

Connor crouched low and tried to listen. But the men's whispers were either too low to make out or, more likely, spoken in a language he couldn't understand.

When Frank's arm extended in the direction of the camp, Connor knew he and his friends had been sold out. He worked the pistol's slide, the metallic ratcheting sound booming loud in the quiet darkness. "Don't move," he shouted, leveling his weapon at the shapes of Frank and his unknown confederate.

The rifle swung in his direction. And fired once. The bullet splattered into a wet pine off to Connor's right. Connor squeezed the trigger on the .45 twice. The gunshots flamed and roared. The rifleman shadow went down as Frank bolted into the dark.

Connor gave chase but hadn't gone far before he heard shouts. More gunshots sounded in the direction of camp. He paused, about to run back to his friends when he realized he wasn't hearing a slaughter so much as a firefight.

The initial exchange of gunfire with Frank's contact had warned his team-mates just in time to arm themselves, and by the sounds of it, they were giving as well as they got. They had been the best of the best after all.

Turning back to the pursuit, Connor realized he'd lost track of Frank in the near total darkness. And the gunfight behind him obliterated any chance of hearing his quarry. "Damn it."

A faint glint of starlight on metal to his right was Connor's only warning. Frank slammed into him with the force of a charging bull, a long hunting knife aimed at his throat.

Connor tried to bring the pistol around, but Frank's blade slashed his right forearm. Bolts of jagged pain raced from his fingertips to his elbow and the Colt fell from his hand.

"I told you we'd take it all back," Frank snarled in the darkness. The Cher-okee's right hand found Connor's throat while the knife-wielding left van-ished from sight.

Connor wrenched to the side as the blade found his midsection. He felt the thick layers of his heavy jacket give in to the puncture, but the knife missed his torso. Connor used his injured arm to pin Frank's left wrist to his side, then delivered a palm strike to the man's face with his own left hand. He felt the cartilage of the Cherokee's nose go in a shower of warm blood.

Frank grunted, his head snapping back from the impact, his knees going weak. Connor hit him again, this time with his fist in the exposed windpipe. The man fell gagging and coughing to the ground.

Feeling and pain crept back into Connor's right hand. He used it to grasp Frank's left wrist until he could wrench the knife from him. Pressing the weapon's tip against Frank's bruised throat, Connor said, "Tell me every-thing."

The guide made a gargling noise that was meant to be laughter. "Suck it, white man."

Connor twisted Frank's captured wrist until he heard the little bones grind and the man screamed. "I didn't hear you."

"Kill me if you have to, but I ain't telling you a thing."

Hearing nothing but his and Frank's ragged breathing, Connor realized the firefight was over. He dragged Frank back to his feet, wrenching his left arm hard behind his back and pressing the knife to his throat. "Let's go. If my friends are dead, you're going to take a long time joining them."

They were halfway back to the camp when a burst of rifle fire came out of the darkness. Connor heard the bullets zip past his head, felt them thump into Frank's body. The captured man went limp with a moan.

"Cease fire!" Connor bellowed as he hit the deck behind Frank. "Cease fire! It's me! It's me! Stop shooting!"

Flashlight beams replaced the gunfire. Goldman called out, "Sarge? That you?"

"No! It's Bigfoot, asshole!" Connor was angrier at himself for nearly getting killed by his own men. He should have known better than to march back to camp after a firefight without announcing his intentions. He'd let himself get rusty, too. His anger turned to disappointment when he saw the wide-eyed stare on Frank's face. The guide's bullet-riddled body sprawled in the wet pine needles. "Shit."

Icky helped Connor to his feet. "Glad you made it, Mac." Icky's shaking flashlight beam roved over Connor's frame, looking for wounds. "You're bleeding. You hit?"

Connor glanced at his forearm. "No. Just a scratch, courtesy of our bullet-stopper, here. Frank sold us out, Icky."

"Jackson's dead," was Goldman's deadpan response. "Took two rounds to the throat and face. I reckon we got some of them, but whoever it was, they took their casualties with 'em when they cleared out."

Connor went cold all over as he absorbed this. Jackson had come along to save his marriage. There was a new widow somewhere in Atlanta and she didn't even know it yet. Connor shook his head, thankful kids hadn't been mentioned. "Anybody else hit?"

"No." Icky gave a nervous laugh and ran a hand through his long hair. "Surprisingly enough..." He looked at Frank's body, then kicked it. Repeatedly. "You son of a bitch! You son of a bitch!"

Goldman helped Connor pull Icky away from the corpse before he could stomp it into a puddle. "Come on. Hold it together, man."

"Okay. I'm fine. I'm cool." Icky shook them off and turned back to the camp. "I guess we'd better fortify in case they regroup and come back."

Connor looked out into the darkness. "I guess you're right." He and Goldman dragged Frank's body a ways into the woods, hoping the black bears were all in hibernation and the red wolves were all in another zip code.

The hours until dawn seemed to take forever. No one slept except for

Jimmy. Hernandez had to dose the kid to keep him from going completely hysterical. Icky and Helena comforted each other while keeping watch. They let the fire go out to help with visibility, so everyone had to endure the night's cold as best they could. Connor and Goldman wrapped Jackson in a sleeping bag, dragged him outside the camp, and buried him under a pile of rocks and tree limbs by flashlight.

"Hell of a way to go," Goldman muttered when they were done. "After all the shit he'd seen. Hell of a way."

Connor nodded and said a silent prayer. "He was a good soldier and a better man."

When the sun finally penetrated the dense canopy, Connor lit the fire again. "I know nobody's hungry, but we'll need our strength to carry Jackson when we get out of here."

Icky looked out from the sleeping bag he was wearing like a hooded cloak. His teeth chattered when he said, "Get out? We're not getting out without the gold, Mac. We've come too far and lost too much. The caves are close, less than a couple hours' hike if I'm right. We're literally a mile or two from all the wealth we could ever dream of. And you want to turn around and walk the other way?"

Connor stared at him. "You can't be serious, Icky. Hicks and Jackson are dead, and there's who-knows-how-many enemy fighters out there, and this is *their* turf. Time to cut our losses and retreat. Provided they let us get out of these woods without another contact."

Icky looked to Goldman and Hernandez. "Suit yourselves, but I'm not leaving without as much gold as I can carry. You guys are welcome to come along, but I'm not going to ask you again. Entirely up to you." He smiled at Helena and gripped her gloved hand.

Hernandez shrugged. "Shot dead in the woods or dead of heat stroke on a roof. Dead is dead. At least here I got a chance at being rich. I'm still in."

Goldman paced around the camp, paused to look at the pile covering Jackson's body. "I reckon if we cut and run, Sarge, then our friends died for nothing. Least we can do is cut Jackson's wife in on his share." He shook his head and gave a half-hearted smile. "Besides, treasure hunts and firefights are way more fun than making porn."

Connor didn't look up from the flames. "And what about Jimmy? What about your cousin, Icky? You going to drag the kid along or leave him out here by himself?"

Icky licked his lips. "When he wakes up, I'll give him the same choice. He's a big boy. He can take care of himself."

"That's bullshit and you know it." Connor shook his head. "Well, if you morons are dead set on it, I reckon I'll have to go along just to keep the rest of you alive... Now somebody start some grub while I go see if I can find my pistol."

An hour later, they climbed the next ridge. The mist was heavy and the temperature low. The forest was eerily quiet; nothing outside the group's movements could be heard in the fog. Trees loomed out of the pale murkiness like ghostly figures before assuming solid shape. Connor took point, leaving Goldman to watch the rear and Hernandez in charge of the still groggy Jimmy. Icky and Helena kept consulting the laminated map and a compass every dozen yards or so, occasionally calling out a course correction. Nobody else said anything, but they all hoped Icky's calculations were solid as there was no visibility to shoot an azimuth.

After three hours of climbing into rockier terrain, Connor finally called for a halt. "Let's catch our breath and hope the sun comes out soon." He looked at Icky and said in his best squad leader voice, "If we don't find these caves by sundown, I'm leading you all out of here first thing in the morning. No arguments."

Icky shrugged. "We'll find 'em." He sat down on a rock shelf and pulled out the map and compass again.

Connor knelt beside Goldman. "You see any sign of a tail?"

The Californian took a swig of water. "Nope. But whoever hit us last night are ninjas. Or at least the best hunters I've ever come across. I never heard 'em moving in or out. If they hadn't left spent brass and a few bloodstains, I'd have thought they were ghosts."

Connor nodded, remembering the assassin who had killed Hicks in Chattanooga. "You're probably not far off the mark, I reckon. I think we're tangling with some Cherokee witches or bad medicine of some kind. The Black Council Hicks warned me about."

Goldman swallowed but he didn't look at Connor like he was insane. "Well, after that giant in Afghanistan, I guess there's all kinds of crazy shit in this world. Only makes sense that a buried treasure would be guarded by some more of it, right?"

Connor nodded at the sunshine breaking through the fog. "Just keep your eyes peeled. And if you even get a hint of that itchy feeling, don't be afraid to sing out."

Goldman smiled. "Sure thing, Sarge."

Connor moved to check on Hernandez and Jimmy. "How we doing this morning?"

Jimmy looked at him, or more accurately through him. "I just want to go home."

Connor turned to the medic. "Pete?"

Hernandez sighed. "His foot's healing..." He looked at the kid who was a step above catatonic. "But I think we need to get him out of here. The sooner the better."

Connor glanced at Icky and Helena. "Well, we'll be out of these woods in about three days. Gold or no gold. He'll just have to buck up in the meantime."

"I reckon we all will." Hernandez pulled his pill bottle from his jacket pocket.

An hour after the break they found the caves.

"I told you!" Icky hopped up and down like he was about to break into dance. They stood outside an outcropping of gray rocks that formed a natural triangle in the midst of the forest. "I told you we were close. Look at those carvings!"

Connor stepped up to the weathered stone and wiped wet sludge from the surface. Ancient pictograms of some sort were clearly visible, but they meant nothing to Connor. They may as well have said "Johnny + Mary Forever" or "Metallica Rules" or some such. But then, the absence of that kind of graffiti was odd in and of itself. Clearly not many folks had found this cave before them, if any.

Dropping his pack, Connor clicked on his flashlight and probed the interior darkness. "Looks pretty tight for a ways. How could somebody get casks of gold in there?"

Icky shrugged, studying the stones. "Maybe they filled it in after? Maybe the rocks shifted naturally over time? It has been over a century and a half."

Connor whistled. "Well, if there is gold in here, it ain't going to be easy getting it out."

Icky grinned as he fished out his own flashlight. "Nothing worth doing ever is, Mac. There's six of us. We can form a bucket line once we find it. Relay it out a little at a time."

Connor didn't point out that could take days to move eight hundred pounds, depending on how deep the gold was hidden in the cave. He decided it was best to make sure the treasure was there first. Icky's rational thought was skating on thin ice as it was. "Okay. Follow me."

It was too tight to wear packs or carry rifles at the cave's entrance, so they descended in single file with flashlights and holstered pistols. Connor would have preferred to leave someone to guard the gear and weapons, but Jimmy needed supervision and everyone else would have balked at being denied the moment of discovery.

They squeezed through jutting rocks and narrow crags, cursing when a head met an outcropping or a jagged edge opened skin. With a steep downward curve, all natural light vanished within a few dozen feet of the entrance. Yellow beams cut through mote-filled darkness, glinting off buried minerals and ribbons of moisture. The air grew warmer with a stale, musty odor. After nearly twenty minutes of the claustrophobic descent, the cavern suddenly opened into a huge arena-like chamber with a surprisingly high ceiling and smooth, glossy floor. No one commented on how the musty smell had grown to an earthy stench. All attention was focused elsewhere.

Reflected yellow light blinded them as their beams fell on dozens of gold bars spilled from rotting wooden barrels. Everyone came to a halt as they entered the cave. No one spoke, barely breathing for a long time. They all just stood there, in awe of the magnificent wealth glittering before them.

"Damn... I'm rich," were Jimmy's first muttered words in almost a day.

Goldman chuckled softly. "As my dear old Bubbeh would have said: *Beseder gamur...*"

"So help me, God, I'll never climb another ladder in my life." Hernadez crossed himself and looked like he might cry.

"It's real..." Helena's voice was barely above a whisper.

"I told you it was." Icky spoke with a confidence he'd never before displayed, his voice thundering through the subterranean vault.

Connor heard an electronic beep. He glanced to see Helena pushing a button on her wristwatch. "What's that?"

Helena stiffened. "Nothing. I was just checking the time, wondering how long this will take..."

"No. That's a GPS beacon signal. You just told someone exactly where we are." Connor drew his pistol and aimed it at Helena.

Icky stepped between her and Connor, his own handgun clearing its holster. "What the hell, Mac? You planning on killing us all and keeping it for yourself?"

Connor blinked at the unexpected accusation. "No, but maybe she is. What do you really know about her, Icky?" He glared at Helena. "Who do you really work for?"

Goldman and Hernandez moved Jimmy out of the line of fire, not sure who to back in the unfolding standoff.

For a moment, Helena's face looked frightened and unsure in the glow of flashlights and gold. The next, her eyes hardened, and her lips set. A Glock appeared in her hand, the muzzle pressed against the back of Icky's head. "FBI, soldier boy. Now drop your weapons or so help me I'll turn Ichabod Crane here into the Headless Horseman."

Connor narrowed his eyes as he safetied his .45 and carefully placed it at his feet. Goldman and Hernandez did likewise. "What does the FBI have to do with all this? Shouldn't you be hunting down angry mothers at school board meetings or telling social media companies what to do?"

"Very funny," Helena said as she snagged Icky's Berretta and motioned everyone to the side wall, away from the gold. "I'm part of a special taskforce assigned to keep tabs on returning combat vets entangled in radicalized movements. Your Anarcho-capitalist friend Hicks led me to this little operation." Her eyes flicked at the gold. "*That's* just gravy that'll put one hell of a feather in my cap. Bringing you bunch of macho G.I. Joes in is the real goal. Nobody in Washington wants leaders with combat skills muddying the waters when it comes time to move the global agenda forward."

"Nice speech," Connor said. "But you're still just one woman against four trained men. Do you really think you can take us all out? Because I, for one, don't plan on going to prison after all I've been through, lady."

Icky looked crestfallen but pleaded with him. "Please, Mac. Don't hurt her..."

Helena laughed. "Hurt me? I'm the one with the guns, *Icky.*"

Connor gnashed his teeth at the mocking way she said his friend's nickname. He could see it hurt Icky worse than the piece of shrapnel he'd taken from a Taliban RPG.

"Besides," Helena said, leaning against one of the kegs of gold. "My team has been following us ever since we entered the forest. They're not more than a couple hours behind us, so just sit tight and don't try anything stupid."

Connor glanced at Goldman and Hernandez, remembering the distant gunfire he'd heard the day before. "You're wrong, sweetheart. Nobody's been following us for a while now. At least nobody that wasn't born and bred in these mountains. I'm betting the Black Council took out your pals before they hit us last night. I think you're on your own."

Helena's face showed uncertainty again. She shifted on the cask, and it began to crumble. Stepping away, Helena kicked something on the floor. It rolled into the middle of the chamber with a dull clatter. Connor trained his flashlight on a yellowed human skull. The others swept the room, the beams illuminating skulls, ribcages, spinal columns, femurs, and more human bones along the cavern's edges.

"What the hell?" Hernandez murmured.

Connor's attention turned to the strange patterns of the rock walls. He hadn't noticed them before as, like everyone else, he had been stunned by the sight of the gold. Squinting, he whispered, "Do those look like... scales to you guys?"

The other flashlight beams joined his, revealing the truth. A low rattling sound slowly grew louder from the back edge of the cavern. The patterns on the walls began to shift, undulate, and move. The earthy stench grew stronger, more intense and viler.

"Oh my..." Helena's eyes and mouth widened as she stared at something above the chamber entrance.

Connor turned just as an explosion of radiant light filled the room. Shielding his eyes against the glare, he saw it. The Uktena's horned head reared up above the cave mouth, its yellow eyes glittering in the fiery glow of the Ulun'suti between its great antlers.

Helena raised both pistols and fired.

Ignoring the bullets, the giant serpent opened its fanged maw and spat.

A stream of smoking green venom struck Helena in the face. She screamed and went down in convulsing agony.

Connor and his friends scrambled for the handguns on the floor. Jimmy tried to run for the cave entrance. Icky shouted, "No! Jimmy!"

The Uktena struck, its huge arrow-shaped head snapping the young

Cherokee in half as its antlers drew sparks from the cave wall.

Thunder, fire, and smoke from gunshots filled the cavern, bullets ricocheting off the giant snake and the stone walls. Flashlight beams swung wildly, pale in comparison to the blinding light of the Ulun'suti.

Icky tried to make it to what was left of his cousin's body, but the Uktena struck like a thunderbolt, taking his head from his shoulders in a shower of gore.

Connor's pistol was empty in a matter of heartbeats. He didn't waste time reloading. He crouched and drew his Ka-Bar from his boot sheathe, feeling a bulk in his coat. He reached into the inner pocket and withdrew the forgotten gas mask of R. Stubblefield.

Hernandez screamed when a jet of poison hit him. The medic clutched his eyes as green smoke billowed from the sizzling wounds. Goldman tried to grab his friend and pull him away from the towering snake. The horned head struck and came away with the Californian's severed left arm in its fanged maw.

His friends falling around him, Connor donned the gas mask and charged the Uktena. It struck, but he dodged to the side, rolling painfully across a scatter of gold bars and old bones. Regaining his feet, he was hit in the chest by the lashing, rattling tail. Connor flew through the smoky air and slammed into the cavern wall.

Shaking the stars and fog from his head, Connor stared through the mask's round lenses. The Uktena slithered into the center of the chamber and reared its horned head above him, readying for another strike. He gripped his knife and tensed.

The giant head lunged. Connor moved. Venom-filled fangs tore chunks from the rock wall. Connor buried the Ka-Bar into the Uktena's skull just below the blazing diamond crest. His left hand grasped one of the long antlers as the monster recoiled, dragging him into the air.

The Uktena lashed and raged, slamming into the ceiling and the walls in a desperate attempt to dislodge him. Though he felt several ribs and a collarbone shatter, Connor held on for all he was worth, continuing to worry at the diamond crest with the knife. Green fumes billowed from the serpent's maw and the bleeding wound, but Connor gulped the filtered air within the gas mask.

Connor lost track of time and space. His entire existence was pain and purpose. He knew most of the bones in his body were broken and some of his organs were finished. But he was not about to let this thing kill him and his friends and live. Somehow his left fist remained locked like a vice on the antler and his right on the knife handle.

At some point, he became aware that the struggle was over. Darkness took him. Not the darkness of death or unconsciousness, not yet. The Ulun'suti lost its fire, and the cave was again plunged into preternatural gloom. The loss of light signaled the end of movement, at least the end of violent movement. As he sank to the stone floor, Connor could feel the writhing death throes of the great serpent beneath him.

Consciousness faded. Connor's right hand closed tight over the big, blood-soaked diamond.

***

He sensed light beyond his closed eyelids.

He breathed in warm air, the kind produced by industrial heat-and-air units in large buildings. Sweet smelling. He grimaced as awareness slowly returned, expecting a crescendo of pain. When it didn't arrive, he thought he'd awakened from a terrible dream.

He sat up in the bed—a king size with clean sheets and a thick, multicolored comforter—and tried to get his bearings. He was in a hotel room: mass-produced furniture, modest flat-screen TV, in-room coffee pot, and mini fridge. The heavy curtains were drawn, a slender plane of gray light sliding between to join the unobtrusive yellow glow of the desk-mounted lamp.

The lamp revealed he was not alone.

Connor tried to speak, but his throat was dry.

In response, the silent man sitting at the desk stood and retrieved a bottle of water from the fridge. He wore an expensive dark suit with a silver-tipped bolo tie and polished cowboy boots. His jet black hair pulled back in a ponytail, aquiline features, and dark complexion identified him as a Native American. Connor tensed, remembering the Black Council ambush in the forest. Or was that a dream?

The man tossed him the bottle and, before Connor could open it to regain his voice, left the room.

Somewhat refreshed by the cold water, Connor got to his feet and examined himself. He didn't have any broken bones, bruises, scrapes, or cuts. No pain whatsoever. He did, however, notice a few pinkish scars he hadn't had before. Stepping to the bathroom mirror, Connor saw that his hair and beard had grown unchecked for at least a week.

After heeding nature's call and brushing his teeth, Connor returned to the main room and checked the closet. A new set of off-the-rack clothes, roughly his size, hung inside. A clear plastic bag was on the closet floor, stuffed with torn and bloodstained hiking gear.

"Not a dream after all..." Connor shook his head, putting the confusion away for the moment. He decided to clear his head with a hot shower before getting dressed...

Someone knocked at the door just as he laced up his new boots. He hadn't found any of his weapons among the articles in the room, so he rolled his shoulders and stretched his arms, back, and legs before answering. If he had to fight, he'd be doing it the old-fashioned way.

"Mr. Mackay." A middle-aged Native American man in a very expensive suit stood outside the door. Two mean-looking young men in dark suits, both almost as big as Connor, stood behind him. The older man smiled. "So glad to see you up and alert. I am John Lisenbe, your current host. May I come in?"

Connor stepped back, opening the door wide, but he kept his eyes on the two bruisers.

Lisenbe half turned to his guards. "You may return to your duties, gentlemen."

The two big men gave Connor some stink eye, but they headed down the hall as John Lisenbe entered the room. "I hope you've found the accommodations sufficient," he said before taking a seat at the desk.

"I don't reckon I can complain." Connor closed the door and followed. "Not that I could make a call one way or the other. I've only been conscious for about twenty minutes. At least the water pressure is good. I'm guessing this is a hotel casino in Cherokee, North Carolina, and you're the head of the tribe."

Lisenbe's smile widened. "One of the heads, yes. And you are quite right as to the location. You've been our guest for ten days now, Mr. Mackay. Of course, it took almost three days to get you out of the woods. Not speaking metaphorically."

Connor opened the curtains to look at the mist-covered mountains. "So I've got you to thank for patching me up, then?"

"Oh, no. The Ulun'suti did that. You have proven yourself quite a remarkable man, Mr. Mackay, by killing the Uktena and claiming the Transparency Diamond. You must have some Cherokee blood in you."

Connor turned. "I reckon most folks from around here do."

Lisenbe's smile became Cheshire-like. "Not as many as you'd think... But if you feel up to it, I'd like to discuss what happens next."

Connor raised an eyebrow. "Why are you asking me? In fact, I'm surprised your boys didn't leave me in that cave to die after they tried to kill us all in that ambush."

Lisenbe's eyes widened, then he nodded in understanding. "Oh, I do apologize. I fear you are under the false impression that I represent the Black Council. No, no, Mr. Mackay. Not at all. We are the White Lodge, the sworn enemies of those vile witches. In fact, my people are the reason you and your friends had no further encounters with them after that unfortunate night before you found the cave."

Connor took a deep breath and paced the length of the small room. "*Unfortunate...* yeah, I guess you could call it that. I just had to put one of my friends—a married man—in the ground because of it. And the rest of them? I guess nobody else made it out of that cave, huh?"

Lisenbe's expression turned somber. "No, I am afraid not. But this entire string of events has not been unfortunate for only you and yours, Mr. Mackay. We lost three members of our lodge in the encounter with the Black Council, and that is nothing to speak of the legal entanglements engendered by the involvement of the FBI. Including the agent who died in the Uktena's lair, a dozen federal officers were killed on or around our land."

Connor sat on the foot of the bed and faced the older man. "So, where do we go from here? Is that what you want to know? Well, you tell me."

Lisenbe reached into his jacket pocket and produced a large item wrapped in a piece of supple deerskin. Setting the package on the table, he carefully unfolded the covering to reveal an uncut diamond about the size of a softball. A deep, blood-red vein ran through the heart of the gemstone. But it did not glow with supernatural fire. "The fabled Ulun'suti, the Transparency. By right of combat, this is yours, Mr. Mackay. Taken to a jeweler, it might be worth quite a few of those gold bars from the cave. But to us, it is priceless."

"You want it? You can have it."

Lisenbe blinked. "After all you have sacrificed to achieve it? You have survived by dent of your courage and skill, Mr. Mackay... but I am afraid that merely seeing the Uktena is... a death sentence for one's family. I am sorry—"

"My family is already dead." Connor exhaled through his flaring nostrils at the confession, hating acknowledging the fact much less speaking it aloud. "Keep the diamond."

"I am sorry to hear that." The old man offered a sympathetic smile and carefully rewrapped the artifact. "In that case, this is most generous of you, and on behalf of the White Lodge and the Cherokee people, I thank you. Now, Mr. Mackay, what would you have of us?"

Connor flexed his hands, which by all rights should have been pulped along with the rest of his body. "I reckon you've already done right by me. But if you could see fit to let my friends' people know what happened to 'em—or some feasible version of the story—and make sure they get a proper burial, I'd greatly appreciate it."

Lisenbe nodded. "That can be done. But what about the gold, Mr. Mackay?"

Connor blinked. "You mean you're not keeping it?"

"Well, possession is nine-tenths of the law, as they say." Lisenbe chuckled. "Or at least, that's what the white man says. I propose an even split. We take half, and the other half is divided equally between you and the survivors of your friends. Our attorneys and accountants can arrange some... *feasible*, as you say, means of making the transfers once the gold is converted into liquid assets."

Connor nodded. Even that split was more money than he'd ever imagined. But it didn't feel right cashing in on the blood of his friends, on Icky's lifelong dream when Icky wouldn't be around to enjoy it. "If you can give me, say... fifty grand in cash now, you can keep half of my share. Give the balance to a woman named Bernice Stubblefield in Dandridge, Tennessee."

Lisenbe's eyebrows shot up. "I know that name."

Connor smiled for the first time in seeming forever. "Somehow, that doesn't surprise me in the least, Mr. Lisenbe."

ABOUT THE AUTHOR

Jason J. McCuiston was born in the wilds of southeast Tennessee, where he was raised on a carnivorous diet of old monster movies, westerns, comic books, horror magazines, sci-fi and fantasy novels, and, of course, Dungeons & Dragons. He attended the finest state school that would have him with the intention of becoming a comic book artist. This did not pan out, so following his matriculation and a brief and unprofitable stint as an illustrator of tabletop RPGs, he embarked upon a whirlwind tour of spectacularly underpaid and uninspired careers. Half a lifetime later, he came to his senses, realizing he was meant to be a professional storyteller.

Publishing his first story about zombies, kung fu, and family ties in Parsec Ink's 2017 *Triangulation: Appetites* anthology, McCuiston has been a semifinalist in the Writers of the Future contest, and he has studied under the tutelage of bestselling author Philip Athans. His stories of fantasy, horror, and science fiction have appeared in numerous anthologies, periodicals, websites, and podcasts, notably Dark Owl Publishing's *Something Wicked This Way Rides* anthology, *StoryHack Action and Adventure* magazine, and *Black Infinity* magazine.

Project Notebook, his first novel, was published in summer of 2020 to critical acclaim. He has since released two volumes of pulp sci-fi adventures with Dark Owl Publishing: The Last Star Warden, Volumes I & II. You can find all of these and most of his other publications on his Amazon page at https://www.amazon.com/-/e/B07RN8HT98 .

McCuiston lives in South Carolina, USA with his college professor wife and their two four-legged girls, Winky and Tonks. Connect with him on Twitter @JasonJMcCuiston.

In the summer of 1947 – months before something fell to Earth near Roswell, New Mexico – the skies above the Pacific Northwest were filled with mysterious lights and strange phenomena. Members of a top secret organization are dispatched to investigate the Maury Island Incident in Washington. The team of elite WWII veterans must uncover the truth behind these extraordinary occurrences... even if it means facing their own self-destruction.

PROJECT NOTEBOOK
BY JASON J. MCCUISTON

Available in paperback and on Kindle
via Amazon

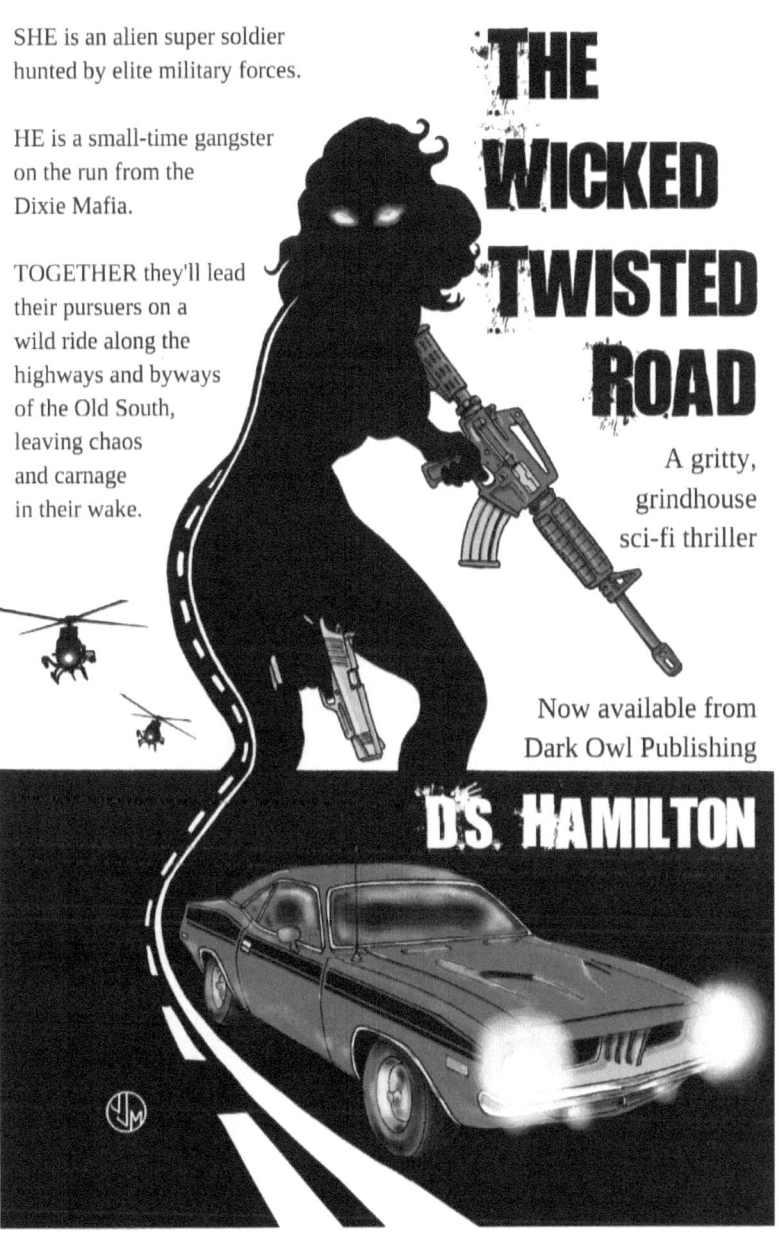

SOMETHING WICKED THIS WAY RIDES

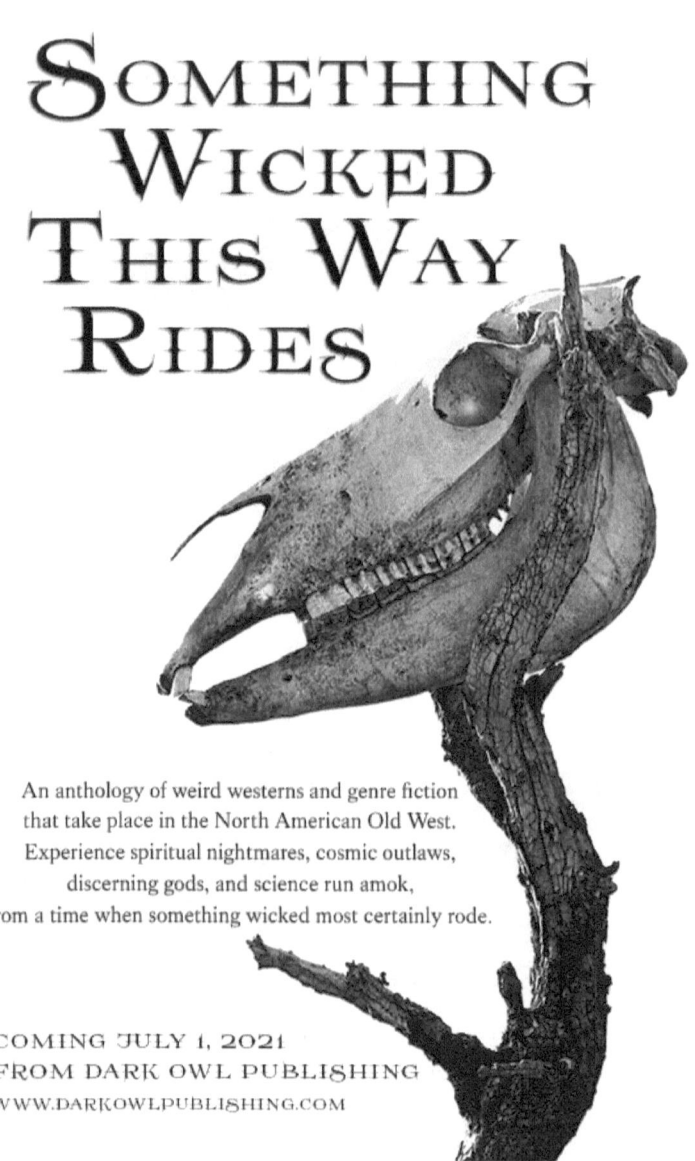

An anthology of weird westerns and genre fiction
that take place in the North American Old West.
Experience spiritual nightmares, cosmic outlaws,
discerning gods, and science run amok,
from a time when something wicked most certainly rode.

COMING JULY 1, 2021
FROM DARK OWL PUBLISHING
WWW.DARKOWLPUBLISHING.COM